LONG RIDE
FOR
JUSTICE

RICHARD O. SNELSON

Cover Painting – Andy Thomas
Publishing Coordinator – Sharon Kizziah-Holmes

SOLANDER
PRESS
Rogers, Arkansas

ISBN -13: 978-1-959548-06-5

ACKNOWLEDGMENTS

I'd like to thank Chelsea Cambeis for her content edit.

Thanks to Kathleen Garnsey for her help with proofing

I'd like to acknowledge the memory and hopeful restoration of the Snelson/Brinker Cabin in Crawford County, Missouri.

Many thanks to artist, Andy Thomas, for the use of his painting for the cover. The Charge of Selby's Iron Brigade, Battle of Marshal, Missouri Oct 13.1863

CHAPTER 1

March 1865
Saint Louis, Missouri

Captain Nelson Paintier walked from the Jefferson Barracks hospital to the barracks corral. When he could stand straight, he topped more than six feet two inches tall. Four years of war battling the Confederate Army had left him gaunt, slightly stooped, and constantly walking with a limp. His faded blue pants looked out of place with the deer-hide jacket he purchased for the trip home.

The pants, and any trace of Federal service, would have to be gone before he reached his home in southern Missouri. Not many there would welcome a former Yankee soldier.

Whipping a lead rope against his good leg, he stopped to look over the herd of horses standing ready for their next call to battle. The day before he angrily watched the troops drive a hundred or more of the surplus horses to a pit and kill them. His big roan mare had been led to the killing pen this morning. No one was going to stop him from getting her out and saving her. He quickened his approach to the corral gate and was confronted by a sentry.

The sentry lifted his rifle in a salute, stepping to his right to block the gate, "You can't go in this pen, mister," the trooper said. "They're killing them horses today."

"Watch me, son." Nelson pushed the young trooper aside and stopped with his hand on the gate latch. "Old friend in there, is coming out with me."

"You have to stop! Told me nobody goes in there. Sorry, mister."

"Not mister, soldier. Rank's captain to you. Damn it anyway, how old are you, kid?"

"Four…four…teen. Lied about that." The boy stared at the ground.

"Stay at your post, son. I'm going in there after my horse." He pushed the gate open and stepped around the guard.

The boy closed the gate and followed close behind, carrying his rifle at his side.

"Over there, the roan mare that's watching us." He gave a short whistle that started the mare pushing through the other horses to walk to his side. "Hello, Blue." He draped his arm over the mare's neck in a hug and slipped his sugar-filled hand under her mouth.

"Bad scar, there on her shoulder," said the trooper.

"Took two mini balls that day. Both meant for me. I kept her wound open for days so it would drain. Slipped a tube in each morning against her breastbone and blew the wound full of iodine. She stood still, like she knew I was trying to help. One mini's still in there. Mare's got a big heart, son. We fought three battles, leading my troops, after she healed up."

"The scar must be why they had her up for slaughter," said the trooper.

"That, and now they don't need her, with the war being

nearly over. You're gonna have to look the other way, boy. I'm taking the horse out of here."

"Oh, shit! My lieutenant's heading for the gate." The trooper again lowered his eyes to the ground.

Nelson tied his lead rope to the horse's halter, scratched the mare behind the ears, and walked leading the mare to the gate where the officer waited.

"General wants you at headquarters," the Lieutenant said, blocking the gate and his way.

"Bullshit!" He pushed the gate open and shoved the lieutenant aside, then walked through with the mare. Without looking back, he led the horse to where his saddle and tack waited. After he brushed the dirt off the mare's back, he tossed the saddle blanket in place, and carefully worked out the wrinkles. He swung the new saddle on, knowing the regret that would soon come from having to break in a saddle on a long ride.

"They need you at command, sir. Now! They're holding up your discharge orders," said the red-faced lieutenant who had followed closely behind Nelson and the horse.

"Do you see what I'm doing? When I'm done, I'm going to ride the hell out of here and head home. I'm going back to what's left of southern Missouri. Are you going to try and stop me, Lieutenant?" Nelson firmed up the saddle's girth and tied the end in place.

"No, but he is, sir." The lieutenant pointed toward General Warren and his aide headed directly for Nelson and his horse.

The General was speaking even before he got close, "Captain Paintier, I see you found that old hero war horse my aides told me about. Let's see, you named her Blue?"

"That's right, sir. My enlistment is up and I'm heading back to Steelville, Missouri," Nelson moved to climb in the saddle.

"I wanted to talk with you about that, Captain." General Warren turned and excused his aides and motioned for

Nelson to walk with him. Nelson reluctantly draped the mare's lead rope over a rail and took several quick steps to join the general's side.

"You're from southern Missouri, Captain Paintier. Are you aware of what's still going on down there?" He did not wait for an answer, he just continued to walk. "The guerrilla troops that pulled off from Quantrill after he burned down Lawrence, Kansas, are still causing my command trouble. Jim Hagan is one of the leaders now. With summer coming on, it will only get worse."

"I've a feeling a lot of those raiders come from around my hometown," Nelson said.

"Things got out of hand for me again last week. One of my damn hot-headed officers, named Turner, from the Rolla command caught some of Bloody Bill Anderson's boys south of Jefferson City. Tied them up to trees, spent the rest of the day killing them one by one. Even his troops tried to get him to stop. Last prisoner he whipped until it looked like he had been skinned, tied him on his horse with a note that said more of this is coming." He stopped and turned to face Nelson.

Nelson shook his head at what General Warren just told him. "I know Lieutenant Turner. He's been trouble ever since he got promoted."

"I ordered him arrested and locked him in the stockade at Rolla. I'll hang him myself when I get him back to St. Louis," General Warren said.

"Looks like I might be riding into some hell."

"We had rumors that the guerrilla raiders were breaking up before this happened. Jim Hagan and his boys had quit Anderson and went on south to Buffalo River. Turns out the man Turner whipped is Hagan's son. He was half dead when they sent him off on his horse, so I doubt if he lived."

"What's this got to do with me, sir?"

"Just this, Captain. I don't have any other man that can ride into that guerrilla territory and survive. I've got two sets of papers waiting on my desk. One is your discharge. The other an extension of duty and pardons to be signed by Hagan and each of his men. I'll sign the pardons when you bring them back. Take your pick. Up to you which you take. President Lincoln wants the killing to stop in the border states. You can help."

Nelson wanted to say what he was thinking, Goddamn almighty generals!

~ ~ ~ ~

Half a day's ride to the west, he left the well-traveled trace for a back woods trail that allowed him to travel without attracting attention. Certain his return home wouldn't remain a secret long, he wanted to delay the news as long as possible. Riding along the ridges and hills of the Ozark Mountains would take a lot longer, but he didn't mind. It gave him time to clear his mind as to why he was really going back to a place where the sheriff had killed his father and tried to do the same to him. He hoped Sheriff Spaid survived the war because he would be facing Paintier justice soon.

With darkness nearly upon him, he found a place to spend the night under a clump of cedar trees next to a creek. After loosening the saddle's girth, he led Blue to the creek to drink. Back at the cedars he unsaddled, then hobbled the mare to graze a small stand of grass close to the trees. The cold of the March night began to chill him, so he gathered an armload of fallen branches and lit a small fire. The hardtack biscuits and jerked beef in his saddlebags would have to satisfy his hunger for tonight. With his bedroll spread alongside the fire, he stretched out and leaned against the still-warm leather of his saddle.

Reaching back to his saddlebags, he took out paper and pencil. For more than a year, he had prayed for the chance to go back to the wrongs he needed to fix in Steelville. He put his thoughts on paper about the guilt that stuck with him through battle after battle, and always brought back the vision of the slave girl standing on the gallows, her stare burning forever in his mind. He had put off writing this chapter.

Steelville, Missouri 1850

They came down the path from the dog-trot cabin toward the spring pool, to where I was hiding in the blackberry brambles, waiting. Shivers crossed my back, my pa would beat me till I'm half dead, if he found out I was here, playing with a slave girl. The master's baby girl clung tightly to the edge of the slave girl's sack cloth dress, the baby stumbled now and then, like all babies that were just learning to walk.

It had been months before that I learned the slave girl's owners called her Mary. When she got close, I jumped from behind the bramble. Mary's hand swept to cover her mouth in mock surprise and the baby girl pulled the edge of the sack dress to cover her face. Mary smiled at my boyhood prank and then leaned over to kiss the child on the head.

I grabbed Mary's free hand and walked around her, turning her and the baby in a slow circle. When the turning stopped, the baby laughed and pointed toward the water. Mary knelt by the side of the dark flowing spring and reached for the tin ladle hanging on a limb. She filled the ladle with the cold water and held it for the baby girl to drink.

I watched as she leaned over the baby and her sack dress fell open. I must have been staring because Mary frowned at me, and quickly closed the front of her dress. It wasn't the first time I saw the fifteen-year old's nakedness. Months ago, I had watched her sitting beside the spring pool, dipping a cloth in the cold water and rubbing it across her breasts, she didn't know I was there hiding behind the bramble bush. I had watched my little sister taking a bath but seeing the slave girl caused me to feel like a man. I didn't tell anyone what I had seen.

Mary hung the ladle back and then turned away from the spring pool to spread the apron she had been wearing on the ground. After she sat the little girl on the apron, Mary took a small cornhusk doll from the pocket of her dress and put it in the baby's hands. When she straightened, she reached for my hand and turned us dancing to the bubbling of the spring water as it went over the moss-covered rock dam. I tugged her arm and backed slowly toward our secret bramble bush hide-away.

I dropped to the ground, pulling Mary down beside me. I reached to feel her, to touch her hair. Black as coal, it would spring right back after I pushed it flat on the side of her head. She pushed my hand away, grabbed a hunk of my hair, and yanked hard, laughing and not speaking a word. I reacted, grabbed her around the waist, and then rolled over her squirming body. The rolling stopped when we hit the bramble stickers. Mary sat up and carefully picked the bramble stickers from the sackcloth dress, only to rise suddenly and leave to check on the baby at play by the spring. I sat behind the bramble and waited for her to return.

Her screams caused me to jump to my feet and rush around the bramble. She stumbled into me, grabbed my arm, and pulled me toward the place where the apron sat empty.

He was unable to continue writing. What came next in the story was difficult to think about, let alone put in writing. He jotted down two names—Sheriff Spaid and Judge Saunders—and underlined them. Aside from Mary, those two names were the fuel behind his pen. Mary deserved justice, and he would make sure everyone knew what had been swept under the rug by that pair of murderous men when he found time to finish those pages. He carefully folded the three pages of handwritten memories and wrapped them in the oilskin cover with the pardons he carried for Hagan and his men. The fire's embers still gave off heat so he turned on his side and hoped sleep would finally come.

The next morning, he saddled his horse, and started again toward southern Missouri and his boyhood home. Three days of riding had brought him close to Steelville. He could always read the roan mare well; her faster pace and alert ears told him a storm would be upon them before the day ended.

A hard-pelting rain started around noon and didn't let up.

"Darn coon oil doing no good on this raincoat," he said to the mare. "I feel the wet trickling to the bottom of my drawers."

After four hours of riding in the rain he dismounted to lead the mare, giving her a much-needed rest.

"Come on, old gal, I know you would like to stop for a while," he said, urging the horse to follow him up a steep rock trail. At the top, he stopped and pulled the slack out of the saddle's girth, the trail had gotten too slick for him to walk, so he climbed back in the saddle. "You can handle it better than I can, horse."

Heading down the far side of the hill, he leaned back in the saddle pushing his feet forward in the stirrups, balancing against the steep descent and the sliding horse. He felt like he was on a runaway train when all four of the mare's feet broke loose. Blue locked her front legs and struggled with her hindquarters to keep her balance and stop the slide. He cleared his feet from the stirrups to keep from being pinned if the mare fell. The slide slowed as the mare gained footing in the rear and ended with them wedged safely against a cedar tree. He leaned over the

8

mare's neck and patted her, a thank you, for again saving his neck. With no place for shelter, he rode on into the night.

The rain continued throughout the night, with the sound of thunder only a heartbeat behind the blinding lightning strikes that seemed to follow them.

He planned by morning when he reached the Meramec River, he could swim the mare across, but the rain didn't stop and now he was sure he would have to wait for the river to fall before crossing. The ridge that he followed would take him alongside the stream in a few hours.

The wind had picked up and changed directions several times in the last few minutes. Frequent lightning strikes with thunderclaps that rattled teeth rolled through the valley. The horse slowed with its ears turned toward the deep Meramec valley they had been paralleling.

"What's wrong, gal?" Nelson stood in the saddle to listen. "Now, I hear it too. Sounds like half the trees in the valley are being yanked up."

He nudged Blue down a trail leading to the river's edge. As they neared the bottom of the hill, the trail ended at a small clearing right at the Meramec River's swollen edge.

He dropped the reins onto the mare's neck. "Easy, Blue. Whoa, gal!"

The dim morning's light caused his tired eyes and mind to play tricks on him. He saw strange shapes that swam in the foaming water, huge monsters that rolled and dived, playing in the currents that blocked his path.

In his mind, he heard the monsters scream as they twisted in the tumbling waters. Screams like others he tried to forget. Screams mixed with blood that gushed from wounded men's mouths. Men left on the battlefield by a Union general too stubborn and proud to ask for two hours of ceasefire to collect his wounded troops.

He pulled his raincoat tight against his neck and started to dismount to wait out the flood.

"Help! Somebody…please! We need help! Please…God!"

A woman's screams and cries for help came from what looked like a floating roof, twisting in the river's current. He jerked the hood off his head, grabbed the reins, and stood in the stirrups. Blue reared, pawing the air. His sudden movements served as a call to battle for the mare.

A tree on the hillside behind them exploded as lightning struck. Stinging pieces hit like fragments from a cannon blast. Nelson didn't hear a bugle sound the charge, but Blue did, he felt the mare clench the bit in her teeth. Blue jumped and plunged far out in the raging river.

The current dragged him from the saddle and swept him into a dark pool of suffocation. He thrashed his way to the top, reaching to find the saddle and Blue. Too far away. Then he saw the mare with eyes wide and nostrils flared. He saw her look toward him. He couldn't help her. Blue was caught in a whirlpool that drew her down.

He struggled to keep his nose above the rolling sea of mud and water. He caught glimpses of the openings between half-submerged trees as the river swept him downstream. The current was too fast. More screams for help came as Nelson hit the side of the roof turning in the currents. The screams stopped, and a woman clutched at his arm helping him climb onto the roof.

"Help us," she pleaded, "Water came up so fast. We climbed out the attic onto the roof."

He shook his head, coughed out the water, and looked around the roof-turned-raft that had saved him. His blurry eyes followed the woman's arm and pointing finger.

"My boy!" The woman crawled frantically across the roof toward the boy clinging to the edge.

"Please…Please, mister. Save him!" she cried.

The roof smashed into a boulder on the river's bottom and threw him to the edge once again. Still, he struggled toward the woman and boy. The woman reached out, over

the edge of the roof trying to grab her son's arm.
A fallen tree lodged across the roof's path swept across
his back and caught the mother's legs in its tangled grip.
Nelson grabbed for her arm and missed. She hung there in
the tree limbs for seconds then vanished beneath the dark
water behind the spinning roof. There were no screams or
cries for help.

"Hang on, boy. I'll get you." He rolled across the roof to
the boy and reached for his hand.

"Take my hand and pull hard."

In one quick pull, he had the boy beside him on the roof.
Only the sound of the water churning in whirlpools came
from behind them.

"I can't see her," the boy stood and looked behind the
floating roof.

"I know, boy. The tree...the river...Keep hanging on."

The boards beneath the roof cracked as they broke away.
It sank still deeper into the brown current.

"Where did she go?" the boy asked, wiping his eyes.

"You've got to be brave, boy, and be ready when it's
time to jump and swim for the bank."

The roof tilted. Nelson shifted his weight to keep it from
tipping over. Somewhere ahead the stream would widen,
and the current would slow. It would give him a chance to
save the boy. He had to wait.

The current slowed, they were rounding a bend in the
river. "Get ready, boy. When we get closer to the bank,
we're going to jump into the willow trees."

The boy still stared back up the river. Nelson grabbed
his arms and lifted him to his feet as the roof brushed the
submerged willow tops along the flooded bank.

"Now! Jump!"

Nelson shoved him with all the energy he had left. The
boy splashed into the willow tops, then sank. He dove after
him, touched the boy's head first and then gripped his
waist, to lift him to the surface. With the boy's weight

holding him underwater, his feet bounced on the willow limbs as the current pushed him over them. He did a strange dance that kept the boy's head from going under the water. All his breath was gone, and he almost forgot the precious cargo that the mother had begged him to save. He kicked to the surface for air. The boy was still there in front of him. His arms went tight around the boy again. Ahead the white bark of the top of a sycamore tree stuck out of the water.

"Grab the limbs. Grab now!"

They hit the tree together, both getting arms around one of the tree's limbs. Nelson's feet bounced on top of the water below. He reached and helped the boy climb up. Nelson still hung over the limb like wet laundry in the wind.

"Climb higher, boy, the water's still coming up."

"I ain't no boy. Name is Joshua."

CHAPTER 2

"**S**tay awake, Joshua," Nelson said. "I feel like an old coon up here in this sycamore, treed by a pack of hounds."

He tried to get the boy to talk during the night, keep him awake, so he wouldn't lose his grip and fall into the water. The boy never answered. Sometime in the night the rising water reached Nelson's knees, and then it started to fall. The river crest passed, and morning found them both safe.

He shook the boy. "You still awake?"

"I was supposed to keep my mom safe."

"This river gets wild when it's flooded." He moved to get a better grip on a limb. He should have been able to help the woman before she was swept off the roof, but he put the thought aside for now. So many times, in battle, he felt the same way when his troops fell by his side. Too many times seeing death had left him hardened and callous.

"Mister, can you find my mom?"

"We can look for her on the way back upriver when the water goes down. I need to get you back home. Steelville's your home, isn't it?"

"I don't want to go…back there," he said, "It's gone. Our home is gone."

"Your dad, won't he be looking for you?"

"No, he won't. He don't stay there no more. Went off to guerrilla fight."

"How long since he's been home?"

"Only time he comes home is when the leaves are thick on the trees."

He understood what the boy meant. The guerrilla raiders needed the thick tree cover for safety and would head south for Arkansas and Texas when fall and winter came.

In the cloudy afternoon light, he saw the fields along the river were full of huge brush piles and heaps of trash washed in by the flash flood. The horse that carried him from danger on the battlefield too many times to count would be there in the piles somewhere. He had to find her and collect the pardons—the purpose behind his current mission.

"River's gone down a lot. We can try for the bank now," he said, sliding down the slick trunk into the knee-deep water.

Joshua followed, but his arms were too short to grip the big tree trunk. He slipped, splashing face down into the muddy water. His head popped up wearing a sheepish look and dripping mud.

"At least I ain't thirsty no more."

Nelson chuckled for the first time since he had taken the mare from the killer pens in St. Louis.

Being barefoot didn't keep Joshua from straying to search around each pile of brush and lumber. "Try to stay up with me, Joshua. This mud is only ankle deep."

"Hey, mister. Look here, sticking out of the boards."

When he saw the legs of a rust-colored cow stuck straight out in death, he remembered always having to milk his family's cow. When he was a boy their cow would stand at the barnyard gate, with a drooping udder and leaking teats, bellowing for him to come milk. When his dad found out he had been off trapping, or hunting, and neglecting the cow, a butt whipping always came after he finished the milking.

The pool of water below the dead cow's udder had turned white from the milk dripping from her teats. He reached and stripped the milk from one of the extended teats of the dead cow, thinking of something to drink.

"You're crazy, Mister. I ain't going to drink no milk from a dead cow," Joshua said.

"One time during the war, we were so hungry, would have pulled that cow out of the brush pile and butchered it for supper."

"I'm glad we ain't hungry yet."

The fields were littered with belongings from the town, wooden buckets, a door to an outhouse, wagon parts, harness, tables and broken chairs all sticking from the huge piles of trees. Nelson stooped to open a leather-bound book lying half submerged in the mud and water and saw land grants and plots that marked-out the town's homesteads. He wondered if all the courthouse records were gone. He glanced up, his eyes fixing on a hand sticking out of the mud and brush on the ground.

"Stay here, Joshua."

Mud splashed on his side as the boy rushed past, ignoring his instruction. He watched Joshua claw at the brush and tree limbs, shoving and pushing them away from the hand and arm.

"It's not her, Joshua. Look! Look here, see, it's a man."

The boy stopped tearing at the pile and stood stooped over staring at the dead man's hand and the small metal object sticking between his fingers. Nelson's fingers slipped off the object as he tried to pull it from the hand's death grip. He pried the thumb up and took the dirty object to swirl it in the pool of muddy water around his boots.

"What is it?" Joshua asked.

He showed it to the boy. "A toy soldier, someone that led the south in battle."

"Is it General Robert E. Lee?" Joshua asked.

"Yes, would you like to keep the toy?"

"It's not a toy, mister. We all have them hid somewhere. They made them secret at the ironworks out of Yankee gunmetal. Then we gave them to the rebs to make bullets."

"Here, keep it, Joshua. Lee is a fine soldier and general. Better than most of the ones the Yankees have."

Nelson and the boy cleared the rest of the brush from the man's body. The man had only one arm, his other missing from a shoulder that showed signs of recent healing. Joshua said he remembered the man from Steelville and how he told them he lost the arm at the Wilson's Creek Battle.

"Remember where we found the man, Joshua, so we can tell the searchers where to find him."

The river valley narrowed, and they were forced to climb up along the bluffs that lined the north side of the Meramec River. The trail there lead to the Maramec Iron Works and the worker's cabin village they called Stringtown. The Stringtown cabins were above the river and wouldn't be flooded so they could get food and supplies there.

When Nelson reached the top of the bluff, he saw smoke rising from a cooking fire close to a mile away. He led the boy across a narrow cut in the bluff and climbed the steep trail leading toward the smoke. In the evening twilight, he could make out the figures of two men sitting up close to a small fire. He heard the uneasy braying of mules. It would warn the men someone was approaching. Sure enough, the men dropped to the ground, and then two shots rang out.

"Hold on, damn it," Nelson yelled. He pulled the boy down beside him.

"Who are you mister?"

"Can me and the boy come on in?"

"Send the boy in first, then you can follow. Get them

hands up over your head so we can see them."

A sideboard wagon sat behind the men with a high-line tie between two trees that extended over eight mules. The two mules on the end paced and snorted with their tall ears pointing at the approaching strangers. He suspected the alert mules were the lead team of the hitch. He walked into their camp with his hands over his head. He could smell roasting meat and heard the boiling of a fresh pot of coffee on the fire. Joshua hadn't looked up since he saw the skewered squirrels.

"By the looks of your muddy clothes, both uns' need some warming up and some eats," said the gray bearded man, "Them squirrels are about done."

"The boy and I were caught in the flood last night. His home got washed away."

"We watched this morning. Looked like the whole of Steelville was coming out of the draw and heading down river."

"Boy and me, we spent the night on a sycamore limb. Name's Nelson, boy is Joshua."

"Me and him, Gales and Lomax. We haul the iron bars and slag iron blooms up to Hermann, where they put 'um on Missouri River steamboats headed for St. Louis. Four mule teams hitched up to two tons of iron aboard. We're headed back to the ironworks. We got to watch who comes around these days. They had us start carrying the Sharps carbines for protection after the bushwhackers hit the company store about two months ago."

"Are the bushwhackers raiding much in these parts?" Nelson asked.

"They ride through town, worse than the damn union cavalry," said Lomax. "At least we knowed what to expect from the Yankees. With the bushwhackers, they hitting their own kind of folks, rob and steal and do worse with the woman folk. They take everything that ain't nailed down. Ain't safe, don't matter where you go."

"Wonder if we could hitch a ride tomorrow? I want to get the boy back into Steelville. His folks there will be looking for him for sure."

"Yep. For now, you two pull off a hunk of one of them squirrels. Bet you ain't 'et all day," Lomax said. "One of us is going to be up all-night keeping watch on them mules. So, eat and curl up by the fire. We're keeping her blazing all night."

The roasted squirrel legs reminded Nelson of meals when he was a boy. He brought home a lot of squirrels for his mother to cook. It was easy to sit under a hickory nut tree and ambush a dozen in one morning, a game he liked to play.

It came back to mind, like it had for years, the ambush, that had burned his house and killed his dad. He would face the men responsible soon. He wondered if Steelville had forgotten the fifteen-year-old boy that disappeared the day they hung the slave girl, Mary.

"Thanks for helping me, mister," Joshua said, "It ain't your fault she's gone. It's mine. I promised my aunt I would take care of my mother."

"It's nobody's fault, Joshua. Some things, we just don't know why they happen. Try and get some sleep now."

The boy turned away, resting his head on a fallen limb and said no more. Nelson scooted lower against the oak limb and was soon asleep.

~ ~ ~ ~

Joshua shook Nelson awake while it was still dark to tell him the men had the teams hitched ready to go.

"Come on, mister. They're waiting for us," Joshua said.

"Name's Nelson, Joshua, Nelson Paintier. I'm coming, get on that wagon, they're headed for Stringtown."

The team driver pushed the eight mules along the narrow trails at a pace too fast and insane. On each corner the back of the wagon swung out of the ruts and into the brush along the side. One hour into the trip, four riders came up fast behind them.

"Lomax got some riders on our tail," Nelson yelled a warning.

"Just saw them, goddamn bushwhackers," said Lomax. "Know how to shoot one of these?"

"Damn right I do." Nelson grabbed the carbine Lomax tossed to him, and then pushed Joshua to the floor of the wagon.

The riders started shooting first, over the flattened ears of their four horses. The feel of the kill was still fresh in Nelson's mind. His saber drawn, splitting a skull, cutting a throat, or cleaving an arm. The rifle was cleaner. He didn't have to look close at what he killed. His first shot pitched the lead rider backward in a somersault over the back of the horse. The three remaining riders were soon joined by four others who seemed to come out of nowhere. Lomax took a shot to the back of his neck and fell forward to the floor of the wagon. A surge of blood stained the wagon's floor.

"Gales, what the hell you fellows packing that those fellows want so damn bad?"

"It's under the seat in the saddlebags. Iron Work's payroll. We picked it up from the steamboat."

"They're going to kill us if they get us stopped, Gales," Nelson said. "Throw the saddlebags on the road. They'll stop for that."

"Can't do that, mister. Lose my job," said Gales.

"Would you rather lose your life? If they don't shoot you, I'm going to if you don't throw that payroll off this wagon," Nelson yelled.

"Throw it, goddamn it. Throw it," said Gales.

Nelson jerked the saddlebag covers open and tossed the money into the air behind the wagon. The coins and bills hit the road in clouds of red dust behind the wagon. The riders pulled up, jumped off their horses, and dove for the floating bills.

"I think that'll keep them busy for quite a while," Nelson said. "Give us time to get to Stringtown." He thought again of his lost saddlebags and pardons. He would have to find his saddlebags and pardons before anyone else did.

CHAPTER 3

In a second-floor office of the Missouri Capital Building in Jefferson City, Senator Saunders stood at the window with his binoculars, watching the side-wheel ferryboat angle against the current and ease into Loman's landing. The steamboat was filled with passengers from Callaway County and points north and east.

"Is your man on the ferry, Judge?" his guest asked as he propped his feet on the senator's desk.

"It's 'Senator' to you. Get your stinking feet off my desk. I haven't been a judge since we left Steelville before the war. Remember, Sheriff Spaid?"

"It's just Spaid now, your highness." He dropped his boots to the floor with a loud clunk.

"He comes every two weeks. Brings me the news of what the high muckety muck army officers are up to in St. Louis," said the senator. "Last I heard they were going after Bloody Bill Anderson and his boys, even if they had to chase them clear into Texas. Relax, have a drink, Spaid. I see him climbing the steps from the landing now." Spaid was always trying to follow in his footsteps. There were too many mistakes in the sheriff's shaded history. He had to get rid of Spaid.

Soon, there was a knock on the door. "Get the door, Sheriff Spaid, get the damn door," Senator Saunders said, letting some of his dislike of Spaid slip out.

Spaid gave Saunders a long look before getting up from his chair and opening the door. He made a gesture with his hand and arm for the man to come in.

"Come in, George. You're out of breath. Lots of steps to climb, coming up from the ferry boat. Have a seat," Saunders said.

"Thank you, sir." George dropped into a chair next to the senator's desk that Spaid had been sitting on.

"Meet my friend from our Steelville days, Sheriff John Spaid," Saunders said.

George stood and shook hands with Spaid, "Glad to meet you, Sheriff Spaid," George said, then dropped back in the chair, sounding even more like he was out of breath.

"Just Spaid, George," he said.

"How are things at Gratiot Street Prison? How many Confederates left in there?" the senator asked, then turned to look out the window again.

"Thinned down some. Yankees pardon them, then send them packing with little more than the worn-out clothes on their backs, and no shoes on their feet. Leave it to the Yankees to try and strip the very hearts out of their prisoners." George turned to look at Spaid.

"It's okay, George. Spaid hates the nigger-loving Yankees as much as we do," whispered the senator, still looking at the river. "Have to keep that kind of talk quiet these days. They have spies and informers all through the capital building."

"I should keep my hatred for the Yankees out of here then," George said.

"Hagan's been raiding down south again. What troops

are they sending against him?" the senator asked.

"They sent one man, undercover, to try and get in with Hagan and his men. Orders are to either capture or pardon him. Pressure is high from Washington to have the guerilla fighters lay down their weapons and go home." George shook his head. "Stop the raiding and killing."

"One man? The guerrillas will have him strung up in less than a week. Know who he is, George?" asked the senator.

"Name's Paintier. Captain Nelson Paintier. He fought for the North but comes from Hagan's stomping grounds.

Senator Saunders turned quickly from the window. "Paintier?"

"Yes, sir, Captain Paintier. He fought the war leading nigger troops back east. Command called him a hero. Some say he's getting a book published about his life when he was a boy in Steelville, when you hanged that slave girl and his father got burned up alive in a fire somebody set."

Saunders stared at Spaid. Killing him was all that came to his mind. "Thank you, George. And please, if you wouldn't care, keep that little story Nelson Paintier's spreading to yourself." Then he took an envelope filled with cash from his desk drawer. "See you next trip." He handed the envelop to his informant and walked him quickly out, then shut the office door.

"You sure were in a hurry to get George gone," said Spaid.

"Paintier? Paintier! I thought you killed that son of a bitch over a decade ago! If he gets his damn book published my run for governor will be over. He's gonna make up some story about us railroading that slave's trial to get her hung. And if he gets it out that we burnt his dad up in their house, we both could hang. Find him, Spaid. Find that damn Paintier and be sure you kill the nigger loving little bastard this time."

Spaid shrugged. "I thought he was in the house, and we

burnt them both up!"

"He sure as hell wasn't, now, was he? You let him get away." The Senator slapped the top of his desk.

"He's a dead man, Senator." Spaid picked up his hat.

Saunders already had the door open for him. He whispered to him as he stepped into the hallway. "It could put both of us behind prison walls for murder if you don't kill him."

CHAPTER 4

The hitch of eight sweat covered mules rounded the last turn on the trace before the steep half mile drop it took into the valley, filled with smoke and haze from the two running blast furnaces of the iron works. Gales pulled the hitch to a stop at a wagon rutted woods path. The body of the second driver lay covered with a tarpaulin tied to the bottom of the double wide seat the driver rode on. Nelson jumped off the back of the stopped wagon and lent a hand to Joshua to join him.

"Where will you take him, mister?" Joshua asked.

"The company men will just bring him back up here to the cemetery near the bluff and bury him today," Gales said, "Glad you two was with us. Drove off those damn killers back there."

"Didn't expect a fight on the way here," Nelson said, "Thanks anyway for the ride."

With a crack of the long reins against the mule team hitch Gales left them and started the decent into the valley below.

Nelson pointed the way for the boy and started the short walk along the wagon path to the bluff and the cemetery. He walked to the bluff's edge and stopped beside a weathered white stone. He had been a proud ten-year-old boy arriving at the ironworks with his family from their Virginia home. He stood behind his mother and little sister, Caroline, on his father's going-west wagon as the oxen strained hard into the yoke, climbing the Stringtown Road that wound along a narrow ridge lined with shanties and cabins.

Caroline leaned on their mother's shoulder singing, like she always did when she was happy. The people along the road watched, tilting their heads, listening to her clear voice singing *"All in the merry month of May, when green buds they were swellin'"* His father walked beside the oxen, urging them to pull harder. Nelson and his sister had named the oxen Bert and Oren.

"Where we going to live?" Nelson asked.

"Your Pa said it was near the top of the hill," his Ma answered.

"Can we walk now, Pa?" Nelson yelled.

"Stay in the wagon. We got a team and a big wagon loaded with ore coming down the hill. It's going to be hard to pass. We got to get way over to the side."

He saw the wagon and the large hitch of oxen coming down the road. The driver had hurried to the lead team and gotten in front to try to stop his lumbering load.

"Get that yoke and wagon off the road," shouted the team driver. "We're carrying a ton of ore. Oxen can't hold her back!"

He felt the panic in his father's voice as he shouted and hit both their oxen hard on the back with the stick. "Gee, ox! Gee over!"

Bert and Oren obeyed his commands, moving far over and knocking down the rails of a yard fence. The oxen were jolted to a stop, hard against the yoke when the front wheel of the wagon jammed against a gate post.

"Ginny, get the kids out. Get away from the wagon," yelled his father.

The ore wagon frame squealed against the wheels as the tongue twisted from the teams not moving together. He heard the crack when the tongue snapped in two. The wagon rolled free and flipped over on its side, skidded past a cabin, smashed into a boulder and catapulted into the air, end over end, down the hill toward them. He jumped from the top of the seat and landed hard on his knees on the rock-strewn yard of the cabin. Looking back, he saw his mother helping Caroline down over the tall wagon wheel. He wanted her to hurry. At the bottom, Caroline caught her foot between the wheel and the rail fence. The thud of the ore wagon tumbling and impacting the road stung Nelson's feet. He saw the wagon spew a red cloud of dust and black hunks of ore into the air. His mother froze, staring up the hill at the wreck coming down on them.

Their oxen broke the yokes and stampeded between the shacks when the lunging wagon and hail of iron ore and dust smashed into the place where his sister had fallen. The red blanket of dust was too thick. He couldn't see her. He could only crawl toward the place he saw her fall. His father was there trying to lift the broken wheel lying across Caroline's chest.

He heard the sucking, wheezing sound that dying cattle make when butchered, except the sound came from his sister, Caroline's crushed throat.

Her eyes looked past their father at her side. They asked for Nelson's help. Her fingers extended and reached for a part of her brother's heart. He reached to grab them, but they fell limply to the ground. He heard his mother cry out, "Caroline!"

There were people all around him crying and speaking to his mother. The women of Stringtown carefully lifted the wheel from his sister. His father lifted her and carried her to the front of one of the cabins. He sat on the edge of the porch with her body across his lap. It was the first time Nelson had seen his dad cry. Two women and a black girl were quickly at his side. The girl reached to brush the dust from his sister's face and open eyes.

His dad pushed her away and shouted, "Get away from her!"

~ ~ ~ ~

It was the next day when the workers placed Caroline's body in a small wooden coffin and buried her in the Stringtown Cemetery. After everyone else had left, Nelson stood beside her grave and looked out across the valley. He noticed the turquoise blue water that flowed from the big spring. She would have liked to sit there smelling the wild blooming lilacs and feeling the wind whip up the valley on its way to lift the hawks soaring above.

He looked again at the turquoise blue water from the spring and then at Joshua stooped in front of the white tombstone.

"Caroline Paintier," Joshua read. "Did you know her?"

"She was my sister." The war had dried up his tears but now some had returned.

"All of those little stones in rows across the cemetery, they're so close together," said Joshua.

"There are a lot of children buried there. Most were only a few months old when they died."

He remembered the weekly prayers his father offered for the dying children. Words like cholera and consumption had little meaning to him then. Whooping cough came and made him sick. His mother had sat through the nights keeping his forehead wet and wiping away the foam from his cough.

"Lucky to have any kids left to grow up," said Joshua.

"Only the strong ones made it, back then in Stringtown."

You made it, Nelson. Must mean you're strong."

"Could mean lots of other things too, Joshua. It could mean I was weak for running away from all of this death when my father died."

"Naw, not you. My ma wasn't strong, was she? Do you think she survived?"

"I don't know. The flood...the current...we should pray your mother is safe with God."

"I want to look for her. Like the man we saw in the brush pile, the searchers need to know where she is."

"I'll help you look for her once we get to Steelville."

The years and the war had changed Stringtown. Only the cemetery had grown. The lean-to huts that the slaves had lived in were crumbled into history, and most of the cabins that he remembered were gone. On the way down Stringtown road, he stopped to brush his hand against a stone fireplace standing in the middle of a bed of charcoal, the remains of the home of someone once his friends. He noticed only a small number of people were still living there to work the forges.

They passed the spot on the road, the spot where Caroline's dark red blood met the bright red clay of Stringtown Road. His eyes were damp. He could still see her reaching, reaching for his hand. He didn't tell Joshua about that horrible day.

"Joshua, go just over yonder and take a look at the ironworks. I've got to get us some grub and a horse."

The boy walked away, looking down, kicking rocks with his toes. Nelson headed over the small ridge toward the company store. The wagon ride had been rough on his leg. His limp was worse.

"Howdy, mister," said a broad-shouldered man who rubbed the side of his face with his leather apron to wipe off the black soot.

"Blacksmith?"

"Yep. What brings you to the ironworks?" he asked.

"Looking for a horse and grub."

"I can take care of getting you something to ride," he said. "See me after you've 'et. Union army took most of the horses from this part of the country. Them the Army didn't get, the bushwhackers took. Do you reckon a mule be okay instead of a horse?"

"Sure, rather have a horse." Nelson said. "Is the mule good and broke?"

"Sure, mister. It's about as broke as a mule ever gets."

Nelson smiled and let that one go.

He headed for the company store. He had a money belt of Yankee dollars but didn't want to draw attention to where he really was from. He took out a couple of gold pieces he'd been carrying before going in.

"Welcome to the Meramec Iron Works, fella," said the clerk. "What goods you looking for?"

"We got caught in the flood. I lost my horse and most else. Boy with me is from Steelville. I'm taking him back there because he lost his mother in the river."

"What's the boy's name?"

"Name's Joshua. He lived with his mother. His dad must have left for the war."

"Would the boy be Joshua Spencer? Some say his dad is traveling with the bushwhackers. His name is Dyer Spencer. He took off right after the war started, came home, found his wife had been bedding down with some Yankee officer guarding the ironworks."

"Boy said his dad just left," Nelson replied.

"'Spect he did. Right after Spencer left, the officer and three escort troopers were shot on the road between here and Rolla. Some say the escort troops had just burned out the Weimeyers and raped their daughter. May have needed killing, some say. Boy's got an aunt, teaches school in Steelville. He stayed with her a lot when his mother was out drinking and such. What you be needing to get outfitted?"

"Lost my sidearm and rifle in the water, so show me one of those new Sharps carbines and that Griswold .36 should do just fine in my holster. I'll also need a skillet, a pan and some food for me and the boy. Reckon that mule the blacksmith is trying to sell me will come with a saddle and some saddlebags, so I'll ride him over to load up."

"That mule! You might be a tad better off and get here quicker if you lead him. You sure know your firearms though, mister. Where did you say you fought?" the storekeeper asked.

He had started toward the blacksmith's barn. "I didn't say."

CHAPTER 5

The mule's stubbornness took hold even more when Nelson and the boy started for Steelville. With both of them on the mule's back, the animal went in circles always turning back to the stable where its long-time mule buddy was braying. Jerking on the reins and pounding on the mule's sides with his boots did little to move it along the road away from the stable. He would have to walk and lead the stubborn animal away from the blacksmith's shop.

About a mile from the ironworks, Nelson stopped and tied the mule up to a fence in front of the old cabin he had helped his dad build.

"Got him far enough away from his mule buddy, we should be able to ride from here on."

"Do you know who lived here?" Joshua asked.

It had been years since he helped carry the flat stones for the foundation and stacked the heavy logs to build the side walls of the cabin. The hard work back then kept the sad memories of how his sister had just died away, for a while.

"Joshua, I want you to stay here for a couple of minutes

and watch that gosh-dang excuse for a mule."

He left the boy and headed down a worn path behind the cabin to an old running spring. He stopped at the edge of the round pool's mirror surface and closed his eyes. The memory of what he had seen there, the baby's face with eyes open, staring at him from below the water's surface — would it still be there when he looked? Afraid to look, he turned and headed back up the trail to the cabin and the boy.

"Whose cabin is this?" Joshua asked.

"Don't know who owns it now. My dad and I built it. We sold it to the Mockbees a few years later when my mother died."

"Mockbee? I've heard that name before. Is this where they lived?"

"Yes. Some of their children are buried over there in the little cemetery with the headstones."

He wished they had time to cross the cabin's field and go there and see the Mockbees' children's graves. The baby he had watched drown lay there next to her older sister. Now he needed to cover the eight miles to Steelville if they were going to make it by dark.

~ ~ ~ ~

Nelson and the boy stopped on the high hilltop ridge overlooking the town of Steelville. It lay spread out along the banks of a stream below. New since he had been there years before, a lot of building had taken place on the valley sides above the creek. He had planned to search some of the river bottoms for the boy's mother and his pardons when they reached Steelville but fooling with the contrary mule had made it too late for that today. Down below the hilltop, much of the town where the two creeks came together had been washed away, leaving only stone foundations and the shell of a former courthouse.

RICHARD O. SNELSON

Years ago, on the day before Mary was hanged, he had climbed a wall to sit outside her cell behind the courthouse. He could still remember the exact words Mary had spoken from the window.

"Sheriff man done told me that tomorrow be the last time I see the morning. What do I believe, with all they done told me this last cold freezing winter and all the hot burning summer? White lawyer man say he gonna save me. Ain't gonna let the sheriff hang no slave child. I tell him he saves me so jail men can bend me over again and poke me. Then they laugh and beat me till the shit done come right out me."

Stumbling from disgust, he ran for home. The next morning, all Steelville and Crawford County stood proud outside the courthouse, as everyone watched the trapdoor drop and the rope snap tight around the fourteen-year-old girl's neck.

Nelson looked at the southwest corner, of what remained of the courthouse, the exact spot he had watched her die. Now there was only bare flood scrubbed ground.

Across from them, on a rise above Yadkin Creek, the bell in the tower of a church pealed out. The church doors were open for the people of Steelville. He knew they were holding a wake for the dead. A wagon pulled up in front of the church. A man ran to the sideboards, lifted a blanket, and fell to his knees, hiding his face. The survivors were praying for the town's dead.

"Over by where the road crosses the creek was a bridge. We lived close by the bridge," Joshua said.

"Where is your aunt's house? Did it get washed away?"

"Up by the schoolhouse on the hill. That's where she teaches."

"Let's cross the creek to the church and try and find her. She must be terrible worried about you."

Joshua led the way down the steep hill and across the creek. The crowd on the church steps got larger, all staring

34

at them, trying to identify the man and boy leading a mule up the hill.

He saw a woman take an uncertain step forward and then another. She covered her mouth with her hands and ran toward them.

"Oh, my God! Oh, my God! Is that you, Joshua?" she cried out as she ran. "I thought you were dead."

Joshua didn't answer. He had stopped with arms at his side and head down. The woman knelt to grab him in her arms. Nelson noticed the beauty of the woman's smile and the radiance caused by the shining tears that crossed her cheeks.

"Say something, Joshua. Say something," she said, hugging him and kissing him on the side of his face.

"I'm sorry. I let her drown," Joshua said.

"Who?" She paused, then said, "Oh, Joshua. You didn't let her drown."

"My ma, I think she drowned...in the river. I was supposed to look after her."

"There was nothing anyone could do. The water came up so fast, so many people are missing," she said, "It's no one's fault. God's will is not always understood." She hugged him tightly and then lifted his chin. "Look here at my face. We can thank God you are safe, here with me," she looked up, "Where did you find him, mister?"

"He found us on the river, rode his horse in, trying to save me and my mom," said Joshua. "His name is Nelson."

"Last name is Paintier, ma'am."

"Thank you, Mr. Paintier. I don't know what I would have done if I had lost this boy. He means more than life to me. His mother is my sister. I'm Ruth Anne Gordon."

"Pleasure, ma'am. Wish it was under better circumstances."

She took Joshua by the hand, "Joshua, come with me. We must go to the church now. Mr. Paintier, is your name spelled P-A-I-N-T-I-E-R?"

RICHARD O. SNELSON

"Why, yes, ma'am, it is. Do you know the name?"

"I can't remember where. Anyway, please come to my house later. I'll fix supper for both you and Joshua."

"I need to find a place to tie the mule, and get cleaned up, then I'll be there."

"Most of the town along the creek is gone, but I have an empty barn up on the ridge by my house," she said, "I won't mind if you use it. I'll send Joshua for you when supper's ready."

"Thanks, Mrs. Gordon."

"Miss." She glanced back over her shoulder as they walked up the hill toward the church, her arm clutching Joshua again and again to her side.

~ ~ ~ ~

After leading the mule up the hill and tying it in the barn, Nelson returned to the church. He wanted to look for his father's grave in the church cemetery. When he passed the church window, he could see Joshua sitting on the floor, his chin on his knees, alongside a blanket-covered corpse. He watched Ruth Anne kneel beside the boy and push his hair back from his eyes.

The lamplight that came through the church windows created a walkway he followed through the granite and limestone markers of the graveyard that crowded against the church on the steep hillside.

He stopped in front of a narrow white stone and ran his finger across a boy child's name, he did not recognize, and then still along the 1Yr 6M 22D, spelling out another short life of the times past. His hand brushed the top of each stone as he walked on, searching.

Nelson knelt at the foot of his father's grave and bowed his head. The lamplight from the church window lit the tombstone's face and caused dark shadows in the deeply carved letters. He looked up to see Miss Gordon standing near him in the light from the church's window.

"I didn't mean to frighten you, Mr. Paintier."

"A bit, Miss Gordon."

"Is this a relative of yours?"

"My father's grave. He was murdered the day before I left Steelville. I wasn't sure where they buried him."

"I'm sorry, Mr. Paintier. You've been gone from here a long time?"

"More that fifteen years," he said, still kneeling by the tombstone.

"Are you back here for a while?" she asked and quickly said, "I'm sorry. That was rude and not any of my business."

"I thought a lot about coming back to this valley all during the war. I plan to stay here. My home will always be here."

"They found my sister's body, Mr. Paintier, Joshua is in the church beside her. I'm going to gather him up, and if you could wait for us in front of the church we'll go up to my house and I'll feed you both."

"Thank you, ma'am. I'm sorry you lost your sister."

Ruth Anne gently pressed his shoulder and then turned and walked away.

~ ~ ~ ~

He waited at the bottom of the church steps for Ruth Anne and the boy to return. Seeing his father's grave for the first time sent him back to the night before he fled north. He had run away when the trapdoor opened, and Mary fell through. The shouting drunken crowd had been pushing and shoving each person trying to get closer to the gallows before she fell. It sickened him. He caught sight of four men outside his home lighting torches. When they saw him, he yelled to warn his father and then turned and fled.

Ruth Anne came down the church steps, "Joshua must

have gone ahead."

She led the way down the long hill and across the creek at the bottom. Going up the steep hill to her house, she stopped and turned to him. The serious look on her face worried him.

"Some of the old timers said you were run out of town before the war. Did you go fight for the north?"

"You get right to the heart of things, don't you, ma'am?"

"School teachers learn to ask pointed questions, Mr. Paintier."

"Yes, I fought for the north." He wasn't sure what to say next.

"It's all right, sir. It's time we all heal from the pain of so much death."

"If you're wondering why I came back, it's partly because of what happened to my father."

"If you're willing to tell me?"

"The sheriff and his gang burned our house and killed my father. They were trying to kill me for trying to help save a slave girl," he said. "I have some of the answers to what happened. I only have to put them together."

"You waited a long time to come back, Mr. Paintier. Why so long?"

"I thought for a while I would never come back, but the war changed that."

He remembered charging over the wounded and dead Negro bodies who had fought ahead at his command. A Negro sergeant dragged Nelson away from the swarm of butternut Confederate troops coming to stick a bayonet through him, the black troops' white commanding officer. The black soldiers had fought bravely and had sealed his fate and conviction to return to tell the true story about slave Mary.

They started again toward her house. She had gotten quiet.

The stoop of Ruth Anne's house sat bare. The windows were dark. She went to the door and called out for Joshua, but no answer.

"I'll get a lantern, Mr. Paintier. He may have gone up to the barn to check on the mule."

He saw the flicker of a match through the window and then the glow of the coal-oil lantern that framed her outline. He breathed in the picture of her standing there. Her youth and beauty had made a strong impression on his lonely heart. She returned with the lantern and turned up the hill to the barn.

"He's not in the house. I wonder why he didn't wait for me at the church?"

"I talked to him some at the river. He kept telling me he was responsible for losing his mother from the floating roof they were on. I think he was ashamed to see you, Miss Gordon."

He noticed the glow of the woman's black hair as she held the lantern above her head to light the way through the barn. He tried not to stare when realizing he was alone in an empty barn with a beautiful woman he wanted to know so much more about.

"Mule's gone. I left him tied tight in the stall."

"Could he have gotten loose?"

"Don't think so."

He reached for the handle of the lantern, her fingers were soft and warm against his. Her fingers lingered before releasing the lantern.

"I put the saddle here on the stall divider. It's gone too."

"We have to stop him, Mr. Paintier. He's gone looking for his dad. Dyers riding with Confederate guerrilla fighters turned bushwhackers. They still rob and kill without reason."

"As soon as its light we can get a search party to look for him," he suggested.

"Mr. Paintier, a search party wouldn't stand a chance of

finding him. The bushwhackers are like a pack of ghosts. If they fade into the deep timber with the boy, I'll never see him again."

"I need to have a good horse. I'll go in the morning at first light."

CHAPTER 6

His nose tingled from the smell of fresh-baked bread even before he saw the outline of the woman walking out of the dark barn, leading a saddled horse.

"I hope this mare will do, Mr. Paintier. I've been keeping her hidden from the raiders," she said.

"Looks like a fine bay to me."

"There's a loaf of bread in the saddlebags and some fried-up bacon wrapped up with it, for when you get hungry."

"Thank you, ma'am."

"Can you find him, Mr. Paintier?"

"I don't know, Miss Gordon."

He grabbed his carbine from the corner of the barn, opened the breach, and chambered a cartridge. He pointed it out the barn door, aiming across the iron sights, and then lowered the hammer before dropping the loaded weapon into the saddle's scabbard. He drew the pistol and checked each chamber for a load, and then slipped it back into his hip holster.

He tugged the saddle horn, and easily slipped his fingers under the girth. The bay had sucked in a big breath when it had been saddled, so he walked the horse outside and then pulled the slack out of the girth. He dropped the stirrups two holes lower to match his six-foot, two-inch frame, slipped his left foot in the stirrup and mounted the bay.

It took only a glance at the path outside the barn for Nelson to tell the direction the boy and mule were headed.

"I see where he went. It looks like back toward the ironworks. Any idea where he might go from there?"

"Mr. Paintier, Joshua's dad has come back only a few times since he had troubles with my sister," she said. "Joshua's mother always kept it kind of secret when his dad was around. I didn't always know he had even been here."

"Has his dad talked any, I mean about quitting the bushwhackers and coming back to Steelville?" The lost pardons and the boy's father might offer a door to a meeting with the bushwhackers.

"I think he would fancy having a wife and family. Union troops have been close to catching his bunch more than one time," she said. "He said last time he was here several of the men riding with him wanted to quit and come home."

"I'll be checking the ironworks first but doubt if Joshua knows where to go from there. I think the best cover for a bushwhacker would be deep in the Huzzah cave areas."

"Bring him home, Mr. Paintier."

"Nelson, just Nelson."

"May God guide you and bring you both back safely, Nelson."

He tipped the wide brim of the hat she had given him and nodded a thank you for her prayer. Kicking the horse into a fast gallop he headed up the ridge toward the ironworks.

~ ~ ~ ~

As he crossed the flat leading into the ironworks blast furnaces, he saw his mule tied in front of the blacksmith's shop. The smithy looked up, holding a steel rod with a bright orange tip in the air. It looked like it had just come out of his charcoal fired forge.

"Boy said you would be coming for the mule. He tied it to the post when he couldn't get it to leave here and took off walking west along the Stringtown Road. Been gone about four hours now," the blacksmith said. "Where's he headed?"

"Looking for something he's lost," Nelson replied. "You can have the mule to keep. I'll get the saddle on the way back."

"Best you keep the carbine across your lap while traveling toward Rolla. Bushwhackers keep outriders posted along the trace in that direction."

"Thanks. If the boy shows up back here, see if you can keep him around until I get back."

He turned the bay and spurred it into a lope up the narrow wagon path they called the Stringtown Road. The rocky ridgeback trail showed no signs of footprints. He could only hope to spot the boy ahead.

After an hour-long ride, he drew the winded bay to a walk. The mare needed to cool out. Sure, the boy hadn't gotten that far, Nelson turned back.

Still slowed to a walk, he saw a broken branch at rider level. Someone had ridden off the trace and into the woods. He slipped his foot out of the stirrup and slid to the ground to check a well-worn deer trail that led south. He ran his fingers over the many scratches he saw on the rocks. Horseshoes. Riders had used the deer trail for cover and turned off the trace to head southeast toward the Huzzah River basin.

The isolated trail and the cover it provided convinced him the riders had been guerrilla raiders. He put his foot in the stirrup and eased back up on the saddle.

He lightly touched the bay's side with his heels and turned past the broken branch down the deer trail going south. Only a couple hours of light remained. Rebel sharpshooters would wait for his kind of fool during the war, and the thought of them brought a tightness in the back of his neck and sent a muscle contraction down the side of his arm.

Boulders the size of log cabins lined the edges of the trail as it wound toward the Huzzah basin. A thick forest covered the trail with limbs high above. The limbs kept out the little light that still remained of the day. The horse would follow the narrow trail on its own when full darkness came.

~ ~ ~ ~

Only a slight breeze coming from the west crossed his path when darkness came. Twice within the last few minutes he stopped the bay to listen for sounds that were masked by the squeaks of his saddle, and the short sniffing breaths of the horse. The third time, he pulled up suddenly, but still, he could not pinpoint any pursuer. He turned off the trail to his right and stopped the bay. Rubbing the horse's neck didn't help to quiet the nervous animal.

He took one foot from the stirrup and stood to swing his leg to dismount. The strike came from behind him. He lunged forward at the shock of the hit to his back and shoulders. The growl behind him from a huge cat still on the horse's rump shocked him. He jumped for the ground at the same time the bucking horse launched him into the air. He tried his best to land on his feet. Instead, he landed bent over smashing his face into the tops of his knees. Stunned, he stood and reached to draw. The holster hung empty at his side. He heard tree branches snap as the stampeding horse bucked to throw the demon on its back off and then the sound came of the horse running hard back up the trail toward the trace.

The crunch of dry leaves directly in front of him sent tremors through his gut. The guttural snarl of a panther came from close to his left, it was moving slowly around him. He waited for the attack. It would come when the cat grew tired of tormenting its trapped quarry. Nelson turned to follow the sounds and keep facing the animal. He swept his hand out over the ground in front, feeling for the big Griswold .36. He froze when a wet blast of spittle peppered his hand and arm. The animal's slowness to attack convinced Nelson that he might have a chance to avoid being eaten alive.

He picked up two rocks he had tripped over and tried to guess how far away the snarling panther was poised. Oh, the hell with it! He crashed the rocks together, stomped his feet, and ran at the panther with the blood curdling yell the charging Rebs had used to scare the hell out of him. He heard the thrashing of the big cat's paws as it recoiled at the sudden attack from the strange prey. He threw both rocks at the cat's sounds, heard them thump flesh, and then backed off from his feigned attack to wait. He heard only the wind. The panther had pulled back.

It took Nelson only a few seconds of sweeping his foot over the ground to find his pistol. Holding his aim pointed toward the last place he had heard the panther. He backed off the trail and against a boulder. The security of the cocked pistol in his hand helped to cut down the churning in his empty stomach.

Finding Joshua had taken priority overeating the fresh-baked bread stored in the saddlebags of a horse that must still be running, headed toward the safety of its barn. Thinking of greener pastures, the beautiful woman back in Steelville didn't help his hurting back. Being pressed up against some cold rock in guerrilla territory waiting for an enemy blacker than night, wanting nothing more than to eat him, was hardly encouraging. The boy's running away had distracted him from searching for the pardons. He wanted to find the boy and get back to the river to search.

His worry increased when he heard the clatter of two horses coming up the rocky trail from the south at a run. He heard the heavy breathing of the two horses as the riders went by and stopped a short distance up the trail. Nelson heard them talking but couldn't make out what they said. Then he heard the horses coming back at a slow walk.

"Hey, Johnny Reb. We heard you yelping up here."

"What you hollering like that for? Come on out. We're your friends."

If he didn't show himself now, the two men would have their whole band out beating the brush for him in the morning.

"I'm here. Panther jumped me. I think I scared his black hide off with that yell."

He could barely make out the two men. They had dismounted and stood behind their horses.

"We can't see much of you, mister. If you be packin' best give it to Charley here."

"Can't see you neither. Reckon I won't be giving up this iron to somebody could be a Yankee."

"Hell, man. Me and Charley be about as far from a Yankee as we can get. Come on out, and we'll take you to meet the rest of our boys."

"'Spect you ain't Yankees. Lost my horse, so I need to double up."

"You can ride behind Charley, he's the little one. For me, mister, gonna' need that pistol. Boys will skin me alive if I bring a stranger in camp still carrying."

He kept his pistol in his hand and crossed the trail to the men and their horses. He reluctantly gave up his pistol to the guerrilla and mounted up behind the one called Charley. They turned down the trail toward the south.

"Ain't far, mister. Couple of our boys was sitting on the cliff over the cave when they heard you yell."

He hadn't planned to be thrown in with the guerrillas this quickly. It would take some leg flipping, jig dancing to get out of the hornet's nest he just got swept into alive.

The ride down to the river took only a few minutes. They turned west along the bank of the Meramec and then up a steep hill to dismount at the mouth of a cave. It didn't surprise him that no cooking fires were burning. Clearly, he had been riding with hunted men hiding from federal troops. Charley led him to the back wall and a flat spot with an empty blanket.

"Here's a place for tonight. Morning, we going to get a better look at you. Figure out what the hell you want, coming down that trail in the dark."

He couldn't argue with a cave full of bushwhackers. He had tried to get an exact count of how many men were bunked in the cave, but it was too dark, Sitting on the blanket with his back to the wall, he watched, trying to see what the men were doing. Someone was coming for him. He could just make out the two men on the way.

"Stand up, mister."

The two men grabbed his coat and yanked him to his feet, pulling his arms behind him, to tie them.

"Charley thought it would be fine, just leaving you sitting here. We don't think so. Want to know who you are and why you followed this trail."

"My name is Nelson Paintier. Started this morning from Steelville looking for a boy. He ran off last night."

"Was it your boy?"

"Nope. Boy's name is Joshua Spencer. I had found him the first time in the middle of the river on top of his house with his mother. I was lucky to save the boy. Took him home to Steelville."

"Gonna tie you right out front to that oak tree, so you get a good look at that river in the morning. Same river we gonna drown your lying ass in before noon comes."

The two men yanked him off his feet and dragged him

across the cave to the oak tree in front.

"We don't take to no strangers coming down that trail."

"Told you, I was looking for the boy. That's all. Then a panther ran off my horse, or I'd be gone."

"Don't do no good making up shit stories. We're gonna kill you anyhow."

He hadn't noticed any hints of recognitions at his mention of the Spencer name. Still, he was sure this bunch knew Dyer Spencer and were probably riding with him, and he settled back against the oak for the rest of the night. He hoped he would stay dry tomorrow.

CHAPTER 7

Nelson didn't like his second time of spending the night against a tree any more than the many other times he had. Dawn showed the Meramec River running clear as glass.

He watched a beaver's wake as it carried a large willow branch toward a deep cut in the bank. He had never gotten over the way he killed the first beaver he trapped in the Meramec when he was a boy. The drowning stake for his beaver set hadn't worked. The big beaver circled the tie staking, dragging the double jaw trap on its hind foot. Nelson tried to push it to the bottom and drown it. Up the beaver would come, and he would have to try again. He wanted to kill it fast so it wouldn't suffer. He could think of no way to get the trap off the animal in the water. Finally, when the beaver's head came up for air, Nelson hit toward it with a stout club. The beaver dove again. The next time it came up, Nelson struck hard. The beaver's nose shattered, and it swam in a darkening circle of blood. Two more times he struck at the animal's nose and head. Finally, the stunned beaver rolled over and floated to the top of the water. He removed the beaver from the trap and carried it to the bank. He waded back to the water-set and removed the stake and trap and threw them into the deep water far out in the river. When he looked back, the shattered beaver had crawled to the edge of the river, trying to reach the safety of the water. This time his blow killed the animal. He felt sick.

The thought crossed his mind more than once during the night that he could be down there under the water fighting for his breath before the day ended. He had enough looking at rivers to last a good long time, and the thought of going back in the Meramec, this time head down, scared him.

Just before dawn he saw a rider leave, cross the river, and head south. The rest of the men were stirring in the cave. They still had built no cook fires. He tried to twist around the tree to watch the bushwhackers behind him.

"Next time I see that head come around the tree, I'm going to shoot it off," said one of the three men headed for the oak and him.

One of the men with a carbuncled face stood with his nose pressing tight to the side of Nelson's face.

"Want to tell us again, about what you're doing on this here trail?"

"Told you, looking for a boy," Nelson said.

"Untie him. Gonna take him for his last swim."

Too many folks had experienced the ruthlessness of the guerrillas still holding out in the southern Missouri hills. They would not need a reason to kill him. They liked to kill. The men drug him down the steep slope toward the cold Meramec waters.

"Tie that rope 'round his feet. Throw it over the limb hanging out over the water. Gonna sink that lying head deep."

The men pulled the rope tight and lifted him across the top of the water into a head-down position.

"Sink him. Sink his sorry ass," the bushwhacker said.

Not certain the bushwhackers were just testing him, he sucked in the deepest breath his lungs would hold before his head went under. He needed it all before they lifted him back out. It took several gasps to get some breath back in his lungs. The dead beaver haunted him again. He didn't want to die this way.

"Gonna give you a last chance, here, mister. You been spying on us, haven't you?"

"Told you, look-"

Nelson took a mouth full of water on the last word. He held back the impulse to choke until his lungs emptied of air. The cough that followed filled his throat and windpipe with water. Still, they didn't lift him.

He saw the beaver with the crushed nose swimming in a bloody circle before he passed out.

Then slaps and voices trying to bring him back to consciousness.

"Shit! I think we killed the bastard."

"What boy? What boy were you looking for?"

The choking and coughing stopped before he could answer, "Steelville boy."

"Tell him what boy. His name."

"Joshua...Joshua...Spencer," Nelson said.

The ropes were off his legs, and someone had sat him up on the riverbank. Four of the bushwhackers were kneeling around him.

"Look at me, mister. My name's Jim Hagan. My men all know I'd just as soon kill you, best you do as well. Now, why are you looking for Dyer's boy?"

"He ran off. Looking for his dad."

One of the men pushed to Nelson's side. "They told me you saved my boy from the flood. Ain't no loss if that whore wife of mine is drowned, but my boy, he was, okay?" Dyer Spencer asked.

"He was yesterday morning. Lost his tracks after the ironworks. I'm sure he was coming looking for his pa."

Nelson tried to get to his feet.

"He may still be up on the trace. Saddle up, men. We're going to tie you back up, so you'll be handy to drown if we don't find my boy," Dyer said.

The sun had dropped behind the river bluff when the riders returned. He didn't see Joshua until the boy slid off the back of his dad's horse. Dyer came quickly to Nelson's side and cut the ropes holding him.

"My boy wants to see you. Come on," Dyer said, heading for the front of the cave.

Joshua smiled when he saw Nelson walking toward him. Dyer stopped Nelson to say, "You know we kill strangers in these here parts. They don't have half the chance of a fat boar pig at a hog roast."

"Is that what happened to a certain Union officer and his escort troops a while back?" Nelson asked.

"Is that what folk are saying about me and the boys?"

"Don't matter to me what you've done, Spencer. God damn war is nearly over now."

"Ain't over for us till we say so, mister. Some of the boys caught those Yankee troops right after they hanged Ralph Biggs. The troops had pulled him out of his house and strung him up in the yard right in front of his wife and kids. Bastards were looking to loot his place," Dyer said.

"You should have turned them in to the troop headquarters at Rolla."

"They'd shot us before we got to the fort gate. Nobody can do no wrong down here, but us Rebs."

"Don't you ever think about coming home? Being a father to the boy?"

"Some of us want to go home bad. It don't do no good thinking about something that ain't gonna happen."

Nelson looked at Dyer, "There's no talk about any money being offered on your head, Spencer. The money is all being offered on Anderson and his bunch." At least that had been the case before Nelson had left for his assignment.

He hoped what he had just told Dyer would sink in. Dyer and the boy left him and walked to the front of the cave and sat talking. Soon he saw Dyer give his son a hug and then head back.

"The boy can't stay. It's not safe for him to be with us. There are still some troops from out of Rolla looking for us," Dyer said. "Take the boy back to Miss Gordon. Ask her to look after his schooling and a place to live. You can head out in the morning."

"You fellows didn't happen to find my bay horse up on the trace, did you?" asked Nelson.

"Joshua had it. He caught the mare coming down the trace right after dark. Some of the boys got her, rubbing some hog grease on the cuts on its flank. Lucky that big cat didn't have you for his supper," Dyer said.

"Scared me so bad I didn't want any supper."

"Nelson, thanks for saving my boy. He told me how you rode into the river and lost your horse and all. Be proud to have you come back and join up with us. Talk is we might head down into Arkansas."

"I'll take him back, Dyer. Won't be joining you now, though. Got some things to settle yet in Steelville."

"They brought your saddle and an extra blanket and put it by the back wall there. Curl up till morning. I'll have Joshua bring you the .36 in the morning, that way my boys won't be nervous about you having it while they sleep," Dyer said.

The dirt floor of the cave would feel like a feather bed after the previous couple of days. With the saddle as his pillow rest would finally come.

~ ~ ~ ~

"Wake up. Damn it to hell, Nelson. Wake up," Dyer kicked his saddle.

"They got Union Troops sitting all along the river with their rifles pointing up here just waiting for morning. Must have followed us when we were looking for my boy."

He stood and tried to reason what Dyer had just said. It wouldn't matter who he had helped win the war to the rifles waiting out front, he would be just another bushwhacker. Shooting their way out while riding breakneck down a steep hill would cost more than half of Dyer's men.

"Keep Joshua with you. We got to hope those Yankees don't know about the back entrance to this cave and how we are going to ride out of it, a long way back up the ridge at daybreak,"

He followed Dyer to the front of the cave. Dyer motioned to stay low, they looked over the rock wall set up in front of the cave. "Those troops are dug in down there. They're planning on holding you here," Nelson said.

"It won't work. When we get out, we're going to lead them away from you and the boy. Take 'em out five or six miles and turn on them when the land is good for a fight. Get the saddle on your bay tightened up," Dyer said, leaving him and going to pick up his saddled horse.

Ordered into a single file line by Hagan, Dyer led the way through the cave passages. Three of the men carried oil-soaked torches that came into view in front of Nelson when the passage straightened out. Each man held the tail of the horse in front of him making a chain of horses and men winding their way through the blackness.

He heard the splashing of water and felt the cold as their path took them through a shallow underground river. Out of the water, the air got colder, flowing around them and coming from somewhere up ahead. The line stopped, and the torches were put out. No one spoke. Not a horse whinnied, a well-trained army of men and animals. He guessed that pickets were being sent forward out of the cave checking for Union soldiers. The line moved again, up a steep, narrow passage that broke out of the cave on the high ridge behind it. The men led their horses on for more than a hundred yards, then stopped to mount on Hagan's command. Nelson saw Dyer headed for him and the boy.

"When you hit the trace up ahead, turn right and ride like hell. We're going to circle back and give those troopers some hell, draw them off west behind us. Take good care of my son. I won't forget you saving him from the flood." He leaned over his saddle and gave his son a short hug. "So long, boy."

Only the soft squeaks of worn saddles and the brushing sound of the horse's tails whisking across their rumps gave away their leaving the cave area on the ride north, up the trail, past the boulder where the panther had attacked. The lead riders broke out on to the Rolla trace when the shooting started, an ambush the bushwhackers didn't expect. The guerilla riders circled back and then spread to the right and left of the deer trail in a skirmish line. They advanced at a gallop on the ambushers waiting on the road. A blood-curdling Rebel yell broke out to his right and spread across the line of bushwhackers. He rode at the back of the advancing line and heard the shots first from the Union riders who snuck up behind them from the river.

He yelled to warn Spencer and turned to see two Yankee troops, in the lead, charging headlong firing as they came. He slapped Joshua's horse on the rump and drew his pistol. Dyer shot first and one rider went down. The second trooper fell from a bullet through his chest. He watched the blue uniformed trooper tumble from his horse. He looked in disbelief at the smoking gun in his right hand.

"I'm hit, Nelson," yelled Dyer.

He spurred his horse to Dyer's side. Joshua followed close behind.

"Took one in the shoulder." Dyer slumped in his saddle.

"Let me help my dad," Joshua said.

"Stay mounted, son," Nelson said, headed east into the heavy brush. "Both of you follow up quick."

"I'll try to stay with you," shouted Dyer.

Nelson reined the horse off the traveled trail and into the timber. He tried to pick a path around the fallen limbs and rotten logs so the wounded Dyer could follow without falling off his horse. Nelson looked back when his horse jumped a dead tree to see if Dyer made it across. The wounded man leaned forward over the saddle horn, holding on with his good arm and following close behind.

"Keep going. Go harder," yelled Dyer, "They'll have scouts looking for us when the shooting stops."

Nelson quickened the pace and pushed aside the low limbs that grabbed and tore at his head and arms.

They traveled on the side of a razorback ridge with narrow breaks that dropped so steeply that the horses kept sliding down the side. The struggle to climb back out slowed the pace. As the ridge got steeper, he had to lean forward over the horse's neck to keep it from going over backward.

"I don't see him," Joshua said. "He was right behind us."

"There's a stand of cedars ahead. We can wait and let him catch up there."

"He's coming," Joshua said.

Dyer's riderless horse struggled up the steep bank behind them and trotted to their side before stopping. The saddle and the side of the horse were covered with mud and dirt. He guessed the horse had fallen climbing out of a gully they had crossed.

"Slide down and grab the horse, Joshua. I'll go back for him."

He found Dyer slowly climbing up the edge of the last steep ridge break.

"Take Joshua and get out of here, Paintier."

"He's waiting up ahead. He caught your horse. He won't leave without you. Come on."

He cleared a stirrup for Dyer's foot and lifted him by his

good arm to the back of his saddle.

Back at the cedars, Joshua pushed his dad's horse over next to a log, so his dad could climb back into his own saddle.

"Get me to Stringtown. I've got friends there," Dyer said.

Nelson took the reins to lead Dyer's horse, then headed along the ridge again toward the ironworks and Stringtown.

"If we're lucky the troops won't follow us. Running the ridge trail to the ironworks is dangerous," Dyer said. "There's a cabin at the ironworks we can hide in."

They approached Stringtown from the valley side of the open pit iron mine at the crest of Stringtown Road. He stopped the horses out of sight of the mine and dismounted.

"Joshua, ride your horse past the iron mine down the Stringtown Road. Don't stop in Stringtown. Ride on down to the bottom of the hill. Circle back from there. We'll wait here for you," Nelson said. "See if there are any Union troops along the Stringtown Road."

"What if troops are there?" Joshua asked.

"Ride by them and head straight for your aunt's in Steelville," Nelson said. "I'll take care of getting your dad someplace safe."

More than two hours passed, and Joshua hadn't returned. The troops had to be searching the Stringtown cabins for the guerrillas. He bandaged Dyer's wound, and the bleeding slowed from the pressure he kept on it. They sat hidden in the thick brush until darkness came.

"Let's get you up on this horse, Dyer. We're going to head around the ironworks. I know a place not far from here where you can hide till that wound stops bleeding and I can get some water and grub for you," he said, helping Dyer get on his horse.

In less than an hour they reached the empty dogtrot cabin Nelson's father had built. He took Dyer around the cabin to a shed built on a rock wall foundation. Inside he motioned for Dyer to stand back. Using his buck knife, he pried away the loose boards in the floor to reveal a large iron gate cover. He struggled to lift the hinged cover nearly frozen in place with rust. With the cover open, he motioned for Dyer to come.

"There are steps going down, and ledges on each side where the slaves slept. Owner locked them down here for the night. No one will find you here."

He went down the steps with Dyer's arm over his shoulder and then lowered him to one of the rock ledges.

"It's too dark to see much. It does feel like your shoulder has stopped bleeding."

"I think the shot went clean through," Dyer said.

"Going to leave you some hardtack. I'll come back tomorrow to take care of your wound."

Nelson had remembered the bacon and bread in the saddlebags and went to fetch it and water the horses. He took the horses down the hill to the spring pool and stood watching them drink.

The memory of the day he caused the baby to drown in the spring pool water would never stop haunting him. Mary had been a good nurse to the baby, always watching it, keeping it away from the spring. A young boy teasing the fourteen-year-old girl had distracted her for just those few minutes. Before her trial, he had tried to tell them that she didn't drown the baby. His pleading for her came too late and did no good.

He tied the horses in the woods and went back to the slave-pit hiding place. He gave Dyer the food and a canteen of water.

"Bringing a doc back here will get me killed. The Yankees will find me for sure then."

"I'll get some things we used for medicine in the war and try and patch you up."

At the top of the pit, he closed the grate and covered it with loose boards.

"Damn, Nelson! You better come back. Don't you leave me in this shit hole place," Dyer yelled.

"I'll be back tomorrow."

He hadn't told Dyer about the lost saddlebags and pardons he needed to find. Nelson flexed the horse around the thick brush and trees that lined the south banks of the Meramec River. The search for his old horse, Blue, and the saddlebags took him through the mud and around the trash left by the flood. He rode past a group of townspeople probing and stooping to search the piles of brush left by the high water. They told him the count of missing and dead had climbed to more than twenty. He didn't ask if they had found the mare and his saddlebags. It would tie him to a roll of Yankee pardons and get him shot.

When he rode past another brush pile, he found his warhorse. The mare lay half covered in the mud. When he tried to get closer, the bay shied at the dead horse. Nelson forced his horse to circle the dead mare.

Nelson sucked a deep chest-raiser breath. "Oh, shit!"

The saddlebags were gone, and a lone set of footprints led off toward the ironworks. Following the tracks in the muddy river bottom would be easy.

Burning her body would be impossible. He'd have to leave her to nature. He swept his hat across his chest in a last salute to his warhorse. "So long, Blue." Finding the saddlebag and pardons could mean he would stay alive.

He turned the horse slowly and then kicked into a fast walk to follow the tracks. The tracks circled several large heaps of trash and brush before continuing in the direction of the ironworks and Stringtown. When the tracks left the muddy river bottom and joined a wagon road, Nelson lost the trail. He circled back a ways to get a closer look at the unevenness in the two footprints, then turned toward the dogtrot cabin to pick up Dyer's horse. Whoever found the saddlebags walked with a bad limp.

CHAPTER 8

When Nelson rode into Ruth Anne's barnyard at daylight, leading Dyer's horse, Joshua stuck his straw covered head out of the haymow door to tell him, "The troops were searching the cabins in Stringtown. I couldn't get back. Is my dad safe?"

"He's safe for now."

"He got shot. Is he going to be, okay?"

"I'm going back, take some clean bandages and food for him." He climbed down from his saddle.

"Can I go?" Joshua asked.

"I'm going alone this time. In a couple of days when he's better, you can go see him."

Nelson slipped the saddles off the horses and led them to the rear stall in the barn. He ran his hand over the deep scratches the panther had ripped in the bay's haunches. He needed to doctor them with a heavy coat of bacon grease. He would darn sure put a quick release tie on his holster before he went on another night ride in Ozark panther country. He had felt naked searching for the pistol in the darkness.

"Joshua, could you slide some hay down? Feed the horses for me."

"Sure. Oh, my aunt said two men were here yesterday. She said they were nosing around asking questions about the stranger. She wanted you to come to the house when you got back."

"Is she up yet?" Nelson asked.

"I saw her feeding the chickens, a while ago."

Nelson needed rest but was worried about the men asking questions. Could they have found his saddlebags and the pardons? He climbed the two steps, crossed Ruth Anne's porch and knocked. He turned at the clanging of a can at the back of the house and looked over the edge of the porch railing.

"Mr. Paintier," Ruth Anne said. She closed the gate to the chicken coop and set the feed bucket on the ground and joined him at the front of the house.

"Miss Gordon, I rode in a few minutes ago and wanted to tell you about Dyer."

"Joshua told me he had been shoot. Is he hurt bad?"

"His wound is going to need some treating. He said we couldn't take him to a doctor."

"I don't think there are any medical supplies left. All of them have been stolen or used up."

What she said didn't surprise him. Left before with little supplies to help his wounded, he had gotten by with treatments from plants and trees. He would find them later to take.

"I was sorry we had to bury Joshua's mother before he got back. I told him we just couldn't wait for him."

"I'm sorry I couldn't get him back in time."

"I think he understood. It helped to cheer him up when he got to see his father."

"Dyer got hit in the shoulder. I found a place for him to hide at the cabin my father and I built, over near the iron works."

"Did Joshua tell you about the men asking questions about you? It worried me and I told them you were just an old friend."

Nelson got the feeling a battle was brewing between him and his past. "I think I know who they are. Someone from my past knows I'm back and writing a book. It has them worried what I might write, I think." If he had to bet, he'd say the former Crawford County judge and his henchman, Sheriff Spaid, were out to make sure Nelson didn't publish their secrets.

He changed the subject, not wanting to scare her, and asked if she would get together some bandages later that day for him to take for Dyer after it got dark. He wanted to tell her he wasn't worried, but the missing pardons would make what he said a lie. He needed to find a place to stay, away from her house and school so she would be safe.

"I'm going to walk through town this morning. See what's left down there," he said.

"I'll have the bandages ready for you this afternoon."

"If the boy could scrape off some red-oak bark we can mix it with water for a disinfectant. It'll help to hurry up healing Dyer's wound."

"I'm sure he would love to help his father."

He walked down the hill past the schoolhouse to the valley floor. Down along the creek he passed the rocks that had supported the general store and remembered the winter nights when the old timers sat with their feet against the pot-bellied stove in the store and told tales about when they were boys. He avoided the courthouse and waded across Yadkin Creek. He walked toward a man and woman prying boards off their wrecked home. The home had been pushed from its foundation by the flood.

"Expect I could give you folks a hand. If you'd let me?" he said.

"Ain't no hurry getting it done. Least ways not till

winter gets here." The man rested the head of his axe on a log.

The woman clamped both her hands to her hips, "Might not be so in a man's eye. We can't sleep in this wreck of a house waiting for another flood to come. It'll wash us clean away next time."

"I can give you a hand with that board, ma'am." He pulled the broken board from the house framing.

The woman said, "We went to bury Mrs. Spencer yesterday. Ruth Anne said your father was Levi Lane Paintier. Both of us knew you and your dad."

"I thought I remembered you. Would it be, let's see, Ellis and May Oliver?"

"You do remember," May said.

"I do, ma'am. My dad always said you were probably kin folks."

"We always wondered what happened to you, son. We thought you might have been killed the same night as your dad," Ellis said.

"The riders that burned our house tried to kill me. I hid and headed out of here the next day."

"You know it seemed peculiar. The fire that killed your dad, it was the night they hung that terrible girl," May said.

His gut twisted, but he let her comment slide. She didn't know Mary like he did. "It was more than peculiar."

"Where you been all this time?" May asked.

He took a deep breath before answering quietly, "Traveling a bit, fighting a war."

Ellis replied first, "You don't have to say that in a whisper. May and me, we wanted to leave things as they were before the war. A lot of the folks here feel the same way."

May stood with her hands on her hips again looking at him, "We've been beat on by both sides. Yankees stomp in here and burn folks out if they think they've been helping the rebels. The damn rebels come at us out of the woods, more bushwhacker then soldiers, I'd say. Kill and loot folks for no reason at all. So, it don't matter which side you fought on, both just as bad as the other. Lots of folks here hate the bushwhackers more than they do the Yankees."

"I understand what you are saying, Mrs. Oliver. We can all pray that the madness ends soon."

"Me and my husband say a prayer like that when we take our evening dinner."

He hated to break into the good thoughts of prayer, but he needed to know more about the men looking for him. "By the way, did you happen to see a couple fellows riding through here asking questions about me?"

"Them fellows stopped up at the teacher's house and then rode off. We didn't see them up close," Ellis said.

"You might ask Ned Gunther. He was up on the ridge when they went by. They stopped to talk to him for a couple minutes." May pointed up the hill. "He lives in the last house, before heading on the trace to the ironworks."

"I think I'll head up there. I would like to know who's asking about me."

"We're glad to see you back." May waved goodbye to him.

He climbed the hill and turned around near the top to study the washed-out valley and what remained of the courthouse and the sheriff's office below. He hated the sheriff and his men for beating the confession out of the slave girl. He hated the beating his dad gave him for wanting to tell what happened. Most of all, Nelson hated himself for not saving the girl.

He guessed the man working in the garden alongside the trace would be Gunther.

"Howdy. Would you happen to be Ned Gunther?" he asked.

"Aye, and would you be the Paintier boy those fellows were asking about?"

"I'm afraid I would be. Did you know those fellows, Mr.

Gunther?"

"One of them was an older fellow I remembered seeing in town."

"They didn't say their names, did they?"

"The younger fellow called the older man Jasper."

Nelson was reluctant to ask too much. It would raise too many questions about why he came back to Steelville. "Did they head off in the direction of the steel mill?"

"They did, and in a hell of a big hurry."

"I expect they'll find me if they come back."

"They're not local folks. Looked like some of the bad law men we had during the war. I'd watch out."

"I will." He needed to change the subject. "It looks like the rain washed away your plantings."

"I'm trying to plant a garden in this here darn clay. Nothing wants to grow like in the old country. Best growing is down in the valley if there's any good dirt left."

He thanked Gunther and started the walk back along the ridge to the barn. He still was thinking about the name Jasper, when he heard the running horses coming up behind him. He turned to face the riders. The horses slid to a stop.

"Come back, have you, Paintier," said the man on Nelson's right.

"Came back to stay," Nelson said, resting his hand on his pistol.

"Sheriff Spaid said he don't want you here waking up no dead black slaves," the man said.

"So that son-of-a-bitch, Sheriff Spaid, survived the war, did he?"

"He and the senator run things around here. He said you staying around gonna get a schoolteacher killed."

So Spaid had linked up with a senator, had he? That sounded like a bad combination. "Why don't you start the killing with me," Nelson taunted.

Both of the riders went for their pistol at the same time. Nelson's first shot got the man on the right in the shoulder just as the man fired. The man's bullet ricocheted off the ground next to Nelson. He fired again and hit the other man's pistol. It went flying out of his shattered hand.

"Hold those horses up, damn you. Tell Spaid he's a dead man for killing my dad, and Nelson Paintier said so. Now, get the hell out of here. I'll kill you both if you ever come back."

CHAPTER 9

Ruth Anne stood in the school yard holding a slate tablet when Nelson walked down the hill after the shots were fired.

"What were those shots up there?" she asked

"Let's go inside. I'm afraid those men might come back with some help." They walked to the front of the one room schoolhouse and sat on the edge of the raised platform in front of the blackboard. He had just a little edge on the two men in the gun fight. Getting no practice with a sidearm needed to change. With things closing in around him, it worried him his skill wasn't better.

"Mr. Paintier, you need to tell me what's going on. Those riders, up on the ridge? Did you kill that man?"

"No, but I shot both of them up some, before they could kill me. They were sent by the man that killed my dad, the night they hung the slave girl."

"What's the slave girl got to do with you?" She stood, walked to her desk and laid the slate on top. "I heard the crowd cheer when they hung the murdering girl."

"I knew the slave girl. It was as much my fault as hers that the Mockbee baby drowned." He stepped to the side of the desk to face her. "I went to Sheriff Spaid before her trial and told him I was there when the baby drowned. I told him it was my fault. He laughed at me and called me a nigger lover. Said for me to go home before someone hung me instead of the girl."

Nelson sighed heavily. "She confessed to killing the baby." He shook his head, disgusted. "I was hiding in the woods when the men came for her. They took her in back of the cabin, tied her to a tree, and beat her till she confessed. The town celebrated the day they hung her, every year before the war came."

"Why didn't you tell the court they beat her?"

"I've tried for years to find excuses for not saving her. None have helped me forget. I went to my dad and told him what had happened. When he found out I had been playing with a slave girl at the spring pool, he beat me. I was afraid of him."

"You went to the sheriff? You still could have spoken up at the trial."

"It wasn't a trial. The judge had planned a lynching from the first word said."

"Is this why you came back here?" she asked. "You must still feel guilty for her hanging."

"I've felt guilty for her getting hanged ever since the day I left. In my mind I've watched Sheriff Spaid drag her up the steps of the gallows, over and over again. I've watched her eyes race across the hate filled faces staring up at her, before they pulled the cover over her head. She had been looking, trying to find my face in the crowd. I may have been the only friend she had ever known."

Ruth Anne came around the desk, closer to him. She rested her hand on his shoulder.

"It's not your fault. With things like they were then. She was a black, a slave. That was enough for any jury to hang her. It's still that way. It's still that way."

"I guess what happened to a slave girl was a lot of the reason I fought for the north."

"I thought you did the first day I met you," she said. "You didn't have the beaten worn-out look the returning men in gray have."

He continued, "Part of the reason I came back was to tell Slave Mary's story. The people here need to know what happened. I started writing it during the war and it's nearly finished. I left most of the manuscript in safe hands in St. Louis with a publisher. It's the story of the ironworks, the slaves that worked there, and the days a white boy and black girl spent playing by the spring pool on the hillside by the dogtrot cabin my father and I built."

"When some people around here learn you fought for the north, they will probably hang you too."

"I'll have to go down fighting. I intend to stay. It's not those people I'm worried about. It's the men that threw flaming bottles on our roof and through our windows when my dad got killed. The men that did it are still here. That's why the riders came to kill me. They know I'll be looking for them."

"I think you should be careful what you say and do here. Some people hate the Union soldiers even more than they hate colored folks. Add that to the men you say are already after you, and that spells a lot of danger for you."

"Ruth Anne, I don't plan to stay silent here. I want to start the first Crawford County newspaper. The family in Saint Louis who took me in as their son, owned a newspaper. They taught me the business and left me their money when they died."

"You're serious?"

"I am. I've several things to finish up before it gets started."

"This town is going to need all the help it can get to rebuild the businesses that were lost," she said. "A newspaper would be a great help to bring new people into the county and the Meramec Valley."

"I hope you're right. I'd better be heading back to where Dyer is holed up, if you have the things ready, I'd like to get started, Ruth Anne."

"They're ready. Would you like to just call me Anne?"

"I would...Anne."

"Stay safe. We need the likes of you in our county."

"There is another reason why I came back, Anne." Nelson explained the orders his Saint Louis General had asked him to carry out and then told her how the pardons had been lost in the flood.

"If you find the pardons, will Dyer get one? The boy needs his father."

"Yes. I'm going to have to get to Jim Hagan first. He's the man Dyer has been riding with."

He saddled the horse and hung the sack with the food and bandages across the saddle horn. He had several stops to make along the trace before darkness came. He wanted to know where to find the ex-sheriff, John Spaid. He had hoped someone had shot the sonofabitch to save him the trouble of doing it, but apparently, that wasn't the case. Now Nelson had to find him, or it'd be the other way around. He made his first stop at the side of the gardener's house.

Gunther stood in the front yard of his house. "Saw those riders come back. It was bad luck for them, picking a gun fight with you."

"Guess I came out the winner from that fight."

"I remember where I saw the one called Jasper," Gunther said.

"Where was that Mr. Gunther?"

"It was at the capitol, Jefferson City. I came on a ferryboat from St. Louis with my cousin. He just arrived from Germany. The man saw his suitcase and started yelling at him about being a dirty German. That's where I saw him, hanging around the ferryboat dock near the capitol building."

"Thanks, Gunther. Do you have any idea what he was doing up there at the capitol?"

"I don't know, mister. He did have some kind of a badge on. That's the only reason my cousin didn't knock his block off. I would look for him at the capitol."

"One more question, sir. Do you know what might have happened to John Spaid?"

"Don't know about that, but there is an old lady that lives up the South Creek branch, about four miles back in there, is where she lives. Her name is Spaid, I go back to see her now and then."

After thanking Gunther again, Nelson headed over the ridge to the South Creek trail. Spaid's connection with the state capitol bothered him. Why would the men come from there to kill him?

The trail sat tucked between a bluff and the small stream that someone had named South Creek. It had been a roaring river a few days before. The trail was shaded by pin oak trees. The hundred-year-old trees were there when he first came to Crawford County. He guided the bay around the many broken pin oak limbs lying across the narrow wagon path. In the few patches of sunlight snakes coiled when he approached, their bronze coats warned him to stay clear of the copperheads.

A loud squeal from the brush alongside the trail surprised him, his horse shied and spun away from the sound. He lost the right stirrup and sat lopsided in the saddle until he pulled the horse's head hard in the direction of the spin, to stop it from running away.

Still squealing, a frightened old sow with two of her litter dangling from her teats ran up the hill toward an old vine-covered cabin. Eight babies followed, they tripped and rolled over each other all the way to the house.

"Last person scared my sow I took a shot at him and

blowed half the leaves off that dogwood you sitting by. Any reason I shouldn't do the same for you, mister?"

The woman that stood by the cabin held about the oldest blunderbuss shotgun he had ever seen. The pair of men's pants she had on looked big enough for at least two of her, a strand of cotton rope tied at her side held them up. Her gray hair hung straight on each side of the slender face. Yes, she belonged with a vine covered cabin.

"Mrs. Spaid?" he asked, still trying to get straight in the saddle.

"Least you know my name. Reckon you're not out here to rob an old woman."

"Reckon not, ma'am."

"Ride on up here. Speak what's on your mind, and don't call me Spaid, my name is Jenny. Just Jenny."

"I'm from these parts, Jenny. Been gone since before the war." He got off his horse.

"You ain't one of them Yankees, are you, mister? Be a shame to have to shoot a man that's as good looking as you."

Nelson chuckled and let her question lay.

"Spent all the war living up here along this creek. Didn't know what was going on, except when I had to go to town for salt and foodstuff. I raise most of what I eat right here."

"Back about fifteen years ago I knew John Spaid, is he your husband?".

"Asking about the high and mighty Sheriff John Spaid, are you! No, he weren't no husband of mine. At one time before he got to be sheriff, he was my brother."

He wasn't sure how to ask where to find Spaid. He guessed the old lady would answer it without being asked anyway.

"Mister, if you're looking for him so you can shoot him, tell him Jenny told you where to find him. Last I heard he was living in the hills south of Jefferson City and working for someone at the capital."

The capital? That fell in line with the riders he had shot and the story that Spaid had linked up with a senator.

"You have a lot of hate for someone that's your kin," Nelson said.

"I suppose you can say I do. He killed the only man I ever really loved. He just didn't like him. He said if I ever told anybody about things he done, his boys would be sent out here and kill me too. So, I ain't never told, just wrote myself notes about all he did. It'll be a cold spring 'fore he ever finds them. Kill the bastard and come back, I'll tell you all he's done. Make the hair stand up all along your neck."

"If I find him, I'll tell him you send your best wishes."

"Best wishes that he's dead, good looking," she chuckled.

CHAPTER 10

Nelson left Jenny sitting in a willow limb chair, beside her cabin. He liked the old woman. It would be fun to tell her he had shot Sheriff John Spaid. She would have a jug of moonshine saved for just that occasion. Anyone else claiming to have so much dirt on Sheriff Spaid would already be dead.

He looked forward to a faceoff with Spaid, but his orders came first. Backtracking down the creek past the copperheads, he headed down the trace toward the ironworks and the dogtrot cabin where he left Dyer. Dyer would be the hook he needed to get a pardon in front of Jim Hagan to sign.

He tied his horse behind the cabin, loosened the saddle girth, and took the saddlebags and the blanket straight to Dyer's hiding place. At the door to the slave pit, he stopped to light a torch made of old rags.

"Dyer, it's Nelson."

"Christ, man, I thought you had left me in this pit to die."

Climbing down the steps, he said, "I told you I'd be back."

He stuck the torch in a crack in the wall and tossed the saddlebags full of food to Dyer.

"Before you eat, I need to have a look at your shoulder and change the dressing."

"Go ahead. It don't matter what you do on my shoulder. I'm going to eat while you work. I thought you left me to starve."

"Hold still. This is going to hurt." Nelson unwrapped the bandage and poured the red-oak disinfectant into the wound.

"Damn! Shit, that stings like a snake bite."

"I should get you to a doctor."

"Getting me to a doc gonna get me caught and hung. Hagan and his men will be headed south after the ambush. I have to get back and join them."

"At least give your shoulder a day or two to start healing. I'll come back and bring your horse the next trip."

"I guess this is as good a place as any to hide as we could find."

"I brought plenty of food and water for a couple days." He wrapped a new bandage tight around Dyer's shoulder.

"You fought good back there in that ambush. Shot that Yankee coming up behind us right off his horse. He was dead when he hit the ground. Why don't you ride with me when I head south?"

Nelson shuddered at what Dyer had just said about the Yankee. He had just left a war where the same Yankee he had killed could have fought alongside him. The men in blue were brave soldiers and killing one had made him ill. Not ready to say his intentions yet he kept quiet on the subject.

He handed Dyer a loaf of bread. "Hold it. I'll cut it for you," Nelson said.

"I'm gonna to have to do it myself soon."

"Are you planning to ride into Arkansas?"

"Got a meeting up place down there. It's deep in the mountains, near Buffalo River and a bluff they call the Hawksbill Crag."

"I'm going up to the cabin, see if I can get a fire started up in the fireplace. Come up if you feel like it." It would lead him to Jim Hagan if Dyer took him along to Arkansas.

"I'm staying here and resting for now. Thanks."

Nelson closed the steel bars and pulled the boards back in place. He walked toward the cabin he had helped build and knelt alongside to feel along the rock foundation. His hand came to a large course stone supporting the corner. That stone had fallen from the cart many years ago. When he tried to unload the stone, it fell and pinned his foot to the ground. He pushed with his other foot trying to get free before his dad saw him. He was too late. His dad didn't put up with him making mistakes, he jerked him up by the arm and dragged his foot out from under the stone. He told his dad he was sorry. That got him the "Sorry ain't a word I want to hear," whippin' of his life.

He pulled the latchstring on the cabin door and went into the dark room to kneel by the fireplace hearth. He found several logs and sticks left by some traveler on the edge of the hearth and stacked them to burn.

When the fire finally flickered to life, he sat, facing the dancing flames. The rustle of crushing leaves behind him caught him off guard. He spun with the pistol cocked in his hand.

"Don't shoot, mister. Lordy', don't shoot no poor nigger man that don't mean you no harm."

"I didn't see you there against the wall," lowering the hammer on the pistol.

"I best go on my way," the man said.

"The chill is on the night. Warm up a bit first." Moving to the side to give the man a place in front of the fire.

The man crawled from his bed of leaves across the

heavy oak plank floor and found a place to sit facing the fire, far to the edge of the hearth.

In the firelight he watched the man's gnarled hands open toward the warmth of the fire. The gray in the man's hair extended down his sideburns and frosted the edges of his beard. Twice the man ran his knuckle over a long scar that crossed his cheek and disappeared under the beard.

"That scar. Come from the war?" Nelson asked.

"Comes long before that. I runs away. Master's dogs caught up to me in the slough, up by the big river. I was took back all dog bit and chewed up."

Nelson noticed the fire had burned to bits of glowing charcoal and stood to look for more logs.

"I'll get some wood, sir," the man said.

The man straightened and went to the back wall of the cabin room. Nelson heard him brush away the leaves that made up his bed and watched him limp back carrying two old boards and a small log.

"How'd you happen to find this cabin?"

"On the way somewheres else, I 'spect," the man said. "I's ain't no runaway."

"Never thought you were, all slaves will be freedmen soon," stoking the fire with a broken stick. "Did you know the slave girl that got brought here to work? Her name was Mary."

"Old nigger man at the ironworks told about the child girl slave that lived in this here cabin," the man said. "I once knowed a child with that name."

"Word, was she came from up in the river bottoms by Jefferson City. They have a holler near there some call Mary's holler." Nelson said. "Are you from up there?"

"I comes from all over and I feels the spirits of that Mary child when I come here."

"When I was a boy, the slave girl and I played together just down the hill by the spring pool. Her spirit is still strong here." He was certain the man knew more about the slave girl then he said. Nelson noted he walked with a limp, and his missing saddlebags took priority. He needed to find out if the man knew more.

"It was a bad flood came through here. I lost my horse right out from under me."

"Saw them horses, cows and goats all dead on the ground."

"Did you see a roan horse with a saddle still on?"

"Yes, sir. I seen that horse."

"Were the saddlebags there?" Nelson asked, still looking at the fireplace.

"Yes, sir. Carried them up to the ironworks. I didn't steal nothing. Horse was dead."

"I know. I saw your footprints along the river. Lost your track on the road."

"I don't have those saddlebags no more. Man working at the iron forge said he would give me fifty cents for them saddlebags. Never had that much money before."

"Would you know him if you saw him again?" Nelson asked.

"Yes, sir I knows him. He works on them mules and horses right as you get to the iron place."

The blacksmith at the ironworks had the wax-covered pardons he had brought from Saint Louis. If they had been turned over to the bushwhackers, he would have been hunted down and killed by now.

As the fire burned down, the old man went back to his pile of leaves in the corner, and Nelson stretched out in front of the fireplace. He remembered the cold nights he spent by his dying mother's side, in the same spot. He hoped sleep would come soon.

~ ~ ~ ~

It was morning when the old man got up and quietly lifted the door latch to leave. He stopped halfway out the door to look back as Nelson turned and sat up. "You knows, I looked at them papers was in the saddlebags. Don't know words, but I just look at all the letters, must mean something. Master wouldn't let no slave have learnin'."

"You've helped me to maybe get those papers back," he said. "Would you want to help building back a town?"

"Yes sir, I be willing to work, long as no man locks me up no more."

"I'll pay you to help us. Need to know your name before I send you off," he said, reaching to shake the Negro's hand.

"My name is Thomas, sir."

"Thomas, a lot of the town of Steelville has been washed away. We're going to need help to rebuild." He told him how to find Miss Gordon and the barn where he could stay. Taking two dollars from his money belt, he gave them to Thomas.

"This money will buy food until I can get back to Steelville. Tell Miss Gordon you'll be working for Mr. Nelson."

Leaving the cabin, he stopped at the slave shed. "Dyer, wakeup. I'll be back in a couple days with food and another horse for you." He heard only a muffled okay from below the grates.

The best way to get to Hagan with the pardons would be to join them. Dyer would soon head south toward the Buffalo River. He would go with him.

On his horse, he headed down the long ridge to the ironworks and the blacksmith's forge. It wouldn't be his first meeting with the blacksmith, still he didn't know which side of the war the man supported. Checking his sidearm on the way, he dropped it in the holster. He pulled up the bay alongside the mule pen and got off. Both of the mules brayed at the bay horse stopped alongside their pen.

"Back again? Not looking for another mule, are you?" the blacksmith asked, setting down his tongs and coming out to meet him.

"Thought you might have something else I'm looking for," he said, adjusting the pocket on his jacket.

"Took me a while to figure out which side you're fighting for, mister," the blacksmith said. "Some say you're from here but fought for the North. Is that right?"

"Yes, sir."

"With you losing your horse and all in that flood, I was sure you would be coming for something I've got," the blacksmith said. "Got the papers hid inside."

The blacksmith disappeared into the forge building and returned carrying the saddlebags. "Here's your saddlebags, mister."

Nelson took the saddlebags without looking inside and reached into his money belt.

"No, sir. All of them papers in there, you get them signed and a lot of folks in these parts will be mighty happy. Won't take no money for that, soldier." The blacksmith reached out to shake Nelson's hand.

CHAPTER 11

Spaid thought back to how good he felt about riding the county as the leader of a militia gang during the war. When the peak fighting had gone on, his men raided and took anything he wanted. With Yankee patrols in the area now, things were getting tough. Most his gang had either been killed or faded away. He harkened back to his old Steelville boss, Judge Saunders for help. With the old bastard running for governor of Missouri, it could mean more work and money if he got elected. Before, he had followed Saunder's orders to steal guns from Yankee shipments coming to the state.

His men would take the guns south to sell to the confederates and the militias. The money Senator Saunders had given him to kill Paintier was almost gone. Finding Paintier and killing him wasn't working out to be easy.

He sat on the back porch of his cabin when one of his riders came back from the mission to kill Paintier. The rider had his gun hand wrapped in a bloody bandage.

"Tell me you found him and he's dead, Jasper!" Spaid

walked to the side of the rider's horse.

"We found him."

"Then tell me he's dead," Spaid stared at the man before him.

"We found him. Right there in Steelville like you said he would be."

"He's dead? Right?" He slapped Jasper on the boot.

"He shot us both. My boy is in bad shape." Jasper wiped his forehead with his hand.

"I told you to kill the bastard. If he ain't dead, I don't give a shit about your boy!" Spaid felt anger fill his body.

"I'll go...back and kill him."

"Back, the hell you will! Them busted fingers is turning black. You ain't going to have a hand to shoot with no how. Get up to Jefferson City and get some of Saunders's men to ride after him. Don't want to see you again till Paintier's dead. Come back and he's not, I'll kill you myself. Understand?"

"Yes, Sheriff." Jasper turned his horse and headed for the capital city of Missouri.

He walked back on the cabin porch and slumped in his chair, talking to himself. He didn't have much faith in Jasper. "War's got all the good men killed. Paintier will kill this idiot for sure," he muttered to himself. "It'll be up to me to end this."

CHAPTER 12

Nelson rode east toward Steelville and turned off the trace every few miles into the deep woods along its sides to watch and see if he was being followed. No one was following him.

Ahead he saw a swayback team of horses driven by a man whose wife sat at his side. Two children stood behind them, squeezed between the wagon seat and a load of furniture. A young calf fighting a lead rope, followed behind the wagon. The load of furniture was too heavy for the old horses straining to pull the wagon.

When he rode up alongside the wagon, the man lowered the driving reins and reached under the seat to bring up a rusty single barrel shotgun. The wagon stopped with a squeal from the wagon's rear wheel.

"Look, mister," the man said, "I'm tired of trouble. Don't want no more. Move on by and we will get on our way out of this hell hole."

"I just stopped to see if your horses are doing okay with that heavy load. You've got a wheel needs greasing bad, on the back."

"Team is old, but all we got," the man said.

"None of my business, but it would be better to lighten that load before the wheel falls off."

"That's right, mister. Ain't none of your business." The man tipped his hat down.

"He's just trying to help," the wife said, tugging at her husband's shirt sleeve.

"Sorry, mister. My wife is right. Seems like the whole damn place is gone crazy. You can't even talk to folks next door, that are supposed to be your neighbors, about what you believe in. When you do, next thing you know, you got a dead cow with her throat slit, and a calf that's left to bottle feed," said the man.

"Lots of hate built up from this war," Nelson took a deep breath. "Going to go on even after the war's over."

"Well, we won't be here when that happens." The woman nodded her head.

"Don't know with which side your feelings lie, but direction you're headed is Kansas. Doesn't make any difference there which side you believe in. If they know you came from Missouri, likely they will kill you."

"Thanks, mister. I'm going to head on up north to Iowa or such." The man snapped the reins on the backs of the two swaybacks, "Hoping this old team can make it up there."

"Give them a rest now and then. They should be okay. Tell the blacksmith at the ironworks I told you to stop, he'll put some grease on that wheel for you. Good luck." Nelson turned and headed again for Steelville.

He had gone a few hundred yards when a freight wagon came barreling around the bend toward him.

"Haw mules! Haw you lazy bastards," the muleskinner yelled, cracking a bull whip over the three-yoke team of six mules.

Nelson rode off the trace into the trees to escape getting

hit by the careening freight wagon, "You crazy sonofabitch!" He shouted, shaking his fist at the muleskinner.

When the dust settled, he rode back on the trace. The loud crash he heard came from the direction of the freight wagon and team. He needed to see if the family he had just passed were safe. He spurred his horse toward the crash.

"God-damn-settlers, taking up all the road," yelled the muleskinner, climbing over the side of his overturned wagon.

"Looks like those folks have as much right as you to use this trace." Nelson rode around the wreck to check on the bucking mules still hitched to the overturned freight wagon.

"They're dragging that shit spewing calf behind their wagon. Dang lead mules wouldn't run over the goddamn calf." The muleskinner pointed to the bellowing brown and white calf, sliding along behind the wagon load of furniture.

"Maybe this will teach you to not drive those mules so damn crazy fast. Lead mules seem to be a bit smarter than you, skinner." He turned his horse back toward Steelville.

"Ain't gonna help me right this wagon, mister?" the muleskinner pleaded, pushing hard to try and get the wagon off its side.

"Reckon not, skinner." He left the wreck behind and rode on toward Steelville.

The last two days had worn at him. In his mind, he was at the dogtrot cabin, walking around the large marble slab that had been placed across the drowned baby's grave nearby. It seemed to sit in his path at every turn. A second slab sat next to the first child's grave. It covered another Mockbee child that had died a year later at five years old. The sorrow he caused that day at the spring pool when their first baby drowned lasted beyond the war he survived.

The nine-mile ride to Anne's barn gave him time to think about what he would do next. He set his goal long ago to come back to Steelville, then the Army asked even more of him, he wasn't sure how to go about stopping the guerrilla raids, yet.

Darkness would catch up to him before he reached Steelville. He reined the bay up in front of the barn and swung down. He dropped a stirrup over the saddle horn, then loosened the girth and lifted the back of the saddle to let air under it. No need to unsaddle, he would leave before morning, sooner if trouble came.

At the water tank, the horse drank long and hard. He remembered being criticized by his cavalry sergeant for letting a horse do that after a long ride, hell with him, horses know what is best when they need a good drink. He led the bay into the barn, feeling his way along the walls to a back stall.

"Drop the reins. Move, and I shoot the woman," a hoarse man's voice commanded.

"Easy. I'm not moving." Nelson tried to see who was there. "Anne?"

"She got some quick schooling on keeping her mouth shut," the voice yelled.

"Let the woman go!" He gripped his pistol ready to fire.

"What do you want with us?" Anne demanded.

"Shut up, teacher. Lead the horse back out the barn door, Paintier. Don't try nothing. The woman is right in front of me."

He had no choice. He turned the bay and walked to the front of the barn and into the moonlight. Anne came out next with a big arm wrapped around her waist. The man behind her was using her as a shield. Nelson couldn't see enough of him to shoot.

"Take your pistol belt off. I want to hear it hit the ground. Then the rifle off the saddle, on the ground beside the belt."

He did as he was told.

"The woman's walking toward you now. She's riding

behind you."

"My saddle's loose, just taking up on the girth."

Anne moved to his side and gripped his arm with both her hands. "He surprise me when I came to see if you were back."

"Both of you shut up and stand there." The man backed into the barn. "Getting my horse. Don't be stupid."

He came out leading his horse behind him. "Both of you, get on that horse," the man commanded.

Nelson gripped the stirrup, stepped into it and swung up on the bay. Anne couldn't reach the stirrup. He easily lifted her by both arms until she could. She sat behind the saddle with her arms wrapped tightly around his waist. Her fingers pinched Nelson's belly. Protecting her was his only thought.

"It'll be okay. I don't think he plans to kill us." Nelson knew he'd lied.

"Turn east at the top of the ridge." The man rode close behind them and urged Nelson's horse into a fast walk.

"Where's the boy?" whispered Nelson.

"Asleep at the house. He didn't know I left."

They had gone less than two miles when the man held up his hand. "Stop here. We're going to walk the horses in slow from here. Anything funny and I'll shoot the woman first."

Nelson didn't need to be reminded. The man pointed out a narrow path for them to follow. The path led to a cabin on a steep hillside about a half mile off the trace. Nelson and Anne dismounted in front of the cabin and stood alongside his horse waiting. Having Anne with them frightened him. Trying to jump the man could get her killed. He would need to wait for the chance to spring at him when she was in the clear.

"Tie the horse to the rail." The man dismounted and stepped up on the cabin's porch.

A man's voice came from the far side of the cabin,

"Don't really think you can ride up here without me knowing it, do you, Pa? Keep them out there, I'll get a lamp lit inside."

Moments later the door opened, and their captor shoved them through it into the lighted room. He motioned with his rifle to a post. "Tie 'em up, boy. Bitch nearly bit my finger off when I grabbed her back there in Steelville."

The boy pushed Anne to the floor. Nelson grabbed the boy's arm and shoved him off of her back. He heard the swish of the man's arm and pistol just before it smacked him in the back of the head. The blow staggered him and drove him down to his knees beside Anne. He watched the boy tightly wrap Anne's hands and arms with rope, then jerk her up and back against a cabin post.

"Hurting this woman is going to get both of you killed."

Nelson hoped they would take his threat serious, but both the boy and the man laughed at him. The man pulled him up off his knees and shoved him against the same post. The boy tied his hand around the post in back.

"Too bad I didn't get the job done on your fingers," Anne said.

"I'm going to hunt you both down for this." Nelson swore he would, still shaken from the pistol blow.

"Don't remember me, boy?" asked the man. "I remember you. You're the nigger loving kid, got run clean out of town."

"You got me. Let her go." Nelson said.

"Not now, they can't," Anne said, "I've seen them both before. They work over at the ironworks. His name is Waldron, the other one's, his boy."

"Want you to know, Paintier. The Mockbees were my friends. I don't ride by that cabin without thinking about carrying their dead baby girl up from that spring," said Waldron. "Then you went crying and bellyaching to the sheriff that she didn't do it. She did it, she drowned the baby. I stripped her and beat her black ass till she said she did it. Ain't forgot, Paintier. Now they're saying you're a turncoat. Fought for the butcher, Grant. He killed my other boy."

"War's nearly over, Waldron. You still working for Spaid, aren't you."

"You and this teacher you've been bedding down, both got your own war right here with me and Spaid and his boss," Waldron shook his head

Nelson needed to figure out what kind of situation he'd gotten himself into. He didn't like hearing about this boss of Spaid's. Back in the day, he and Judge Saunders were a callous, deadly pair. He wasn't too keen on the idea of someone powerful enough to back Spaid's ongoing crimes being back in the picture.

"Did you say Spaid's boss?" Nelson was stalling, but also looking for the information they might be willing to give if they thought he'd be dead in no time.

"Yeah. The senator." Waldron put his hands on his hips.

"This senator have a name?"

Waldron scoffed. "Quit your stalling." Then Waldon looked to his boy. "Check them ropes, son. Then pull them burning coals out of the fireplace onto the floor. We're leaving 'um to burn."

Nelson and Anne watched the cabin door slam shut, then heard the sounds of the men's horses clatter up the path they had come down. The hot coals the men spread had the wooden floor ablaze.

"Sorry I got you messed up in this." He tugged at the ropes that held him. The flames spread across the floor toward their feet. His pulling and twisting did little to free his hands.

"It was my fault, for going up to the barn in the dark of night, looking for you." She struggled wildly. "The fire is getting close to my feet." She coughed and choked on the smoke.

"Nelson? Aunt Anne," came the voice from outside the

window.

"Joshua, we're tied to a post in here, hurry," Nelson said, fighting to kick the fire away.

The door crashed open, and the boy came in holding his hands up to shield his face from the flames. He ran to them, and Nelson felt him struggle to find the ropes tying his hands.

"Behind the post. Our hands are tied." He tried to see through the smoke, but it filled his smarting eyes. "Cut her free first. Get her out of here. She's choking bad."

The boy cut fast. Both of their ropes fell to the floor at nearly the same time.

"Come on, get out of here." He grabbed Anne and Joshua's hand and rushed for the door. Not stopping on the porch, they went for the dirt yard of the cabin. He stooped to put out the smoke coming from the hem of Anne's long dress.

"How. . .how did you find us?" She could barely got the words out.

Nelson went to the saddlebags on the bay and got a canteen of water for her. "Here just a sip. It should help clear your throat." He turned to Joshua after a minute and reached to shake his hand.

"I saw the man take you both off. I run behind following. I couldn't keep up. Then I saw the mare coming back empty. I rode her till I saw the fire."

"Saved us, son." He headed over to lead the frightened horses further away from the burning cabin.

"Found your pistol on the ground, would have shot them if they were still here." Joshua held up the gun. "Reckon this makes us kind of even, you saving me and all, don't it?"

"I reckon it does. Can you ride now, Anne?" She nodded yes and went to the horse.

"You two ride the bay, I'll walk along side, back to the barn," Nelson said. "Oh, and maybe you better give me that pistol."

They were less than a half mile from Steelville when Nelson saw another fire light up the night sky.

Anne pointed. "My house!"

"Joshua, slide off the horse. Anne and I need to get to her house fast!" Nelson mounted as soon as Joshua was off. He pushed the horse into a fast gallop for the short ride. He pulled up in the front of Anne's burning house. Smoke poured out of the broken front windows, and the flames surged from floor to ceiling in both front rooms. They had gotten there too late to save anything she owned. Out of breath, Joshua ran down the hill to join them.

"Why'd they do this?" Joshua asked.

"The old man and boy hate me for my past. I'm certain they're also working for Spaid," Nelson said. "It's my fault your house is burning, Anne."

"It's not your fault." She turned her head away from her burning home. "It was only a matter of time until someone burnt it because of my sister's husband, riding with the raiders. Will it be safe for either of us in Steelville now?"

"Is there someplace, someone Joshua can stay with if you leave?"

"Yes, the Olivers." Anne nodded. "He'll be safe with them."

"You and I need to ride out of here then and pick up Dyer on the way." Keeping Anne safe had pushed any thoughts of the pardons aside. He wanted her close to him.

"They will come looking for me when they find out I'm alive, won't they?"

"They'll be back for both of us, Anne. Can you get two other horses?"

"I'll get them. Come on, Joshua. I'll take you to the Olivers."

CHAPTER 13

Only the smoking embers of Anne's house remained when she returned, having borrowed a riding skirt, a white blouse, and a short leather coat. She led two more horses. They were saddled and ready to ride.

"Joshua wanted to go with us, Nelson. I hope he doesn't follow this time."

"Lucky, he did last time." He took her arm and gave her a small boost up into the saddle before handing her the lead rope for the third horse she had for Dyer. Turning, he clucked to the bay to move off, running two steps alongside before swinging up into the saddle in one smooth motion. At the top of the hill, they turned west toward the dogtrot cabin where Dyer was hiding. "Push the horses hard, Anne. We need to be at the cabin before daylight."

The morning light caught them loping their horses for the last mile of the ride from Steelville to the ridge just above the Maramec Iron Works.

"Ride behind the cabin. We'll tie the horses in the woods. Dyer's hiding under the smoke house. It's a place where the Mockbees locked their slaves up at night."

With the three horses hidden in the woods, he led the way to the smokehouse, giving a whistle to signal Dyer.

"Dyer, we're here." He lifted the floorboards and grate covering the pit.

"Someone with you?" Dyer asked.

"It's Anne, Dyer."

"Anne, what the hell are you doing here?"

"A couple of men tried to kill us last night. They burned down her house."

"Is Joshua, okay?" Dyer asked.

"Yes, he's fine. We left him with the Oliver family," she said.

"Your boy saved us last night. An old man got the drop on me and took us to a deserted cabin about two miles east on the trace," Nelson said. "He and his boy tied us up and set the place on fire. Joshua got there in time to cut us loose."

He checked Dyer's wound and settled in to tell him the details of earlier that night. Dyer knew old man Waldron and told them that he didn't ride with the guerrilla raiders.

"Can we ride south and join your friends down there?" Nelson asked him.

"That may be safer for Anne than staying around Stringtown or Rolla. I think Hagan will be glad to have us join up with him."

"I'm going to ride over to the ironworks and pick up the supplies we'll need for the next few days." Nelson looked around the cellar. "I'll be back in a couple hours."

He climbed the short steps leaving Dyer and Anne to wait in the slave pit hiding place. He carefully pulled the floorboards over the opening and left the smokehouse. Walking across the clearing alongside the dogtrot cabin, he stopped at the hickory tree where Mary had been tied. He ran his hand over the rough scar in the tree bark carved there years before. "MURDERER." Time still hadn't healed the wound.

He loped the bay down the long hill and didn't slow until he reached the river crossing. The flood had eroded the banks, leaving broken and fallen trees stretched all along the shore. The spring fed river ran clear again, and he could see the deep ruts where many freight wagons had crossed. He dropped the bay's reins across his saddle and let the horse pick the path across. The horse stopped at midstream and struck the water several times with its front hoof, finally dropping its head to drink.

The horse getting a drink gave him a chance to study the two riders headed toward the river from the direction of the ironworks. He nervously touched his rifle and lifted it slightly to be sure it would slip from the scabbard if he needed it. With that, he settled back in the saddle, to wait.

The riders pulled their horses up before reaching him and touched the brims of their hats in a greeting. He got a quick glimpse of a gold badge on the closest man.

"You fellows from the ironworks?" Nelson asked. He still rested his hand on the rifle's stock.

"We're lawmen. About the only law, if you don't count the Rolla garrison Union Troops," said the man with the badge. "I'm Sheriff Turner. Bill here is my deputy."

"My name's Nelson Paintier. Glad to meet you fellows."

"Paintier? You're the fellow saved the Dyer boy in the flood? Clerk at the ironworks told us what you did." The sheriff looked at the man before him.

"Found him and his ma on the roof of their house, coming down the river out of Steelville." Nelson still felt cautious about the two men being lawmen. He had heard nothing about law enforcement being elected in Crawford County.

"Glad you saved the boy. We're heading over to the county seat. Heard the boy's aunt's house burned last night. We wanted to see if we can help there," the sheriff said.

"When I came through there folks said the house was

empty. Teacher got out just fine. Fire burned so fast it looked like it had been set on purpose," Nelson said. "Hope you catch the guys that did it."

Seeing that he was smack dab in the middle of the most lawless part of Missouri, he felt surprised that anyone would claim to be "a lawman."

He nodded to the men lifted his horse's reins and headed for the ironwork's store.

He rode past the blacksmith shop and past the iron smelter being fired. He rode up to the store tucked back against the south hill of the valley. The store was empty except for the clerk Nelson had met on the day of the flood.

"See you're back again, mister," the clerk said.

"I need to stock up on some supplies. There's not anything available in Steelville. The stores along the creek got all washed away."

"I'll be glad to help you out. By the way, two men were in here a day or so ago asking where they might find you. I told them you might be staying in Steelville."

"Any idea who they were or might work for?"

"I don't, but one of the iron workers said the older man was from Jefferson City. Might work for some of the government folks up there." The clerk scratched his head. "They acted like someone had told them you were headed back to this part of the country. Sure, were straight on their facts."

"Couple of their cohorts from Jefferson City found me the other night. Wasn't a very friendly meeting. I almost ended up roasted." Nelson looked the man in the eye. "If they come back, how about telling them I'll be looking for Sheriff Spaid to pay him a visit."

"After what you did to save the boy, I'll be glad to do that."

Nelson walked around the ironworks grounds the rest of the afternoon. The furnaces had been stoked and the glowing hot billets of iron were being flattened. The ringing sounds of the drop hammers hitting the red-hot iron echoed throughout the valley. No one seemed to notice a stranger making a visit.

After he climbed the hill to the cemetery and visited his sister's grave, he walked back down the steep Stringtown trace and stopped in front of the burnt-out cabin where his sister had died. An old negro man passed him, headed up the hill toward the carpenter's shed. He remembered him from years before at work at the shed. The man was a carpenter and made the small wooden coffin for his sister. The time had come to head back to the cabin for Dyer and Anne. They all had a long trip ahead of them.

CHAPTER 14

When they left Missouri and crossed into Arkansas, Nelson felt sure they were far enough away from the men who were hunting him for Anne to be safe. The ride had taken them several days, each night they had slept in caves and old barns along the way.

"How's the shoulder doing, Dyer?" he asked.

"Can't move the arm all that much, but I feel like I'm getting stronger," he said, lifting his arm a few inches. "There's a friend of Hagan's lives half a day's ride ahead. He always welcomed me and the boys to stay in his hayloft. We should be there before night."

"A hayloft sounds really good after where we've been sleeping." Anne rubbed her backside.

Dyer took them across a steep ridge and down a rocky trail that led into a creek bottom. At the bottom, he turned to follow a small stream. In a half mile it flowed into a wide valley where they picked up a well-traveled dirt road.

~ ~ ~ ~

Later that day, Dyer pointed to a house and barn that sat on the west side of the valley near the creek. Smoke from a wood fire hung in the still air around the gray clapboard house. The unpainted barn sat to the side of the house that was dug into a hillside. As they got closer, Nelson noticed the hayloft's front stood open with a double strand of rope hanging from a pulley at the top. He remembered when he was a young boy helping a farmer use a four-prong hayfork fastened to one strand of a rope for lifting loose hay into his loft.

"That hay loft has got to be full of hay. It's sure looking good for a place to rest." Anne pointed up at the opening.

"Hang back a little. I'll head in first. I don't want Joe to greet us with some double ought buckshot," Dyer said.

Two coon dogs in the yard had started barking at them before he got closer than a quarter mile to the house. They still hadn't let up as he rode through the gate and stopped in front of the house. Both dogs were making their stand under the front porch. "Joe," shouted Dyer. "It's Dyer Spencer. Got two other friends with me." Nelson and Anne had followed and held up just outside of the yard fence. Both coon dogs came out from under the porch and stood watching the approaching riders, sniffing for their scent.

"Reckon it is you, Dyer," Joe said, stepping through the door. The heads of two boys popped around the door jamb behind him to stare at the riders in their yard, "Some of Hagan's men came through last week, said you'd been shot, fighting the blue coats up on the Rolla Trace."

"They didn't get me this time, Joe."

Joe went on, "Been keeping an eye out for strangers, still got some of those crazy bastards from Kansas seeking revenge over here for what we did to Lawrence. They can't seem to get over the whippin' we gave them in sixty-three."

"Will it be okay if we borrow your hayloft for the night?" Dyer asked, as Nelson and Anne rode up alongside him.

"You bet you can. Unsaddle and tie up the horses in the barn. I'll have Martha fix you some grub," Joe said.

"I'll go in and help your wife." Anne swung from her horse, then handed the reins to Nelson.

"Martha already been cooking for us four, so I'm sure she can add on a bit for the three of you," Joe said, opening the cabin door for Anne.

"How many of the boys made it out of that fracas up on the trace?" Dyer asked.

"Couple of them got shot up bad. Said they lost two at the first volley. They counted you being dead too," Joe said.

"I would have been captured or dead if Nelson here hadn't rode me out of there." Dyer pointed at Nelson. "He saved my boy, Joshua, too."

"He's more than welcome to sit down and eat with us." Joe turned to look toward the cabin. "Come on in when you get unsaddled."

Dyer led the way to the stall area at the back of the barn. He tied his horse and the other two, as Nelson dropped the girths and slid the saddles off. The ride had been slow for the last hour, so they didn't need to walk the horses to cool them out.

"Joe rode with us till his wife had their second kid. Then he started doing more farming and hog raising to keep food on the table for them." Dyer lifted his straw hat and ran his hand over his hair. "It'll be nice to slip into the creek back there, it's down the slope off to the side of the barn."

"Food's on the table, boys." Anne's voice came from the front of the barn.

Both men joined Anne and headed for the house at a fast walk. Nelson felt hungry enough to eat a bear.

The cast iron kitchen stove had a red glow under the edge of the stoker door. A big skillet filled with fresh cooked sausage with gravy simmered on top of the meat sat on the fire. Joe's wife put a final stir on the gravy and carried the skillet to set it on a round burnt board in the middle of the table. The gravy and home cured sausage would be more than enough to fill all their hungry bellies.

"Just baked a batch of biscuits for Joe and our boys this morning. I sure can do another batch later, so dig in, folks. Help yourself," Martha said. "Our boys can eat later. They're gone up in the cabin loft thinking up mischief. We got no school round these parts to keep them out of trouble."

"How old are your boys?" Anne asked.

"Young one is two, other going on ten, ain't he, Martha?" Joe said.

"Be ten in September," his wife said.

"Anne was teaching school up in Steelville," Dyer said, choking on the big mouthful he had tried to swallow. "Big flood came and nearly washed the town away."

"Are you heading south to join up with Hagan and his boys?" Joe asked. "Last I heard they were somewhere down 'round Buffalo River."

"Yes, it wasn't safe around Steelville and the ironworks for any of us," Dyer said.

"Welcome to stay here long as you want, 'fore you move on," said Martha. "Maybe Anne can give our boys some learnin'."

"I'll say hello to them in the morning before we leave," Anne said.

After supper the three guests thanked Joe and his wife then headed for the barn.

"Still warm enough. I'm going to head down to that creek, wash away some dried blood and clean up a bit," Dyer said.

"We'll check on the horses, get them some hay, and head up to the loft," Nelson said.

Anne climbed the board ladder into the loft and pitched down several forks of hay into the stall mangers. Nelson led the horses to the windmill water tank to drink, then led them back into the barn. He looked forward to time alone with Anne in the loft. He wanted to be a lot more to her than her protector. He climbed the ladder to join her. A small handful of hay came dropping on his head from above. Anne laughed at him wiping off what she had tossed at him. He settled in beside her on the hay.

"Anne, you know Joe and his wife would be glad for you to stay here with them, till we come back," Nelson said.

"I'm sure they would. They're such nice people."

"You don't sound too keen on it."

"I feel safe with you. I'm going on with you and Dyer." She scooted a little closer to Nelson in the hay.

"Safe? I nearly got you burned at the stake. Your home has gone up in flames, and here we are headed to meet up with some of the meanest guerrilla raiders outside of Quantrill and his bunch." Nelson shook his head. "You have a good reason for being here. Let me help all I can."

He flattened out a larger place for them to lie. She pulled up an arm full of hay for their heads and they both laid back on it.

"I don't want anything to happen to Dyer. Joshua needs his dad. It'll be hard enough without his mother."

"Dyer tells me some of the men that were riding with him want to quit raiding and get back to their families," Nelson said. "I think that could happen soon."

"And you, Nelson. What do you want?" Anne moved closer and their hands touched.

He closed his hand over hers, and with a gentle urge, she moved to press against his side. His other hand slid along her neck under her hair. Then she turned to face him. The kiss came... he didn't know who moved first. He loved the feeling of someone he had started to care about deeply lying against his side. Their closeness only got to last for an hour.

"Really quiet up there. You guys asleep?" Dyer started up the ladder into the loft.

"Nope. Just talking about Joshua. Hoping he's ok," Anne replied.

She slipped her hand from Nelson's and moved to another area of the hayloft to make a bed for herself. Dyer crossed the loft, climbed high in the loose haystack. A spark had been lit when Nelson first saw her, and now the kiss. It warmed his whole body. He had worried she might not like the fact he fought for the north, but that fear had left him. Soon his thoughts faded into dreams. Later, the same nightmares of charging ranks of gray-coated soldiers trying to kill him came.

"Wake up," whispered Anne, shaking his arm. "I'm worried about the hounds. They're growling, and I think I heard a horse whinny close by."

"Wake Dyer. I'm going to slip up to the front of the loft," Nelson said. "Maybe those Kansas Jayhawkers came back."

He stood, strapped on his pistol, grabbed the rifle, and moved to the side of the large hay-loading door at the front of the barn. The pale light from the moon made it hard to make out any danger in front of the house and barn.

Awake and at his side carrying his rifle. Dyer whispered, "See anything out there?'

"The dogs seem to be bothered by something out by the fence." Nelson pointed in that direction.

A flicker of light, and then the light of a torch outlined two men. Another torch was lit from the first, then the two men started running across the yard.

"Wait," Dyer said. "They might be friendly."

The first torch flew through the air toward the roof of the cabin. The second swung back over a man's head, aimed straight at the open door of the hayloft.

"I've got him," Nelson said. His shot dropped the man on top of the torch. A shotgun blast from the cabin porthole aimed at the other man caught him head high, he fell flat on his back.

All hell broke loose in the barn yard. Four mounted raiders charged in, firing at the house.

"They don't know we are up here," Nelson said, "Take them out."

Three more were dead on the ground before the last rider turned and headed for the gate. A rifle shot from the other side of the loft door knocked him from his saddle. Nelson and Dyer both turned in surprise to see Anne crank the action on her rifle to reload.

"The fire is on the cabin roof. I'm going after it. Holler at Joe, tell him we got the last of them," Nelson said jumping onto the hanging hay rope and sliding to ground.

"He knows, coming out of the house now with buckets," shouted Dyer. He followed Nelson from the loft. "Anne, make sure those fellows on the ground stay there."

The fire lasted only a few minutes after the buckets of water reached it. Nelson slid down from the house roof and lifted a lantern to join Dyer checking on the attackers lying on the ground.

"This one's dead. Buckshot took off a lot of his face," Dyer said.

"Got one here still breathing. He's just a kid. The shot hit him in the gut." Nelson knelt beside the boy. "Why're you crazy bastards trying to burn down a farmer's home?"

The wounded boy lay with his hand pressed against the hole in the side of his stomach.

"I wasn't supposed to get shot up this way," he said. "We're traveling, raising hell with the damn people that killed my mom and dad in Lawrence."

Joe's wife had come up to try and help. "Let's get him in the house."

Before anyone could speak, the last shot of the day came from behind them and went straight to the middle of the boy's forehead. "We can't let none of this bunch live,

Martha," Dyer said. "They'll come back with all of Lawrence and kill all of you. You got a place in mind to bury this bunch, Joe?"

"I'll get the team hitched up in the morning, load them up and haul them down the valley about a mile, quicksand bog swallow them up quick," Joe said.

"I might trade out the horse I've been riding for one of theirs," Dyer said, "Mine's a little gimpy on his right front."

"Gonna take the rest of the horses over by the White River next week, folks there always looking for good animals and don't care where they come from." Joe smiled.

~ ~ ~ ~

Next morning, Dyer and Joe loaded the bodies in the wagon and headed for the quicksand bog. It gave Anne and Nelson a chance to slip away to a deep-water hole in the creek Martha had told her about.

"I'm taking you along, sir, but not to watch me," she said, "I expect you to stay up here watching the path while I take this soap Martha gave me and get clean."

"Can I at least say I'm disappointed at that order, Miss Anne?"

"You can say it, but it won't make any difference." She looked into his eyes. "And keep those eyes toward that creek unless you hear me drowning."

Anne finished her bath in the creek without being interrupted. Back on the sandy bank she slipped on a white cotton shirt she had borrowed from Nelson's saddlebags and took her dirty clothes to wash in the creek's running water. The drops of water falling from her wet hair softened the cotton shirt she was wearing, making it transparent. All of the beauty of the shape and shadows of her firm breasts were waiting for Nelson to see.

"Finished down there yet?" Nelson started to fidget over

the scene he was missing on the sandy bank of the creek.

"You can come down now." Anne turned toward him.

His wait had been worth it. He took her hand and pulled her to him, gently moving her wet hair from her lips to kiss them softly and tenderly.

"That's all for now, mister. You stink worse than that horse of yours."

"Must be my turn to jump in that creek."

"Oh really? I might have to sneak just one little peek, you know."

"Not allowed. I have too many scars I need to hide."

"Here, rub some of this lye soap on them. It should help to soften them up quite a bit, if it doesn't burn the rest of your skin off."

He left his gun belt and pistol at Ann's side, stripped off his pants and shirt, and kept his long johns to take off when he got in the water.

The spring fed creek water felt good, and the strong lye soap peeled off the layers of dirt from his neck and arms. He was afraid to try the soap on his hair, so he just ducked under for a minute and scrubbed his hair and head hard. With the long johns off, he gave them a once over with the lye soap and then wrung the water out of them.

"Coming out now," he called.

"Not before you toss me those long johns," she said, "You don't really think that little washing got them clean, do you?"

He tossed the underwear to Anne and stayed in the water to watch her give them a second and third scrub down before she hung them over a bush beside the creek.

The spring fed creek water had started to make him shiver. "Not going to give them back?" he asked.

"Oh, I thought after the look and kiss the white shirt got me, maybe it would be my time to look and stare." Anne giggled.

He paused a moment and then waded slowly from the

waist deep water to Anne. She let the white cotton shirt slip from her shoulders and fall to the wet sand. She pulled him down onto her, onto the white cotton shirt below.

Later they sat pressed against each other, the shirt hung loosely over Anne's shoulders. They talked of the fire and how Joshua had saved them. She gripped his arm tightly when he spoke of her home burning. She tried to hide the tears flowing across her cheeks. He could tell she had fought to keep them back.

"I would like to rebuild the house for us." Nelson waited for her reaction.

"Come on, time to get the sand off." Anne slightly gasped, then pulled him behind her into the cold water.

"Was that too much?"

"It surprised me. Maybe you should wait to know me better before making plans like that."

"I'll be glad to do that." What he said had just slipped out from deep in his heart. It had been before the war since he felt so close to someone.

On the walk back up the path to the barn, Anne asked, "Where is Dyer taking us? Do you know?"

"Dyer tells me we aren't far from the Big Buffalo River Valley. There has been a lot of Federal troops pushing down into that area. They caught a bunch of locals mining saltpeter from a cave, making gun power for the Confederates. Shot them all dead on the spot. We'll have to be careful down there."

"I know the valley," she said, "My folks were going to homestead there when we first came west. Since all the good bottomland was settled, there was nothing left but patches of land up on the benches of the mountains. Daddy took us back north."

"Dyer's been saying we would find Hagan up around an area he calls the Hawksbill, big rock ledge sticking out over the valley. He said their camp is in the deep woods just before the cliffs, with escape routes off in two different directions." He looked into her eyes. "It'll take us about two more days to get there at least."

"Any idea what you're going to do then?"

"How about staying alive, to start with?"

CHAPTER 15

The tall burr oak and hickory trees closed in around them as they rode a narrow ridgeback trail toward the Hawksbill Dyer had told him about. A few minutes before, Dyer had taken the lead. He had warned them to stay alert since Hagan's men would be quick to shoot and ask questions later. Dyer pulled them up to a stop. He cupped his hands in front of his mouth and blew a loud bellowing tone. Two long blasts and then a short. When he got no response, he turned to Nelson and Anne, "We won't hear nothing back. They know it's one of them and we're close." He motioned for them to follow and started ahead.

"I saw a reflection off something in a tree up ahead." Nelson pointed out the tree.

"Best shut up. Just follow me close. Keep your hands on the reins, don't be pointing." Dyer looked at Nelson "I saw him up there back a ways."

Nelson had started to think riding into a bushwhacker camp with Anne might have been a bad idea after all. He turned to her and said, "Stay close. Ride up to my side."

"Camp should be just over that ridge."

Dyer's voice was little more than a whisper.

"Lookout has a rifle leveled on us," Nelson replied.

"Hey, Dyer. You ain't been killed?" shouted the lookout.

"Yankees tried hard. Fellow riding with me had a lot to do with keeping me alive," Dyer yelled.

"Ride on in, Hagan will be glad to see you're alive," the lookout said.

When they crossed the ridge into the camp, Nelson picked out the leader from a line of seven men headed for them. He had three men on each side of him and they stood ready for a fight. Each of the men carried two or more revolvers, some holstered, others stuck in their belts.

"Dyer, what the hell do you mean bringing strangers to this camp?" Hagan's hands moved with the word "strangers" to rest on their pistol's grips.

"This woman is my wife's sister. The other one's Nelson Paintier, we about drowned him at the cave. He saved me from the god-damn Yankees when we rode out of there." Dyer shrugged his shoulders. "He shot one clean off his horse as the soldier had me in his sights."

"I heard about what he did. I still ain't sure he didn't just shoot that Yankee to save his own skin," Hagan said. "Get down. I'll need to know more about this Yankee killer later."

"Thanks. Another Bluecoat shot me in the shoulder after I got a shot in him." Dyer carefully and slowly dismounted.

"You look tuckered. The gals been riding with us got some coffee brewing," Hagan pointed to his right.

The three joined Hagan on the log benches around the campfire. Waiting for the coffee gave Dyer time to tell him about the flash flood that had hit Steelville, and how Nelson had saved his boy.

"Know about floods on that river, got some family living about five miles downstream from Steelville." Hagan nodded slowly. "They got flooded out of that valley once before, moved their cabin up the ridge, case it happened again." He moved the pistol on his waist and the one sticking in his belt around a bit.

"We had a bad flood there after my dad moved us to the ironworks," Nelson added.

"Notice you walking with a limp, Nelson. Some Yankee get a shot into you?" Hagan asked.

"Nope, horse went down, took two hits to her chest. Stopped it cold in her tracks. I went over the top. Hurt my leg." He wasn't ready to tell him a man in gray had shot the horse.

"If you shot a Yankee to save this old sidekick of mine, that makes you good enough to ride along with us," Hagan said, "Coffee up, then get unsaddled. Your horses look worn out and needing to graze. I'll have the boys take them over to some grass once you get them unsaddled."

After drinking the strong coffee, they unsaddled the three horses and tied them to the camp's picket line.

"Thanks for speaking up for me, Dyer. These boys got mighty fast hands when it comes to thinking about their guns."

"Wait till you see them really pissed. They break out their black flag and carry it up in their front row. It scares the hell out of anyone we attack. Men know we'll follow that flag into the gates of hell." Dyer smiled.

When they returned Anne sat waiting at the campfire circle. Dyer told Anne and Nelson that the camp sat only a few hundred feet from the Hawksbill crag. Both wanted to see it, so Dyer led the way through the woods to the bluff.

"Walk careful along here. There's lots of loose rock up ahead," Dyer said.

"Look at that, Anne." Nelson pointed toward the huge ledge sticking out over the Buffalo River valley.

The three of them walked halfway out on the ledge and stood looking at the valley, and river far below.

"Would hate to fall off here." Anne stood and looked down.

Dyer pointed to the end of the cliff, "Legend tells of a preacher that stood out near the edge of it every day. Lifted his arms to the sky and shouted his prayers to God. On a stormy Sunday morning, a lightning bolt hit the preacher. Lighting so strong, no one found any of his remains. He was just gone. The congregation argued for weeks, some said the devil, others said God took the mean old bastard. It's a scary place."

"Heard rumors that bushwhackers had thrown men off the Hawksbill," Nelson pointed down. "More than a rumor," Dyer said.

~ ~ ~ ~

A cold wind blew across Nelson and Anne that night.

"Don't think you're going to get all that bed of pine needles do you, Captain?" Anne moved in tight against Nelson's back, pushing for even more room.

"Hope those arguments going on across the camp aren't going to keep you awake." Nelson chuckled softly.

"What's going on with the men?"

"Men are playing poker to see who is next with the girls." He chuckled again.

"Guess I'm lucky you've got the best poker hand in the game, Captain," Anne said

Back-to-back didn't last long. Nelson turned toward her first, "You know, lady, my heart glows warmer each day you're with me."

Anne turned to face him, her arm felt for him and pulled him close. Her deep kiss drove away the cold of the night and erased his memories of the war that haunted him day and night. Near morning he awoke to feel the warmth of her breath as it touched the side of his face.

"Only you, no other has ever made me feel this way," he

whispered in her ear. She woke at the sound of his voice and kissed him again and again.

The sun came up fast on the mountain top and found Hagan and his men packed to ride. Dyer had their horses saddled and ready when Nelson and Anne joined him. By noon they were ten miles north of the Buffalo River and hungry.

"Smell coming in on the afternoon wind," Hagan's top sidekick, Red said.

"It's coming right off fresh hams and side meat that's being smoked, I reckon. It's making my mouth water," Jim Hagan said.

"I feel hungry, like an old hound that's been too long on the trail without even a bone," Red said, "Smell coming from close by."

"Too bad they didn't name you Red Bone after the hound dog. You can smell meat cooking a mile away." Dyer laughed.

"Gather the boys around, Red." Hagan lifted one of his revolvers and checked the loads. "Nelson, you and that Griswold ride up here with me. Dyer, you hang back and give that shoulder a rest."

"Circle up, men, over here!" yelled Red.

"Them Yankee troops have pushed us as far as I'm going to let them. We need to split up and head on down into Texas," Hagan said to his twelve men. "We got to get some provisions before we split up for good. Smell of that smoking hog meat drawing hard on me. I need two of you to get up there. Scout out the place." Two of the men pivoted their horses and were gone before he had finished speaking.

"Give them five minutes and we'll follow. I've got folks on down in Texas. My boy went down there when I made him leave. The fighting was getting real bad up here. Ain't seen him in quite a while."

"Them wanted posters were popping up all around town

on us 'fore we came down here." Red shook his head. "No place left for us to go."

"Doubt if I can ever settle again." Hagan looked around the area. "Too many people know my face. Let's close up on the boys."

~ ~ ~ ~

Hagan had led the way north from the Hawksbill for more than twenty minutes when he pulled up to meet two riders that rode up in front of them.

"Might not want to ride in there, Jim. String of blue coats got the man stretched out by his neck. He's pulled up to the hayloft. Woman screaming somewhere back in the barn."

"How many blue coats?" Hagan demanded.

"No more than a dozen. Some drinking the man's shine," said the rider.

"They're for sure going to kill that man. Do worse with the woman," Red added.

"I know. Then they go tell the county that Hagan's boys did it. Maybe we can head that off before it happens."

The barn and farmhouse lay on a flat hillside up from the river bottom. Nelson could hear the laughter of the men, and then a woman's screams came from the open doors of the barn. He and Anne tied their horses with Hagan and his men and crept to the edge of the woods overlooking the barn with them. Hagan's men were talking and pushing him to let them rush in and kill the blue coats. Nelson couldn't be sure if they wanted to save the woman or get to the meat cooking on a fire in the cabin's yard.

"Sounds like a bunch of them's got the woman in the barn. Red, you and Nelson see if you can get in the back of that barn. We'll get the drop on the ones in the yard."

Not sure Anne wouldn't rush in the barn to help the woman, Nelson asked Dyer to be sure she stayed safe with him. Nelson and Red crawled to within a few feet of the back door of the barn without being noticed. Nelson stood and then ran to the door and swung it open to go in first. Red followed close behind. The woman's screams had been choked into whimpers.

Two of the three Yankees in the barn, held the woman's legs to the ground, her dress had been ripped apart and twisted around her neck. The third man stood between her legs, his blue pants dropped to his feet, his penis still dripped from the rape he had just committed.

Nelson's first shot blew away the soldier's manhood. The second went straight through his heart. Red fired twice. Both soldiers that had headed for the door fell dead in their tracks.

Nelson went to the crying woman and covered her with what was left of her dress and his jacket. He lifted her in his arms and carried her through the back-barn door to meet Anne coming down the hill.

"She's alive. Them blue bellies in here ain't," Red shouted out the door.

The eight Yankees in the yard had been caught drunk or asleep. Hagan had them sitting in a row with their hands pulled hard and tied behind their backs. Only one of them had on a full blue uniform.

"What are you men doing this far south, riding without an officer?" Hagan kicked the closest one in the back.

"They sent us out on patrol. Our sergeant got us lost," said the man twisting from the pain of Hagan's kick. "We ran out of food."

"Ran out of luck too," Nelson said. "They're deserters."

Hagan slammed the soldier's head with his pistol's side, "I didn't ask for a damn lie, shit brains."

Hagan's men had cut the barn ropes and lowered the strung-up man to the ground. He fell unable to stand, with his hands on his throat. The only sound he could make was a groan. Anne walked around the barn supporting the man's wife. She was trying to run to help her husband.

"Damn, Hagan, Nelson's shot took the raping bastard's dick and balls clean off in there. Then he plugged him in the heart as he was looking to see where his parts had gone," Red said.

"I would have let him stand there for a bit to think about what he was missing." Hagan laughed.

"What we goin' to do with prisoners?" Red asked.

"Think about ways to kill them in the morning. Need to get you boys fed, so we can think on that."

Hagan's men were quick to raid the farmer's smoke house to get meat for cooking on the fire in the barnyard. Several of the men searched the farmer's house for anything else they could cook to eat.

~ ~ ~ ~

Nelson took Anne a plate of fresh cooked bacon and grits and joined her alongside the empty barn.

"I'm not sure where I stand with Hagan. It had to help taking down those raping deserters."

"I heard some of his men talking about wanting to go home," Anne replied.

"That's about the only thing I have going for me." Nelson sighed. "Probably going to kill me if he finds out I fought for the North and am carrying these pardons."

"Is Hagan going to stay here tonight?" Anne asked.

"Believe he's going to. Afraid it's going to be a sleepless night for me, sitting with my back to this barn," Nelson wrapped a blanket around Anne's back and had her slide her head and shoulders into his lap.

Nelson was still awake when the rider come in a little after midnight. Hagan's guards were the first to meet the rider. He could hear the rider talking to the guards.

"Been looking for Hagan and you boys for over two weeks now," said the rider. "Have some news he ain't gonna want to hear."

Hagan came out of the farmhouse and hurried to the rider. "You look worried, something you don't want to tell me? Spit it out, damn it!"

"It's about your boy." The rider shook his head. "Yankees caught him and the others up east of Jefferson City a couple weeks ago. Killed all his men except your boy. They skinned him like a buck deer, beat the hide right off his back, put him on a horse with a note saying they would do the same to any bushwhacker they caught from now on. Another bushwhacker found the horse carrying him wandering in the woods up by Rolla. Your boy must have only lasted a few days."

Hagan grabbed the rider by the shirt. "Who? What troops did this to my boy?" Hagan demanded, pushing the rider against the wall.

"One of our men got away. He told us it was the officer that cut up your son. Company pendant looked like they were from the Rolla command," the rider squeaked. Hagan relaxed his grip and eased him off the wall.

"Get everybody up. We're going to drag those goddamn blue bellies to the Hawksbill and throw them to hell," Hagan yelled. "I'm going to find that sonofabitch that skinned my boy. He'll think hell fire and brimstone been poured all over him when I get through."

The fate of the deserters was sealed for sure. With the deserters roped together in a line to walk, Hagan and his troops headed to the camp near the Hawksbill crag. Several of the captured men in the rope line kept slowing the group down.

"Cut them out," Hagan yelled, "Tie a rope round their waist. Going to drag them behind my horse."

Seeing the two men being dragged behind Hagan's horse did a lot to speed up the rest of the prisoners.

At the Hawksbill camp standing over one of the bound-up Yankees, Hagan taunted the prisoners, "What's your name?"

"Johnny Brant," the man said.

"Well, Johnny, too bad for you you're not a Johnny Reb. Where would your home be?" quizzed Hagan.

"Wisconsin."

"Wisconsin. Folks in Wisconsin be proud of you? Deserting? Your momma going to miss you? Won't ever know what happened to you." Hagan laughed.

"What you mean?"

"Mean! Mean today I'm going to throw you off the highest place around here. That's what I mean, you bluecoat bastard," Hagan laughed louder.

"You can't, we're prisoners of war," Johnny Brant said.

"Can't! Don't tell me can't!" Hagan drew his knife from his belt and cut the man's ropes. "Stand up, I'm giving you a chance, run for it."

The prisoner's knees buckled twice before they could hold him erect. He glanced around the camp for a way to run.

"Run that way, Yank. I'm going to count to ten." Hagan pointed to a path up the ridge.

Dyer shook his head and looked at Nelson in disbelief. The other prisoners all watched and struggled with their rope ties. After this, Hagan would probably let them sweat through the night before pushing them off the cliff.

"Now run, Johnny. Run for your life. One... two...three."

Hagan's count only reached five before he shot the man in the back of the head.

CHAPTER 16

Nelson had commanded and ordered the death of deserters more than one time in the war that was just ending. The deserter's executions happened quickly by firing squad or hanging. Today, death would not come quickly. It would be at the end of a two-hundred-foot screaming fall off a cliff.

"What's going to happen to the men?" Anne asked.

"They're deserters and rapists that sure as hell deserve to die. Still, they're soldiers and should hang for what they did."

"Would talking to Hagan change his mind about how they die?" Anne asked.

"The bushwhackers have been brutal and rarely showed any mercy all through the war. So, I doubt if he would change how he plans for them to die. I can at least try."

"Are you sure you want to do that?" she asked.

"Stay here when they take the prisoners to the Hawksbill. Walk off, down toward the creek we crossed just before we got here. If he takes me too, stay close to Dyer," Nelson said.

"It's all happening too quick. You come back to me, Nelson Paintier." Anne kept her hold on his hand.

"I've got to tell him about the pardons and why I brought them, Anne," Nelson said, pulling away and handing her his pistol and holster. "Weapons won't do any good when he hears what I have to say."

He walked across the camp and stopped directly in front of Hagan, "I knew about your boy."

Hagan slowly looked up and in a harsh voice, "Knew what?"

"The son-of-a-bitch that did it is named Turner," Nelson said. "Union Army command has him locked up, at Rolla. He's going to hang for what he did."

Hagan sprang to his feet with his pistol in his hand, and smashed Nelson in the side of the head. The blow dropped him to his knees. "Get up, you son-of-a-bitch. Who the hell are you? How come you came riding in here with Dyer?" Hagan asked.

"Didn't come here to do you harm," Nelson said, as he struggled to get on his feet.

"You must be God damn tired of living then," Hagan said. "Might as well stay down there on your knees, 'cause I'm going to blow most of your head off."

"I came here to try and end the killing. My home used to be in Steelville, just like Dyer's. We might have fought on different sides, right now it doesn't matter. It's time it ends, for both sides," Nelson said.

"Mighty fine speech for a Yankee," Hagan said. "Going to let you watch me push these deserters off the cliff, then you're going to follow them. Red, get some rope and tie him up with the rest of the Yankees."

"I heard you say you want to get this war over, Hagan. I'm your chance to do that. I can send you and your men all home with a pardon."

"Pardon? Whose pardon?"

"Pardons straight from Washington. President Lincoln

wants to stop the killing in Missouri and Arkansas."

"You're about to see five more killings, right before I make it six," Hagan said.

"Shoving those men and me over the Hawksbill is just going to keep the war going on down here," Nelson said.

"Don't think you understand. A Yankee officer skinned my boy. Peeled the hide right off his back and tied him to a horse to die. That bastard's going to pay when I catch him," Hagan said.

"You want the officer that did that to your boy?" Nelson asked.

"Want him? I'm going to ride into that fort at Rolla and drag his sorry ass out. Burn what's left of the place." Hagan took a deep breath.

"I'll get him for you." Nelson stared at Hagan.

"What?"

"I'll get him. You'll lose most your men storming a fort like that. What happens to him after I get him is up to you." The torture Turner had put Hagan's boy through turned Nelson's stomach.

"Hold on with the rope, Red." Hagan held up his hand.

"The Command will move him to Jefferson Barracks in Saint Louis for court-martial." Nelson looked at Hagan. "With six of your men in Yankee uniforms, I'll be able to march into the Rolla Fort and get him."

"Red, tie him up," Hagan yelled. "Gather up our men out by the Hawksbill and drag those raping bastards with you."

The five men whimpered as each of them were led out to the edge of the Hawksbill. They either had to jump or be shot in the testicles. He heard the screams as all the men chose to jump to their death. The dull sound of each body smashing far below echoed across the face of the bluff. Their bones would spend eternity, scattered across a mountain valley. Hagan returned, walking up the path toward him, his pistol in his hand.

"If we try this and it don't work, I'm going to make you sorry as hell, Yankee." Hagan stuck the end of his pistol barrel against Nelson's forehead. "I've got the uniforms we'll need. What else do you want?"

"I'll draw up a general order for his transfer to Saint Louis." Nelson felt the pain when Hagan pulled his ropes tighter.

"We'll talk about those pardons, if I let you live. I have the uniforms stowed away on the way north," Hagan said. "If you don't get that sonofabitch for me, I'm going to hang you! Right after I skin your backside just like they did my boy."

"I'll get him." Nelson wasn't certain the offer he had just made would work or not.

"Red, he needs watching till we move out in the morning. Best tell your girlfriend over there goodbye, Nelson. Mess this up, and she's going to be a lot of fun for my boys. Tie him to a tree, Red."

Red yanked Nelson's arms around the tree trunk, tied him fast, and then left to join his men around a newly started fire. Anne walked to Nelson's side.

"I can cut you lose when it gets dark," she whispered.

"I'm afraid I got you into the middle of some quicksand." Nelson looked into her eyes. "You heard about Hagan's boy and the man that did it. Only way this is going to play out for me to live is for me to grab the bastard from the Rolla stockade."

"What about Dyer? Is he going with you?" Anne took a deep breath.

"Don't think so. He's your best hope if I don't get back. I think he'll keep you safe."

"Did you have a death wish coming back to Steelville?"

"I don't have a death wish. Maybe I have some guilt for a promise I made to a fourteen-year-old slave girl in the days before her trial. I couldn't save her. I promised myself someday the truth would come out. I would make sure of that." He left out his wish for revenge against the sheriff and the judge.

"Best get some rest, Anne. They'll be moving you north in the morning."

CHAPTER 17

Morning found Nelson alongside Hagan and six of his best men. He had watched Anne and Dyer heading out with the rest of Hagan's men for a hideout in the Ozark Mountains. Dyer gave Nelson his word he would keep Anne safe until he returned.

"Ok, Nelson. It'll be your play when we get to Rolla. Meantime, I'm going to keep you right beside me. Any trouble and I'll shoot you so quick you won't even see it coming," Hagan said.

"It's going to take a couple cool heads to ride into that stockade wearing Yankee uniforms," Nelson warned.

"One's going to be me," Hagan said.

On fast horses, the group of seven left the Hawksbill crag high above the Buffalo River and headed north toward Rolla. Hagan set the pace and pushed the group well into the night before they stopped at the bottom of a bluff. Two of his men tied their horses and went toward what looked like a fallen tree. They lifted some of the branches aside and disappeared into the bluff wall.

"The uniforms are hidden back in that cave," Hagan said.

"Won't be the first time they were used to fool Union troops," Red said.

"What are you going to tell that post commander when we get in there?" Hagan passed around some jerked beef to his men and Nelson.

"Tell him we've come to move the captive to Saint Louis," Nelson said. "We need to get to Rolla fast before the Saint Louis troops come to take him to hang."

"You better goddamn well hope he's still there, Yankee," Hagan said.

"We're going to look a little rough in those uniforms, so we need to ride in there at night." Nelson waited for Hagan's response.

"We'll stop and get shaved up, before going in." Hagan rubbed the hair on his chin.

"I'm going to need to write a general order for the prisoner's release."

"Got paper and ink in my saddle bag. Do that when we stop," Hagan said.

~ ~ ~ ~

After detours to avoid known Union outposts, they pulled up the horses in a wooded area three miles south of the Rolla Fort. He watched the bushwhackers struggle to get the tight-fitting Union uniforms on. It was a sight he never thought he would see, and it didn't sit well with his gut feelings. Putting a forged signature on the general order to release the prisoner, he folded it and put the paper in his uniform breast pocket.

Several minutes before midnight, Captain Paintier, with Sergeant Hagan riding beside him, approached the fort's gate. An alert sentry on the fort's wall gave the order to stop while they were still twenty yards out.

"Troop couriers, from Saint Louis," Nelson said.

"Advance to the gate, sir," said the guard, turning to call out the fort's guard troop.

"Stay calm, Hagan. No matter what happens in there. We're going to take that sonofabitch out of there before you screw him up, understand?"

"Get on then."

"Open the gate," the guard ordered.

Just inside the gate, the Sergeant of the Guards with six of his troops were standing at parade rest to meet Nelson and Hagan. "Captain, Sir. What brings you to Rolla this time of night?" the sergeant asked.

"We're here to pick up the prisoner, Turner. We have orders to escort him to Saint Louis for court-martial," Nelson said.

"You came a little late for that, Captain. He escaped. The troops here was never going to let a hero like him hang for what he did to that murdering shitbag son of Hagan's," the sergeant said.

Out of the corner of his eye, Nelson caught the motion of Hagan going for his pistol. Nelson kicked Hagan's horse in the side and turned into it, forcing the horse toward the still open gate behind them. The guard at the gate leveled his rifle at Hagan a second before Nelson rode into him and knocked the guard off his feet. Both Nelson and Hagan were through the gate and into the darkness before the firing behind them started.

Three miles south of the fort, they joined up with the other six men and pulled up to circle the horses.

"Troops will be going crazy back there. Won't take them long to come after us," Nelson groaned.

"I'm going after that sonofabitch. Follow him to hell," Hagan said. "You saved my life back there, Nelson. I'm going to thank you for that, rather than shoot you."

"There aren't many places he can go. The troops from Saint Louis will be looking for him if he goes east." Nelson looked around the area.

"He'll go west and find friends with the Jayhawkers in Kansas," Hagan said. "He must be at least a day's ride ahead of us by now."

"He'll stay north of Springfield, most likely. Shouldn't be too hard to get a handle on where he's headed in that direction," Nelson said.

"We've got lots of friends around there that will give us a hand tracking him," Hagan pointed at his men. "Head 'em. up, boys. We're headin' for Kansas."

"Hold on, Hagan. Eight of us riding off in that direction will leave a trail wider than a set of wagon wheels." Nelson watched while Hagan thought about what he'd said.

"Guess you're right. You're coming with us, Red. Rest of you men lead the Rolla troops off south, set up a running ambush when they least expect it." Hagan raised his hand and pointed again. "Get your regular riding clothes on, one of you men bury all these Yankee uniforms. Get caught with them, you'll hang. Might anyway."

~ ~ ~ ~

Having ridden throughout the night, the three men pulled up their mounts and dismounted for a rest alongside the Big Piney River. Patches of white foam oozed out from under the horse's saddles and around the edges of their bridles. The horses had been ridden hard and were taking deep breaths from being winded. Red gathered up the reins of the three horses and walked them along a river pathway. It would be a while before he would lead them to the river to drink, they had to cool down first.

"I doubt if he's pushing this hard to get to Kansas," Hagan said. "He doesn't know the devil himself is on his heels."

"If we guessed right about where he's headed, there's only a couple traces through here for him to take. Are you thinking the same, Hagan?" Nelson asked.

"You're right. He should be only a half a day ahead now. He'll be stopping to bum or steal some food before today is over. His doings will give us a chance to find out if we're on him."

"Until we find some sign of him for sure, what do you think of splitting up on these two traces?"

"Good idea. If you screw me up, you know what's going to happen to that pretty schoolteacher been riding with you."

"I know, Hagan. I told you I'd help get this guy and I meant it. Leave Anne out of this."

Hagan nodded. "We'll just have to see. There's a good place to meet up north of Lead Town on the rail line that runs through there. If you find him holed up somewhere, don't kill him! I'm going to do that slow and make him suffer like my boy did."

"He's yours, Hagan."

"Take the north trace, Nelson. Red, you're riding with me."

~ ~ ~ ~

Riding the trace, Nelson crossed dozens of deep valleys with steep descents. Holding the horse back going down the valley sides got harder as the animal tired from the many climbs to get through the area. He had been walking his horse in a valley creek area for the last few minutes to give the mare a rest when he came upon a shack alongside the trace. Burlap gunny sacks covered the side window of the sagging clapboard structure. A rusty tin stove pipe stuck through the wall and turned its nose to the sky as if it was trying like hell to get out of the shack. He felt surprised anyone could live there. An old man sat in front of the shack on what could hardly be called a porch. The man picked up the crutch lying beside him and used it to push himself erect in his chair.

"Can I ride up?" Nelson called to the man.

"Looks like you're comin' anyway," the man said.

The man's long heavy beard and yellowing white hair made him look over sixty, but as Nelson got closer, he placed him to be much younger. The wounds of war did terrible things to age men. When he let the reins slump, the horse walked the rest of the distance to a hitching post in front of the shack and stopped.

"Get down, mister. Sit a bit," the man said, pointing with his crutch to the edge of the porch.

"My name's Paintier. Have you been sitting out here long today?"

"Been out here since they took my leg and sent me home. I still think about killin' all them that was coming at us in that fight," the man complained.

"Those kinds of battles are hard to forget, ain't they?" Nelson more than agreed with the stranger.

"Ain't a matter of forgetting," the man said. "Matter is there ain't nothin' else to think about now and hardly nobody to talk to 'bout it."

"I've been following a Yankee soldier a couple of us want to catch up with really bad." Nelson paused a moment. "I think he might have come through this valley." He wasn't surprised when the man didn't respond to what he said. The wounded and scarred man only stared off into the distance. He waited, giving the old soldier time to answer. Nelson still could have minutes of not talking himself when he got wrapped up in the war thinking.

"I sit out here most of the night. It don't do no good going inside and trying to sleep. I just end up fightin' all those battles over and over. At least out here the air smells good. I'm not shut up no more like when the Yankees had me in prison. The man you chasing a Yankee?"

"He's a Yankee officer. He's done some really bad

things."

"The rider you're after came through here about dawn. He stopped when he saw me sittin' here. Seen his dirty Yankee uniform, had my shotgun up to shoot him 'fore he took off. Hope you catch him."

"Why they take your leg?" Nelson asked.

"Yankee doctor cut it off. Said it was rotten anyway and I was going to die if he didn't. Funny thing, first their army tries to kill you. Then along comes their doctor and tries to save you. Don't make no damn sense to me," the man said. "Them Yankee's savin' me from dying and all."

"War's a crazy thing," Nelson said.

He thanked the man and headed his horse west again. He would close up the gap before night if Turner stopped for food, or to steal a gun.

Nelson saw only a few scattered houses along the trace during the next four hours of riding. For the last quarter mile, the winding road had descended into an even deeper valley. He heard running water even before he saw the wide blue spring flowing from under a bluff and into a narrow stream. A well-kept barn, set on the bank of the stream, had a water wheel turning in the current.

A dozen wooden barrels sat in front of the barn, each one with smoke coming out the top. The barrels were being seasoned. Before he got to the barn the sound of a water driven saw inside stopped. Two rifles were pointed at him from behind stacks of barrel staves in the doorway.

"Easy there." Nelson held up his hand. "I'm looking to stop for a drink of that spring water and anything you keep in those fine barrels." It had been a long time since he had a drink of some good home-grown whiskey.

"The last fella stopped here, stole one of our rifles and more than a quart of our whiskey," a woman said.

"Was he wearing a Yankee uniform?" Nelson asked.

"It could be. He had on a blue shirt and some pants a foot too short for him."

"It sounds like the fellow I'm chasing got a change of clothes. He's a Yankee that needs killing really bad."

"Then you're welcome to climb down from that horse and get that drink. Whiskey gonna' cost you a nickel, Mister. You ain't that far behind the stealin' Yankee," the man added.

Nelson led his horse to the creek. After the mare drank, he went back to the barn for a shot of Ozark whiskey and something to eat. He wasn't disappointed on either.

"If that Yankee drinks much of that quart you'll find him lying beside the road somewhere up ahead. Our whiskey got a kick in it like a mule." The man laughed.

A half hour later Nelson rode out with a warm feeling in his gut, not only from the whiskey, but also knowing he was pushing the escaped Yankee to a meeting with his maker. The light from the full moon helped him keep riding through the night.

CHAPTER 18

Once he rode out of the steep valley country of the Ozark Mountains, the trace settled onto level ground, where the virgin timber crowded each side of the narrow pathway and made an ambush possible from either of the sides. He wished Hagan and his men were with him, leading the way with their black flag flying, throwing fear into all who saw their symbol of give no quarter. Turner could be waiting ten feet to the side and out of sight. Nelson spurred his horse into a run.

After two short stops to give the horse a rest, he rode into a settlement of half a dozen houses and a general store. Tying up to the hitching post in front, he climbed over the two broken steps leading to the porch and went in.

"Howdy, young man," came a man's voice from in the back. "Be up there in a minute."

Nelson looked around the counters, noticing the short supply of food items on the store shelves.

"Not a lot to eat on them shelves, is there," stated the store clerk.

"The damn fighting making it hard to get food down here, I bet." Nelson looked around the poorly stocked store.

"Folks that raise their own food are still going hungry. Both sides of this fight have come raiding and stealing from all of us."

"My name's Nelson. I've been traveling for a couple days looking for a murdering Yankee."

"I ain't seen nobody much. We only had one fellow stop in this afternoon, besides you."

"Mind telling me what he looked like?"

"He's a tall man, wearing a blue shirt," said the storekeeper. "Traded me a quart of good whiskey for an old six shooter I kept here under the counter."

"That's the fellow I'm looking for." Nelson shook his head. "How long ago did he leave?"

"He ain't left, as far as I know. Took up with our town whore and headed up the street with her about twenty minutes ago. He should be about done by now. The woman is known for getting things done fast. He was riding a dark bay horse. Her house is just up the street. He should be easy to find in this little town."

"Thanks mister. I'm going to have a look for that horse." Nelson left quickly.

~ ~ ~ ~

The bay horse stood beside the white house at the end of the street. A military saddle with an empty scabbard sat on the horse, ready for someone to ride. Nelson rode up quietly and dismounted to stand across the street waiting, using his own horse to hide behind. He slid the action on his rifle to chamber a round and backed up alongside a tree to watch the house. The front curtains on the house's only window were drawn tight. Twice he felt sure he heard a woman in the house laughing. When the front door of the house opened halfway and then slammed shut, he knew he had been seen and a fight was on the way. The front window of the shack shattered when someone knocked it out. A volley of shots from the window hit around him. His mare shuddered when a shot hit her. The wounded animal reared and stumbled, knocking him to the ground. The horse fell pinning his foot under the edge of the saddle. He caught a glimpse of Turner pulling his blue shirt on and running for his horse. Turner passed him half out of the saddle on the other side of his horse. It made a small target. He jerked his foot from under the horse and stood, firing at Turner, now out of pistol range. Nelson ducked when two shots came from the rifle a woman held standing in the door of the house. They ricocheted off the dirt in the street behind Turner.

"God damn it, lady!" Nelson yelled. "You're going to hit me with that wild ass shooting."

"Ain't shooting at you, mister. Just the runoff bastard that didn't pay me nothin' for my pussy!"

The woman at the door stood stark naked with her red hair draped over her shoulders covering only the top half of her breasts. He couldn't believe what he saw. "Too bad you didn't hit him. He just shot my damn horse!"

The woman had stopped firing at Turner and stood in the doorway with the butt of her rifle on the floor and the barrel in her right hand. She had her other hand holding one of her breasts and shaking it at him. "Heard you say something about wild ass? Why don't you come on in here and get some? You can finish off what that prickless bastard started."

"Lady, best you get on back in that house. I've got to shoot this mare and I ain't happy about it at all," Nelson said. Looking at the mare's shattered leg, before he walked in front of the shivering horse to put her down with a pistol shot to the head.

"Damn it to hell anyway!" Nelson knelt beside the mare's side and felt to be sure there wasn't any heartbeat.

"Any idea where I can get another horse?" Nelson asked the woman still watching from her door.

"See the man at the store. He keeps a couple horses at a farm just up the road." The woman waved at the man. "Fix you right up. Sure, you don't—"

"Hell no!"

~ ~ ~ ~

More than three hours had gone by before Nelson settled with the storeowner for a sound horse and paid him to take care of the dead mare, up at the end of the street. The man he chased didn't give a hoot about shooting a man or his horse. He would need to watch for an ambush on the trace ahead.

An hour out of town he heard a train whistle off to the south. From the direction of the sound, the trace ran parallel to the tracks and would lead to the meeting place with Hagan and Red.

"Don't like riding another horse straight into an ambush, boy," Nelson said to his new mount. "Tracks look like he's riding full out."

Turner would have several more days before he could reach Kansas and the safety of one of the Jayhawker towns. He followed at a steady trot, letting the fleeing Turner push ahead and wear out his mount.

He heard another train to the south; it was closer this time. The trace would soon join the tracks at the place he hoped to find Hagan. With luck he hoped Hagan might have caught Turner by now.

He rode up a steep bank to the railroad line built along the top of a swell. A short distance west, Hagan surprised him and came from behind a stand of willows to the south of the tracks.

"Didn't have any luck on the south trace. You?" Hagan asked.

"I've been close on him for a ways. He's not far ahead, now. I had a run in with him when he had stopped for some Ozark pussy. I tried to wait him out. The bastard must have seen me. He shot my horse. I've been only a couple hours behind him all day."

"I got here about an hour ago. I didn't see nobody pass," Hagan said.

"His tracks are still showing on the trace. His horse lost a shoe back there five miles or so," Nelson said shifting in the saddle to look back to the north where he'd been riding.

"Lead on back to the trace," Hagan said. "It's getting too late to corner him and fight it out in the dark."

"He'll need to get another shoe on, riding on all this rock. I've been letting him string out a bit so he wouldn't be sure how close I'm getting," Nelson said. "He'll have to find a blacksmith. His horse is starting to favor that right foot."

"We're close to Lead Town, he'll slip in there for the night," Hagan said, dismounting and taking a hoof pick to each of his horse's feet. "I picked up some shale crossing that track."

"There's only one trace out of Lead Town that heads west." Nelson followed Hagan's example and checked his horses' hooves.

"What you got in mind?" Hagan asked.

"I'm thinking you might ride hard on past Lead Town, and I follow him in there and run him out. Let him start out on the trace, we could have him boxed in." Nelson lifted his hat and brushed his hair back from his forehead.

"I want to see his face when he finds Jim Hagan blocking his path." He lifted his pistol from the holster and pushed it back solidly and securely into place. "I'll be out about ten miles on the other side of Lead Town. What's this bastard riding?

"He's hard to miss, wearing a blue shirt, sitting a big, dark bay horse. I'll be tight on his ass out of Lead Town.

He'll be pushing the bay hard. Watch him, he picked up a pistol back there, and he's not going to go down easy."

"We'll see about that. Take Red with you this time, I want that bastard to myself," Hagan shouted, joining the trace at a gallop.

~ ~ ~ ~

With little daylight left, Nelson and Red rode into the mining town. The dark buildings sprouted a wooden plank walk along their front. The light shining from the door of the last building lit the end of the town's business buildings and the sidewalk. Sure, the light came from a tavern, they rode around behind the first building to tie their horses out of sight. Back on the rickety plank walk, Nelson stopped and pointed out the glow coming from a blacksmith's forge on the other side of the street.

"The smith is working late on somebody's horse," Red said. "I smelled the forge out a ways."

"He's probably got the shoe on by now. If we're lucky, Turner stopped to get something to eat in the saloon."

"Hagan will be mad as hell if we kill this bastard." Red adjusted his hat.

"I want to try and just run him out of town, if we can." Nelson said. "He'll head west on his own."

They had passed the front of the hardware store when they heard the shots up ahead. They ran toward the noise and saw the powder flashes from the pistols' barrels pointed over the edge of the saloon's balcony. The light coming from the doors and windows behind the balcony lit the women standing at the rail firing and cursing at someone on the street below.

"Ladies are mad as hell at somebody." Nelson tried to see who they were shooting at.

"Somebody coming from the blacksmith's barn. He's going like hell to get out of here," yelled Red as the rider passed them.

"It's hard to see, but it looked like the bay Turner was riding." Nelson pointed at the horse that just passed them.

Up ahead, men were hanging lanterns in front of the saloon.

"Come on, Red. We need to find out what went on up there." They hurried the rest of the way to the door of the saloon.

"I'm needing to form up a posse over here," shouted a man just clipping a badge on his night shirt.

"Did anybody get a look at that guy?" Nelson asked stepping into the light of the lanterns.

"Ask the gals upstairs," the sheriff responded. "He herded all them whores in one room and took all their money. It's too bad them gals didn't catch him, would have been some serious cutting going on."

"You see the horse he rode out on?" Nelson asked. "I've been chasing a Yankee riding a big bay horse missing a back shoe."

"He came in before dark and rode the bay down to the smithy to get the shoe on. When he came back to the saloon to eat, he finished and took the nigger gal upstairs. Next thing I knowed, he came ripping down the steps with the gals all screaming. Them girls took to the balcony to try and kill the bastard!" The sheriff took out his pistol, pointed it at the ground and turned the cylinder to check his loads. "Did you see which way he headed out of town?"

"It looked like he rode off to the east." Nelson lied. He didn't want anybody chasing Turner but himself, when the unlucky bastard rode up on Hagan's ambush.

"The ladies will want me to mount a posse up quick, they worked hard for those earnings he stole." The sheriff snickered.

"You help on those earnings too, sheriff?" Nelson kidded, turning to go into the saloon to look for something to eat and drink.

"I'd be glad to have you boys ride out with us in the morning, mister," the sheriff said.

"Thanks sheriff." Nelson knew that would never happen. No way in hell! He planned on pushing Turner right into Hagan's grasp.

Nelson and Red went on through the double doors of the saloon and just inside found the way blocked by three women, each wearing nothing but an open robe. Each of them carried a smoking pistol.

Red reached for Nelson and held him back from passing them for a moment, "These ladies look hotter than them pistol barrels."

"We ain't no ladies, gents. That bastard got the drop on our Molly. He threatened to shoot her if we didn't cough up our earnings." This gal stood out, taller and wider than the other two.

Moving aside to let them pass, she walked up to the bar and picked up a half-empty bottle of whiskey. After she filled three glasses, she cussed and smashed the empty bottle across the edge of the bar. Turning, she handed two of the glasses to the ladies that had joined her. They had backed up to the bar. He was surprised the big gal hadn't torn Turner's arms off by herself.

"Did we hit him?" asked a dark-skinned girl, looking hopefully at Nelson.

"I don't think so. He rode by me headed out of town fast. He's a hardass Yankee I've been chasing," Nelson said.

"Buy us the next drink, sweetheart? We're done bare ass broke, see," said the redhead opening her robe and turning her bare butt into Nelson's side. He turned away, reached into his pocket for a coin, and slapped it down on the bar. It would buy several drinks for the girls.

He needed rest. They would need daylight to track the horse with one new shoe. He and Red could pick up the trail in the morning.

"Get something to eat, Red. This will take care of that and any other thing you might like." Nelson flipped him a coin. "I'm going to rest on the bench out front till first light." He grabbed a jar of pickled pig's feet that sat on the bar and headed for the swinging doors. He chewed around two of the pig's feet before he stretched out on the front bench. He was glad the girls hadn't followed him. He fell quickly asleep thinking the girls would surely give Red the ride of his life upstairs.

~ ~ ~ ~

Before dawn Nelson climbed the steps into the saloon looking for Red. He found him sprawled across a double bed draped with womanhood and smelling like he just took a bath in a pig pen.

Back with the horses, Nelson began picking out the dirt and small rocks lodged under their steel shoes. As he finished, Red came around the corner of the hardware store, still tucking in his shirt and buttoning his pants.

"Them three women soft as melted butter on the outside, but harder than them steel horseshoes inside," Red said.

"I know what you're saying, Red." Nelson packed the half-empty jar of salt pork into his saddlebag. "Let's push that bastard...hard. Hagan will be waiting for him west of here."

"Should be light in a few minutes. Be able to follow his horse easy with that new shoe," Red said.

It didn't take Red long to find the horse's tracks. Falling in to follow Turner, they settled into a gallop, slowing only to check they were still on his tracks.

"His track showing...he slowed down...." Red pointed at the tracks. "He's thinkin' no one is chasing."

"He must have waited till daylight to do that so he can't be that far ahead now." They covered the next half mile at a gallop.

Slowing his horse, Red pointed at the trace. "He pulled out quick though here, he must have heard us coming. Tracks show he's going at a hard run now."

"Then he knows we're back here," Nelson said. "Watch if he slows again, he might try to waylay us." Both men spurred their horses into a run.

CHAPTER 19

The thunder of their own running horses drowned out the noise of the gun battle coming at them from around the next bend. A single rider came first, his horse stretched out in a run, turning to glance behind and waving a pistol in his hand. "It's Hagan," shouted Red, pulling up his horse.

Hagan passed Nelson and Red and slid to a stop. "They're coming...get ready...about six left, Yankee troops...been shooting at me for the last two miles."

The mounted troops rounded the bend, coming through the dust from Hagan's horse, each one firing blind at the guerrilla they chased. They pulled their horses up at the sight of the new opponents.

Hagan yelled, "Come on, Red, good place as any to die." Taking his second pistol from his belt, he charged headlong toward the surprised troops. The guerrillas rode with their reins in their mouth and a pistol in each hand, their well-trained horses holding their ears flat on their heads and running headlong into the stunned Federal troops. Hagan's first shot took down the lead rider. Red's hit a trooper who fell backward from the saddle onto the trace. Nelson rode beside them and fired, his shot going over the head of his target on purpose. The four troops that were left turned and slumped low in their saddles as they headed back west.

"Let 'em go," Hagan yelled. "They won't stop till they get to Kansas City."

The pause gave Nelson time to think. What in the hell was he doing, riding and helping the guerrilla leader he had been ordered to kill or pardon? Quicksand was closing in all around him. With Anne traveling with the rest of Hagan's men, and Hagan meaning to skin the guy they were chasing there were way too many things to go wrong if he didn't help Hagan get Turner, even if he didn't like playing a part.

"Red, find his track again. He had to come through here," Hagan said. "He didn't get past me."

"Turner's horse has a new shoe on the right rear, Hagan," Nelson added. "He had to turn off somewhere close by when he heard the gunfight coming at him."

Nelson rode slowly along the north side of the trace, Red along the south, each of them looking for some sign of where Turner had turned off. Hagan rode picket, watching the trace out in front for danger.

The second time Nelson dismounted to walk up deer paths that crossed the trace, he found the spot about twenty yards up where Turner had stopped and turned his horse, watching the fight back on the trail. Nelson gave a sharp whistle that brought the other riders to his side.

"He came through here...headed on north," Nelson said, pointing at the steep hill in front of him.

"He can't be far ahead." Not pausing, Hagan led the way up the climb in front of them. The tracks on the rocky trail were hard to follow, so Hagan motioned for Red to take the lead.

"He can track a coon swimming in water," Hagan said.

"I've been following behind that red top of his for four years now. Ain't never let me down on following a track."

Hagan pulled his horse up beside Nelson, waiting for Red to pick up the track.

"I told Red if anything happened to me out here, for him to go back with you. Take the pardon and get home," Hagan said. "I fought in the war like you did, only I broke away before surrender and formed up with these boys to keep bushwhacking you damn Yankees. We done some bad killin', but nothing like Turner did to my boy. I'm going to make him pay for what he done."

Hagan wouldn't stop until he got the revenge he was calling for. Problem was, Nelson was right in the middle of helping him get it.

"I figure I've been lucky some Yankee like you ain't shot me," Hagan said.

"Now one is helping you shoot Yankees. It ain't worth even a chuckle, is it?" Nelson said, shaking his head and looking down at his saddle horn.

"Red's on him again," Hagan said, starting up a steep trail to their right. "There's a river bluff up ahead a ways. We might have him by the balls real soon."

Duty had driven his urge to kill for three years of battle. Now, after one of his own army's officers had torn the skin off a captured rebel, Nelson's desire to capture and kill someone had never been stronger.

Nelson urged his horse on. The three horses stopped nose to tail. Hagan pointed to their left at two elk, their heads up sniffing the air.

"I'm afraid he's got a lead on us," Hagan said. "Those Elk wouldn't be just grazing this close behind him." Both elk broke into a run at the sound of voices. They went off down the hill crashing through the brush and trees.

Red dismounted and knelt beside the trail. He picked up a broken chunk of moss. "This moss is still damp on the back. His horse went through here less than an hour ago."

RICHARD O. SNELSON

"He must have turned the horse loose...He's going on foot now," Nelson said. "The elk would have smelled a man."

Hagan caught on quick, "Sonofabitch knew we would track him down on horseback. We'll never find him in here on foot...shit!"

"His horse will stop to graze...I'll make sure that's what he done," Red said. He left to follow the horse's trail on up the ridge. He came back in less than ten minutes. "The horse is up there...bridle...saddle both gone."

"Head back. We'll start where he left that saddle and Red can pick up his track," Hagan said.

~ ~ ~ ~

A quarter mile back down the trail, Red found the saddle. Turner had left the horse's tack covered with leaves and brush so they wouldn't see it right away. Red quickly found Turner's foot trail.

"He started off west," Red said. "He won't be in a hurry. Knows we can't follow him on horseback through that thick brush."

"I'm going in and find his sorry ass," Hagan said. Climbing off his horse, he handed the reins to Red.

"Rather you get back up there," Red said. "Leave his trackin' to me. I'll push him out somewhere up ahead."

"He's going to come out of there desperate. He'll need water, food and another horse, if he's able to lose us," Nelson said. The thick brush and woods would make it a hard track to follow through. Hagan had told him Red was the best. His hopes were high they would have Turner before the end of the day.

Hagan took the watch from his pocket and handed it to Red, "Fire a pistol shot every hour. Nelson's got a watch and keep track how far along you get tracking him."

After an ammo check, Red disappeared into the brush,

leaving his horse to Nelson.

Back on the trace, Nelson and Hagan walked their horses west. Nelson led Red's horse alongside his. The first pistol shot from Red came right on the hour. They could only guess how far west the sound came from. Stopping, they waited for the next hour's shot, it would tell them how far Red had followed Turner.

"There's bound to be a stream crossing up ahead, we can ride up stream half a mile or so and wait till Red runs him out," Hagan said. He spurred his horse into a lope.

In less than two miles they found a stream crossing the trace. They waded the horses up the streambed, swimming them across deep holes of water. Hagan pointed out a place on the bank for Nelson to wait, then rode on north. In less than an hour, Nelson heard the next shot. A rifle shot. He rode up the stream to find Hagan. Three more shots followed. They were from a pistol.

"Red's in trouble...that's our signal," Hagan said. "I need to get back to where we found his saddle so I can track him." Both men headed back to the place where Red started following Turner.

At the start of the trail, "Nelson, stay with the horses. That sonofabitch doubles back, kill him."

He didn't like waiting. Especially holding three horses and not sure what might come out of the brush. He carefully tied the three mounts on the side of the trail and found a place to hide and watch just off the narrow trail.

The wait seemed forever before Hagan came out of the brush carrying Red over his shoulder. Nelson hurried to help him lay the wounded man on the ground. The front of Red's shirt was stained dark with blood.

"He's hit...bad," Hagan said.

"Leave me here...,damn it, go after him." Red gasped and passed out.

Nelson cut Red's shirt off and ripped it into long strips. "Shot didn't come out," Nelson said. He headed for the jar of salt pork in his saddlebags. "Get this wrapped tight with some pork skin against the hole… It should be enough to stop the bleeding. It will sting like hell when he wakes up. "

"Nelson, you're going to have to take him back to Iron Town. The closest doctor would be there."

"You know the way Turner's headed, straight for Lawrence, Kansas, don't you?" Nelson said, "They'll welcome him like a hero out there."

"Lawrence? Shit…," Hagan said. "Wasn't much of the place left after my last visit with Bill Quantrill."

"If they catch you there…do more than hang you," Nelson said. "I'd have a lot better chance of dragging Turner out of Lawrence than you would."

"I've been putting a lot of trust in a damn Yankee, Nelson, but you do make some sense," Hagan said. "Best not do me wrong. I'm still thinkin' about you missing that trooper back on the trace this morning."

"I'll see if I can get Red awake." He ignored Hagan's comment and slapped both of Red's cheeks without any reaction.

"Wake up, goddamn it, Red. Can't lose my best tracker to some son-of-a-bitch murdering Yankee." Hagan leaned over Red's face to yell at him.

Nelson winced at the disparaging remark. After what Turner did, he couldn't blame Hagan, but at the end of the day, Nelson was a Yankee too.

"Have to tie him in the saddle," Nelson said. "I can wrap a blanket around him."

Red groaned as they tied him half-sitting up onto his horse. He'd die before night if he didn't get to a doctor to remove the bullet and stop the bleeding.

"I'll get him to a doc, then come back out to wait for you," Hagan said.

"Wait along the border. I'll come back along the place the Federals tried to head Quantrill off on his way out of Lawrence," Nelson said.

"I know that place too damn well," Hagan said. "I'm not going to ask how you know it too."

"If something happens...I'll drag him back to your Buffalo River den."

Alone again, he planned the next couple of days, and his ride to Lawrence. Turner would have to steal a horse soon and then travel through a lot of burned-out land before he got out of Missouri. Speaking to the wind, "I'm going to beat you to Lawrence, you son-of-a-bitch." With a sense of urgency, he spurred his horse toward the guerrilla ravaged town of Lawrence, Kansas.

CHAPTER 20

He knew the Lawrence folk would welcome a wounded Yankee officer, so he put on the blue pants from his saddlebags and wrapped a bandage around his leg. More than a couple days passed while he waited on the porch of Lawrence's only hotel for Turner to show up. The Kansas Jayhawkers would welcome Turner as a hero when they found out what he had done to a bushwhacker.

Turner didn't look much like a hero when he showed up riding an old skin and bone mule. The mule had patches of black soot all along his side and looked like no one had fed him for months. The mule must have been left to roam on the burned out no man's land along the Missouri-Kansas border.

Turner didn't look much better than the mule. He rode right past the hotel without noticing the man slumped on the bench with a bandaged leg. The deception had worked. Turner urged the mule up to a hitching post in front of the Lose It Here saloon.

"Hope that fellow just passed ain't no Johnny Reb," said

the man standing to the side of Nelson's bench.

"I expect he ain't," Nelson said. "Hear the good folks of Lawrence would likely offer him lunch and then hang him."

"Lost my wife...when the bushwhackers come...I was out tending my field. They caught her coming out of the hardware store and just rode her down. Found her lying dead in the street," the man said.

"We killed some of the bastards when they headed back toward Missouri," Nelson said. "Your welcome to sit."

"Reckon I can, for a while. My name is Mesman. Yours?" the man asked.

"Just Captain will be fine. I've been fighting for so long I almost forgot the rest that goes with it. Yes, just Captain."

"My wife and me, we're Dutch. We came out here from Pennsylvania back in fifty-six. Never thought much about slaves and such," Mesman said. "We came through Missouri on a steamboat."

"I think a lot of the folks came here the same way. They saw how the slaves were treated along the Missouri River towns," Nelson said. "It got their tempers up, some of them took to raiding the southern sympathizers back in Missouri."

"I never done none of that. Back in Pennsylvania some of us Dutch were treated bad," Mesman said. "I brought my wife out here to get away from it. I'm sorry now I ever come."

"Lucky in some ways you didn't stay in Pennsylvania. The fighting there wasted away a lot of the people just trying to get out of the way of the war," Nelson said, watching as a unit of Federal Calvary passed the hotel.

Nelson made a quick excuse and left Mr. Mesman sitting on the hotel porch. He needed to find another horse before nightfall. No way would he take Turner back to Missouri on the worn out mule he rode in on.

Before looking for another horse, he made a stop at the

saloon to check on Turner. There'd been too much distance between them when Turner shot his horse, so he wouldn't recognize him if he found him. He saw him as he went in the door of the saloon, surrounded by half a dozen Lawrence, Kansas, Jayhawkers who were buying him drinks and listening to him telling about killing some of Bloody Bill Anderson's boys in Missouri. He was already staggering drunk, carrying him out of there later tonight would be easy. He left the saloon and walked on up the street toward the stable sign at the end of the street to get another horse.

"Howdy, mister," said the stable owner, "You look mighty sore to be walking."

"You could be right, sir," Nelson said. "I need a sound horse."

"Most horses out there in my corral are work horses. The cavalry buys up all the rest. Too many of their horses get shot. I've got mules around in the back. You would have to take both mules if it's a team. One won't go without the other."

"I would rather have a buffalo than another mule."

"I'm keeping a mustang for my brother. He's afraid of all the horses' spirit. It's a big roan horse. We'll take fifty dollars for the horse. Take him and ride him out good before you decide."

Getting a roan with spirit cheered him. He had wanted another horse that would fit his riding like Blue had. Blue was always willing to go where he commanded. She would climb a rock shelf, clawing her way up. Always giving her best to her master.

"Let's saddle him up. I think my leg can stand a little spirit from a horse."

The mustang sniffed hard when they approached his stall. His ears laid flat against his head.

"Has somebody been treating this horse mean?" He picked up a lead rope from the rack and draped it carefully along his side so as not to frighten the animal.

"My brother ain't easy with horses. He never had no business owning a stallion. So, I had the horse cut a while back. He's still got plenty of fire in him," said the stable owner, "Brother took a chain to him couple times. The horse broke out of the stall and chased him clean out of the barn."

"Just set out the saddle for me. I'll get to know this fella alone." He opened the stall door, watched, as the horse backed to the far corner, facing him with ears flat.

"Easy fella...not going to hurt you...," whispered Nelson, walking slowly toward the side of the mustang's head. "Easy, boy, get my smell." He slid the lead along the outside of the horse's neck and then stroked his front shoulder. The ears came up a bit, one turned toward the stranger at his side. He attached the lead to the horse's halter and rubbed his hand along the horse's side before leading him into the barn's aisle.

"Ain't seen nobody with courage enough to do that for a while," said the stable owner. "Not after he stomped my brother's dog to death. Named him Killer right after that."

"Anything else you want to tell me now, before I ride Killer?"

He walked around the horse, lifted his feet and pushed the center of each hoof with a hoof pick to check for soreness. The horse didn't flinch. He took a curry brush to the gelding's sides and croup before saddling, and then led him to the street before mounting the fifteen hands tall animal.

"Easy, just a walk for now...," always talking to the horse. He could feel the horse loosen up and relax. Someone had done a good job breaking the mustang. The horse flexed on command, bending each direction, and then changing leads without queues into figure eights. He rode at a full gallop, and then half a mile from town, slowed before he reined the horse down into a deep ditch. The mustang climbed out with the power and agility he always looked for in a mount. Back at the stable, Nelson handed the owner four twenty-dollar gold pieces. "Need the saddle and bridle too." He waited for the answer.

The man rolled his finger over the gold pieces in his hand. "Okay, reckon I'm a lot happier to get that horse out of my brother's hands, than you might be to get him," the stable owner said.

Back at the hotel stable, he loosened the horse's girth and walked the fine animal for a few minutes to cool him out from the workout. He tied him and asked the stable keeper to saddle his other horse and keep them both ready to ride.

Nelson paced his room and finally went down to the hotel dining room and ordered the first steak he had eaten since the war started. He drank a cup of strong coffee before leaving his room key at the desk and going to be sure the horses were ready. When he passed the saloon, he saw Turner had passed out in a chair near the front of the drinking establishment.

At closing time for the saloon, Nelson entered, telling the bartender he was looking for his friend. The bartender pointed him out in the corner and offered his help to get him out.

"Come on, buddy...stand up...taking you to your room," Nelson said, getting Turner to his feet and guided him out the door. Turner could barely walk, but Nelson managed to get him out of the tavern and around to the back of the hotel.

"Where...we...goin?" Turner sputtered, leaning against the saddle.

Nelson grabbed Turner's belt and hoisted him flat across the saddle. "There, go on back to sleep." With only a couple of moans coming from the drunk, Nelson had him tied across the saddle and covered with a blanket. Climbing on the mustang, he led the horse and his captive toward the border. "We'll have him back in Missouri by morning, Killer," he said to his new horse. "Gonna have to change that name."

CHAPTER 21

"**G**et...me...the hell...out of this," mumbled Turner, struggling against his rope ties and the pain of being strung across a saddle while traveling at a trot.

"Shut up, Turner. Want to stay tied up like that all day?" It felt good to be traveling on Missouri soil again. When he had crossed into Missouri, he looked for Hagan but there was no sign of him. "I'm stopping just ahead. Then I'll set you up on the saddle," Nelson glanced at Turner and shook his head.

"I don't have any money. Why did you kidnap me? Who the hell are you?"

Nelson didn't answer the questions. He pulled up in a thick stand of trees and stopped to untie the ropes holding Turner in the saddle. When Turner slid off the saddle his leg folded under him, and he slumped to the ground in a heap.

"Stay down there," he said pulling the cover from Turner's head and pushing him flat on his belly with his boot.

"Shit…tying a man on a horse like that. It ain't human!" Turner tried to reach for a stirrup to pull himself up with. "I pissed all over myself an hour ago."

"You might be doing a lot more pissing if I shoot you." Nelson took his own aim next to a tree. "Going to need those legs working, so walk around, before I tie you up straight in that saddle for the rest of the ride."

"Damn it. Who are you?" Turner demanded again.

"Captain Nelson Paintier to you, Lieutenant Turner." Pointing his pistol at the man. "Get your hands out in front. I'm tying you back up. You're going to ride along side of me. If you make a break for it, I'll kill you."

"They ain't never going to hold me in that Rolla Stockade." Turner tilted his head up. "Most of the troop at Rolla know I'm a hero."

Nelson let the hero idea fly, knowing Turner was going to wish like hell he was back in Rolla, when he got to the Hawksbill. Leading Turner's horse, Nelson urged his mustang into a trot.

Nelson had filled both his saddlebags with food before leaving Lawrence. He would stop midday to feed them both and rest the horses.

Nelson wasn't surprised that all the houses and barns along the trace were gone. There was nothing standing but rock walls and blackened fireplaces, monuments to the Union Army's Order 11, in 1863, by General Ewing to clean out the guerrilla supporters in three Western Missouri counties. General Ewing burned out all the people living there regardless of who they supported. Only a few people had returned, most were unwilling to sign a pledge to support the Union and the constitution of the USA.

The trip to Lawrence had taken more than several days. Having to deal with Turner on the way back would take longer.

"We're riding late tonight." He nudged the lead on Turner's horse to keep up.

He had been leading Turner's horse in the dark for two hours when he heard the sound of water rippling across the trace. After riding downstream along the creek for a short distance he stopped the horses and got Turner out of the saddle before tying him to a tree.

"You've got room to sit or stand, Turner. It doesn't matter," Nelson said. He loosened the girths on the saddles and led the horses to the creek to drink. He didn't want to risk a campfire attracting attention so out came the hardtack and jerked meat.

"You chased me clear to Kansas. Thought I had killed you back in the brush," Turner said.

"You shot a friend of mine back there." Nelson checked Turner's ropes before thinking about sleep. "If you give me any trouble, I'm going to tie you up sitting in the middle of this creek. You'll get mighty cold before morning."

"Damn you. Why you doing this to me?" Turner demanded.

"I'm doing it for something you did up Jeff City way. It got right under my craw," Nelson said, "You took the pledge to be an officer, not a murderer."

"I took that pledge before the confederates killed my Pa. He taught me an eye for an eye." Turner pulled against the roped that held him.

Nelson looked at him in disgust, thinking he'll change his mind about that when I get him to the Hawksbill. "Pa teach you to skin a man too?"

"He was one of Bloody Bill Anderson's bushwhackers. It don't matter how he died. They were doing worse raiding and killing all along the Missouri River."

"That boy you skinned was Jim Hagan's son," Nelson said. "Have you ever heard of Jim Hagan? He's looking for you all over southern Missouri."

Turner got quiet.

~ ~ ~ ~

"Come on Turner, get on that horse. We've got a long ride ahead today," Nelson said.

"Paintier, you better get me the hell back to that stinking Rolla stockade," Turner said, "If Hagan catches us out here, he'll hang us both."

"Oh! Now you want to go back to the stockade? There will be plenty of time for hanging when I get you back." Nelson remained quiet about where he was really headed. Turner would be twice as hard to drag along if he knew the truth.

"The Yankees will never hang me. When they find out the confederates killed my Pa, they'll acquit me," Turner yelled.

"Your Pa. Is he the Turner who ran the grocery at Loose Creek?" Nelson looked Turner in the eye.

"Did you know him?" Turner looked surprised.

"Yep. Stopped in there and met him about two weeks after you killed that boy," Nelson said. "You lying sack of shit." He pulled up the horses at the sight of what was ahead.

A troop of mounted Federal Calvary stood their horses blocking the trace. Nelson was afraid he was in trouble for the incident at Rolla. No way could he outrun the Calvary, and still drag Turner along. Instead, he rode right to their front and stopped to salute the officer in command.

"Captain Nelson Paintier, sir. I'm returning my prisoner to Jefferson Barracks for court-martial."

"Raise your hands, Captain Paintier. Both of you are our prisoners," the federal officer said, ordering his men to strip Nelson of his weapons.

"Hold on, what the hell, I have written orders in my saddle bags to return this man to Jefferson Barracks," Nelson said.

"That the same order you tried to hoodwink my Rolla troops with, Captain Paintier?" the officer asked. "It's a two-day ride back to Rolla. It will give you time to think about the visit to the stockade you'll have there."

With troops on both their sides and chains on their wrists, Nelson and Turner began the trip back to Rolla. There wasn't much doubt he had gone too far in helping Hagan get his revenge.

Turner soon started in on Nelson, "Going to like sharing a cell with you. I'll catch you asleep some night. Make up for that real comfortable ride tied across this damn horse."

"Shut up, Turner!" Nelson said, "We aren't back there yet."

"At least it ain't you taking me." Turner laughed.

The officer in charge pulled the troops up midafternoon by a small creek. With orders to water the horses, Nelson and Turner were allowed to dismount. Nelson quickly sided up to a tree to relieve himself. When he turned away from the tree the officer stood waiting.

"Captain Paintier, I'm leaving my first sergeant in charge of getting Turner to the Rolla Fort. I'm under orders to investigate who burned a family out of their house and hung a man in the yard in Sedalia. I'm leaving with the main troop."

Paintier furrowed his brow. Why in the hell was the captain telling him this?

"If Turner doesn't get to Rolla, things will get a whole lot worse for you, including a hanging. I don't like counting on a prisoner to help, but in your case, I'm all right with it. You can help if Turner tries to turn one of my men."

Without waiting for a response from Nelson, the captain left and ordered his troop to mount. They rode off, leaving the first sergeant in command of the prisoner detail, with Nelson to assist.

~ ~ ~ ~

An hour of daylight remained when the first sergeant ordered the troop off the trace into a clearing that appeared to have been used as a camp before.

Relief came when they unlocked his chains to get him down from his horse. His relief didn't last long. They chained him up again with his arms around a tree. Turner was on the other side. He watched as the sergeant posted two of his men as sentries, out twenty yards from the camp. He ordered two-hour rotations for the guards. The other two started a small fire to make coffee. No one offered coffee or food.

Tied to a tree again for the night rubbed him the wrong way, he couldn't sleep hugging a damn tree. Finally, he found a way to get his arms low enough on the tree to sit down. Turner kept chuckling and jerking on the chains to torment him. It didn't matter, there would be no way to sleep.

"Sergeant, take these chains off long enough for Turner to take a piss," Nelson said. "Captain, sir, I'm sure he can piss just where he is. The word is, they are going to hang him back in Saint Louis. He'll for sure know what warm piss feels like running down his leg then!" The sergeant chuckled at his own humor.

It got quiet after that. Sometime after midnight, Nelson heard the sound of two head splitting blows at the perimeter of the camp. He watched a shadow cross the campfire and stop with a pistol to the head of the first sergeant. Hagan had returned.

"Get up, tell your two men to keep their heads under their blanket if they don't want to die tonight," Hagan said, shoving the sergeant toward Turner and Nelson. "Unchain both of them." Hagan's men were quick to bring up Nelson and Turner's mounts. Nelson recovered his pistol and carbine and saddled the mustang. Hagan had put the chains back on Turner's arms.

"Who the hell is this?" Turner demanded, not realizing

the short path to hell he was traveling on.

Hagan hit him on the side of his face with his pistol. Turner spit blood and a broken tooth from his mouth before saying anything. "Yankee troops are going to hang all you son-of-a-bitches!" Turner yelled.

Hagan yanked the chain tighter around Turner's arms and shoved him down on his face.

"We gonna kill this bunch, boss?" one of Hagan's men asked as he held a gun against the Yankee first sergeant."

Nelson didn't say anything, only shook his head no. Hagan had what he was after.

"Tie them up. They get to live, today at least," Hagan ordered.

With the five soldiers hogtied and left at the camp, Hagan led the way south. They had Turner's and his horse wedged in between two of the riders.

"Head for Buffalo River and the Hawksbill," Hagan told the riders. "The men gathered back there waiting for us to show up. Your woman is there waiting too, Nelson."

CHAPTER 22

Nelson could see Anne leave Dyer's side and break into a run when she saw he was with the men riding up. He jumped from the saddle before his horse stopped to meet her and take her into his arms.

"I wasn't sure you would get back!" She held him tight in her embrace. "Dyer brought me back here because it wasn't safe anywhere else for me to stay."

"When they left with you, I thought I would have to search all of southern Missouri to have you back in my arms." Nelson lifted her hair to caress her neck.

"What are they going to do to Turner?" Anne asked.

"They'll kill him for what he did to Hagan's son."

"It won't be a quick death, will it?" She tightened her hold on Nelson.

"Hagan will make him suffer just like his son did. I don't think Hagan will listen to me about taking Turner back to hang. I'll try talking to him." He left Anne and crossed the camp to find Hagan.

~ ~ ~ ~

"Hagan, can we talk about this?" Nelson looked Hagan in the eye. "I helped you catch this bastard, so at least give me a chance to say my piece."

"Stay out of this, Nelson. He's mine now." He started to walk away, but then stopped. "Go ahead say what you got to say."

"We can take him back to Jefferson Barracks and they'll hang him in front of the whole Yankee army. It'll set an example to stop things like this from happening. The General will sign your pardon on the spot."

"Ain't gonna be no pardon, till I kill this bastard. You understand? It don't matter if you don't." He walked off leading the chained Turner toward a log circle in the center of the camp. "Sit, damn it." He yanked the chained man to the ground.

Hagan's men sat, waiting for the already set-in-stone trial to start. Nelson and Anne stood behind the men, not sure what was going to happen next.

"Red, are you able to stand long enough to give this piece of shit a trial?" Hagan asked, watching as Red pushed himself up with a rifle from the log seat.

Red leaned on the barrel of the rifle. "Have you got anything to say, dead man, before we start this trial?"

"It won't make no difference...all you just like the ones we killed," Turner said, in defiance and shook his fist at Hagan and spit toward him.

"Difference is we got you," Red said. "You would be dead now if we wasn't being fair."

"Hagan says we got a witness...to what you did," Red said pointing to Nelson. "Tell him what you know, Nelson."

"Hagan said for me to stay out of this." Nelson stood his ground.

"Still a Billy Yankee, ain't you, Captain." Hagan said.

"You brought him out of Lawrence. You should have something to say at his trial."

"The Western command had him put in the stockade for murdering your son." Nelson paused. "No man should die the way your son did, not even the one you have on trial." Anne tightened her grip on his side.

"That's good enough for me to get a vote." Red looked around, each of Hagan's men showed Turner a thumb down.

"You got anything to say, Turner?" Hagan asked.

"It won't make any difference what I say," Turner said.

"Might make a difference about how quick you die." Hagan stared Turner in the eye.

"I'm glad I skinned the little bushwhacking son-of-a-bitch. I'd do it all over again!" Turner said.

"Take off his chains," Hagan ordered. "Give him a pistol with one chamber loaded."

Turner stood staring at Hagan, holding the pistol between both of his hands.

"You got one hour, before we come after you," Hagan said. "Best use that shot on yourself. If you don't, I'm going to drag you back here and hang you over the cliff upside down with your guts hanging out."

"Run, your only chance, Turner," Red said.

Turner shook his fist at Nelson, "You're nothing but a bushwhacker now!" Turner disappeared running down the ridge toward the valley.

"Nobody goes after him till I say so," Hagan said. "Get the pole ready to hang him out over the Hawksbill."

Nelson tried again to talk to Hagan and convince him that Turner should hang at Jefferson Barracks. Hagan listened but wanted more than an eye for an eye from Turner. When the hour had passed Hagan turned to Nelson.

"Bring him back, Nelson," Hagan said. "If I go, I'll kill him out there. I want him to die here on the Hawksbill."

"He's not going to use that bullet on himself, he's a

coward," Nelson said, "He doesn't believe what you threaten him with."

"You bring him back and he'll find out, won't he," Hagan said.

The broken branches along the path led Nelson down the valley toward Buffalo River. Turner was running like a crazy man. He left a trail anyone could follow. Twice he found spots of blood where Turner had taken a hard fall on the path. Two hours passed before Nelson reached the river. Turner wouldn't try to cross the raging white water of the Buffalo.

"So, it's you that came after me!" The voice came from behind Nelson. Turning he came face to face with Turner no more than thirty feet away, holding the pistol cocked and aimed.

"Hagan warned you...it would be best if you use that shot on yourself," Nelson said, "He's not going to show you any mercy."

"I'm not going back. I'm gonna kill the sonofabitch that got me in this mess."

"Then take your shot...the way your hand is shaking...I'm waiting." Nelson saw the smoke from the shot even before hearing the sound. The shock of the bullet passing his side moved the edge of his shirt.

"My turn now." Nelson pointed his pistol at Turner's chest. His finger tightened on the trigger. He paused before firing a shot that would surely put Anne in danger. Hagan waited at the top of the ridge for his revenge on Turner.

"Head back up the trail, Turner. I'm not going to drag you, instead I'm going to shoot you in the arms if you don't do what I say."

"He's gonna skin...me."

"Walk, Turner."

Turner stumbled into the guerrilla camp with Nelson pressing him forward. Several hands grabbed for Turner forcing his back to a tree.

"Drag him to the Hawksbill." Hagan said. "The turkey buzzards already circling waiting for your stinking guts, Turner."

"Don't follow, Anne." Nelson held out his open hand.

"Just shoot him out there on the Hawksbill, Captain," whispered Anne.

"Hagan would never let us leave here alive if I do." He was surprised at Anne's bluntness.

Hagan's men dragged the sobbing Turner through the woods to the waiting precipice. A long pine pole braced against two boulders stood ready to swing the upside-down Turner out over the edge of the Buffalo River canyon. Nelson stared at the fall from the Hawksbill and wished Hagan would just throw Turner over the edge instead of gutting him first. It turned his stomach and drew up memories of battlefield wounds, and men left to try and push their guts back inside in hope life would stay. Still, they prayed and cried out, *"Ma...Ma...I'm coming...coming home."* Nelson shook his head. No way could Hagan be stopped from getting his revenge and hard justice the bushwhacker way.

Hagan's men stripped Turner's clothes off and held him flat on the ground before tying his feet to the end of the long pole.

Hagan approached Nelson first.

"I'm telling you again, stay out of this. Understand?" Hagan stared at Nelson. "I'll kill you on the spot."

Turner shook and twisted from side to side trying to get the ties on his feet loose. Hagan walked to Turner's side and took a skinning knife from his sheath.

"Lift the pole. Get him off the ground and hanging," Hagan said.

The pivot of the pole raised Turner's feet and body into the air, only the tips of his fingers touched the ground.

"Look at me, Turner. I'm going to split open your belly wide. Your guts gonna fall right over your face," Hagan said. "Then I'll leave you hanging out there over the Hawksbill alive. Them circling buzzards know what's coming. They'll land on your face and start with your eyeballs and pick you clean to the skull."

Hagan reached across Turner's belly; the edge of the skinning knife pressed against bare flesh. Nelson lifted his pistol. The snap of the rifle shot came at the same time Hagan's knife ripped the belly open. The back of Turner's head went flying out over the canyon. Hagan dropped the knife on the ground and spun toward Nelson.

"You bitch!" Hagan shouted, racing past Nelson and slapping the rifle from Anne's hands, before he knocked her to the ground.

"There...the terror you caused him paid for your son!" Anne held the side of her face.

Hagan pointed his pistol at Nelson, "Take her...get out of here. Before I kill you both."

CHAPTER 23

The moonlit night found Nelson and Anne more than fifteen miles from the Hawksbill camp. They had ridden the horses at a run, wanting to get far away from Hagan and his men. Their horses were too tired to climb the trail over the mountain to leave the Buffalo Valley, so they had pulled up on a river sandbar for the night. Neither had spoken for the last hour.

"I saw you go for the pistol," Anne said, "He would have killed you."

"I almost died anyway...from the shock of seeing you standing there with a smoking rifle," Nelson said shaking his head from side to side.

"Will they come after us?"

"No, I think Hagan is glad it's over with Turner."

"What about the pardons?" Anne loosened the cinch on her horse's saddle.

"I think he understands the pardons are his only chance to ever go back home and start over. We'll have to wait and see if he comes for them." He took the two horses to drink and returned to hobble them to graze the higher riverbank grasses.

"I haven't been near a bath for way too long," she said dropping her clothes behind as she ran to the fast running stream.

The image of Anne's tall body and long midnight black hair bathed in the moonlight erased all the bad things that had tortured him for the last weeks. He dropped to the sand, sitting quietly with his arms wrapped around his knees, watching, trying to see way more of Anne than the flowing river would allow. He loved watching her duck her head and come up to throw the long strands of hair over her shoulder.

"Are you going to sit up there alone forever, Captain?"

She didn't have to ask that question twice. His boots were already off sitting in the sand behind him, the rest of his clothes were strung between the boots and the river's edge. The cold water stung him, but only for a second. When he got near, he wrapped her in his arms. Too much had happened that day, both only wanted the embrace. A naked embrace he would never forget. They held each other tightly for more than a few minutes.

"You know I'm going to be a scandal, in Steelville, don't you?" Anne laughed. "They'll kick me out of the school for being with you, but I'm still glad you came into my life, Captain Nelson Paintier."

"I'm glad too, Miss Ruth Anne Gordon. Now kiss me again, scandalous woman."

~ ~ ~ ~

The war, Union Soldiers, and guerrilla troops had all stripped the farms of cattle and crops making things hard for families that had to hide what little food they had to survive. Nelson had buried most of the gold he had been carrying on his person from Jefferson Barracks, but he still carried enough to bring out some of the hidden food on the way north. It would be dangerous approaching farms for help, even families with the same name were divided in their support of the north or the south. Ambushes were frequent, bitter killings of cousins had happened throughout the Buffalo River Valley.

With morning's light, Nelson again went swimming in the river. In a few minutes he had four large freshwater mussels lying on the bank. If they were going to have anything to eat it would have to come from those shells for now. He watched Anne shake her head from side to side, indicating no, no.

"The racoons eat them, you know." He slipped back into his pants, then went to work with his hunting knife to open the hard-shell mussels.

"Enjoy your morning meal." Anne laughed. "Is this all we're going to have to eat today?

"It just could be, my dear. Sorry." He lifted the mussel from the half shell on his knife and offered the dripping bite to her.

"Go ahead, you first."

He didn't wait but took the whole mussel down in one swallow.

"It's not bad. Best you try some."

"All right, don't laugh if this slime gets stuck in my throat."

They were both hungry, so twice more Nelson went back into the river for mussels. After they forced down the mussels, and saddled the horses, they headed over the mountain to leave the Buffalo River behind them. He rode hoping to find a farm with a big garden. They were not that lucky. The day ended with both of them still hungry.

~ ~ ~ ~

With no need to delay since they had nothing to eat, they were saddled and riding at dawn. Nelson preferred the lesser traveled trails that led north, hoping to find farms that had been spared the wrath of the war.

It was midday when they topped a ridge and saw the weather-beaten house with broken panes in both front windows. A heavy moss layer had started to fill in the uneven spaces in the wood shingle roof. The open front door made the house look like it had been deserted for years. Only part of the corral fence on the north side of the house was there, empty fence posts stood alone, the rails to keep livestock in were gone.

"Looks like they used part of the corral for firewood last winter," he said riding to the edge of the fence.

"Nelson, there's a woman on her knees, working a little garden." Anne pointed ahead.

He took up the slack in his reins. "Get ready to ride. I just heard a hammer being pulled back inside the house," he whispered.

A child's voice from the house, "It ain't no garden she's doin'. She's trying to bury a dead baby. You best get on out of here. Ain't nothing here to steal no more."

"Talk to him, Anne. A woman's voice will be better."

"I'll help your mother to bury her child." Anne took a deep breath. "We didn't come to steal. We're just hungry like you must be."

A shirtless skin and bones body of a boy carrying a rusty muzzle loader came around the house. Rings of dirt circled his chest and his bare feet had taken on the color of the red clay yard. The boy stood the musket against the clap board side of the house, and walked up to Anne and her horse, stopping with his hand on her boot. His tears made puddles in the dirt that covered both his cheeks.

"Ma just been sitting looking at that dead baby all night," the boy said. "She killed him 'fore he starved to death."

Anne and Nelson both swung down from their mounts to the boy's side.

"She killed her baby?" Anne asked.

"All us are starving. I've been hidin' thinking she's going to kill me too."

"Your mother won't kill you; she needs you, son. You can help with hunting for food," Nelson said.

"I had the gun hid, when they come. They took the little bit of powder and lead that was left with them. So, I can't shoot nothing to eat anymore."

"Who came? What else did they take?" Nelson asked the boy.

"Ma called them neighbors, before they came. They called us Secesh traitors. They beat Grandpa to death with his own walking stick."

Nelson didn't know what to say, only slowly shook his head. Many times, before when he had advanced his troop into the southern areas, they had found families just like this one. Because they had to keep moving ahead fast, there had been little they could do for the stricken wives and children. This could be different.

"I'm proud of my Grandpa, mister. He cussed that man, before they killed him. He told him hell would be too good for the man and his kin."

"I'm going to try and help now. We can help your Ma bury the little one," Nelson said.

Anne went to the mother and took her to sit on a rock ledge alongside the house. Nelson walked with his arm over the boy's shoulder to join them.

"She told me they buried her father over by the edge of the field. She wants to bury the baby so it will be near him," Anne said, sitting next to the grieving woman.

Nelson found a broken shovel in the yard and headed toward the pile of stones and the narrow plank-cross carved to mark the boy's grandfather's last resting place. Without asking, he dug the shallow grave for the child beside the pile of stones. When he finished, he walked back to Anne and the mother.

"When she's ready," he said softly to Anne.

Without a word, the mother stood, walked to the body of the baby and lifted it from the quilt.

"Ain't got no other way to keep the boy warm when winter comes to this mountain, going to need this quilt," the woman said, carrying the naked baby in her arms toward the fresh dug grave.

At the edge of the grave, she passed the rigid body to Nelson's arms. The decay that had begun in the day's heat gripped his stomach. It was the smells of death he could not forget, or ever escape, it flowed over every battlefield he had fought on, and it lasted for days. He knelt at the side of the shallow grave and slowly lowered the baby to the bottom. He stood and backed away to the side of the boy.

"Go ahead, you cover him up," the mother said, "There's no need to pray. All that praying we done since the start of the war, it brought us nothing but death, and nothing to feed my brats. It brought a church praying neighbor to kill my pa and steal all we had to eat. I ain't praying no more."

With tears in her eyes Anne gripped Nelson's arm whispering, "Wait." She turned and ran to her saddlebags, taking out a clean white blouse she had been saving. Returning to the side of the grave she handed the blouse to Nelson.

"Please," she said.

Again, he lifted the lifeless body and placed it inside the blouse. Nelson and Anne scooped a small handful of red clay and slowly sprinkled it over the baby's body. The little brother followed their lead. The mother turned away and ran into the house.

"My momma is sad. She just don't know how to show it anymore, mister." the boy said.

CHAPTER 24

After Nelson and Anne finished the burial, they walked back to the house arm in arm.

"Do you think she killed her own baby?" Anne asked.

"She probably hasn't eaten for days. They must have taken her cow, and her own milk dried up, there wouldn't be anything she could do to feed a baby."

"We have to help them. Can we take them with us?" Anne asked.

"We could if she would go. I'm thinking of paying a visit to her thieving neighbor. Maybe getting some food back for them," Nelson said.

"You might ride into more than you can handle doing that," Anne said.

"I'll see if I can hunt up some squirrels or a deer before doing that."

Nelson unsaddled the horses and hobbled them to graze the sparse grass, then drew his rifle from the scabbard. Digging to the bottom of his saddlebags, he came up with a ball of heavy string that he handed to the boy.

"What's your name, son?"

"I'm Joseph, sir."

"Okay, Joseph let's see what's left of the wildlife here on this mountain," he said, heading off with the boy toward the woods. Within a half mile he motioned for Joseph to come sit by a tree.

"Looks like a spot squirrels will be coming to feed." He sat down beside the boy and showed him the acorns lying on the ground that had been split by the squirrels.

In a few minutes, pointing to a large oak tree just in front of them, he whispered, "Hear the scraping noise? It's a squirrel climbing on the bark. He's up there on the other side of the tree hiding from us. Slip around to the other side, make a little noise and he'll come around for me to shoot."

The red squirrel was quick to move around the tree away from the noise Joseph made. Nelson leveled the rifle and with a shot to the squirrel's small head harvested the start of dinner.

"Wow dang! Wish I could shoot like that." Joseph reached to touch the stock of Nelson's rifle.

~ ~ ~ ~

Joseph was smiling and carrying the rifle for Nelson when they headed back to the house with four cleanly shot squirrels. "Thanks for letting me shoot, mister," he said, "Sorry I missed him though."

"Lots harder to hit a squirrel with a rifle than a shotgun. Takes even more practice to shoot them in the head." Nelson chuckled.

On the way back, Nelson showed Joseph places where rabbits had made paths going through the brush and grass. Using the cord, he had brought, he showed how to set snares that would not fail to catch rabbits.

"Be sure you check the snares twice a day, otherwise a fox or wolf will steal your catch."

"I will, maybe even more often when we get really hungry."

"Can you clean squirrels?" Nelson asked knowing that he needed to hunt for bigger game for the family to live on.

"Sure, cleaned them all the time, 'fore running out of anyway to shoot them."

"Ok, I'm going to reload and head down the ridge toward the water. May get lucky and spot a deer when they move near sunset. Tell the ladies to go ahead and cook the squirrels, don't wait for me."

Both armies had done their parts in cleaning out most of the big game in the Buffalo River Area. He hoped to kill a deer to provide lasting food for the woman and her son. He reached the river and followed it upstream for a quarter mile before finding what he had been looking for, a worn trail of deer tracks to the riverbank. He backed off from the trail about twenty yards and crawled into a thick bunch of willows for cover. Night found him still watching the river's edge for prey. He settled back against the willows to wait for the morning.

Well before dawn, he sat alert and watched the trail. His luck got better at midmorning when a doe came down the trail and lowered her head to get a drink. His shot dropped the deer at the water's edge. After bleeding and gutting the kill, he headed up the mountain to get his horse for the carry. Anne and the boy met him halfway leading the horse.

"I heard the shot and thought it must be you," Anne said, handing him a stick through a skewered squirrel. "Roasted the squirrels last night, saved this one for you."

"Hungry enough to eat raw deer, luck was with me, bagged a doe too big to carry out," Nelson said, giving Anne a hug and greeting the boy. "Might need all of us to get the deer up on the horse, it's heavy." He chewed the squirrel meat off the bones as they went down the hill to the river.

With the doe finally loaded over the horse's back, they

climbed the steep hill back to the cabin. In back of the cabin, he hung the deer from a tree to finish butchering it. He cut two steaks and carried them to Anne to cook for dinner. After he filled a tub of meat to be ground for sausage, he cut the rest into thin strips and took them to the woman to dry for jerky.

He said to her, "I need to know where to find the man that killed your father and stole your food."

"No more killings going happen over me," she said.

"Then leave with Anne and me. We can take you to any other family you have."

"This is our home. He's coming back to us, soon."

"Your husband? How long has he been gone?" Nelson asked.

"It's been two years now. They took him away to fight."

He didn't ask about the baby. The scars she must be wearing came with the baby's inception, but still, she didn't want to leave her mountain home.

The next morning, they waved goodbye to the woman and boy. The large deer kill and the renewed spirit of the boy to catch rabbits would at least keep them alive for a while. They rode toward the Missouri Ozarks and Anne's burnt-out home.

~ ~ ~ ~

Joshua shouted his hello when they started down the steep hill into Steelville. "Nelson, I was afraid you wouldn't come back," Joshua said. He dropped his rake and ran to meet them. "Where's my pa? Is he Ok?"

"He's okay, Joshua. I don't know when he'll be coming back though. He stayed with the men he had been riding with," she said, leaving her saddle to hug the boy.

"Joshua, I see you have some help cleaning up the burnt-out house," Nelson said. He walked to Thomas and gripped his leather-hard hand. "Glad you decided to stay and give us a hand, Thomas."

"Might you help me learn to read for staying to help?" Thomas asked.

"We both will, Thomas." Anne said, "Guess we'll have to fix up the barn to live in till I can get a house built."

"Mind if I lend a hand, young lady?" Nelson asked.

"Counting on it, mister," Anne said.

~ ~ ~ ~

The next three weeks went fast, Nelson made several trips to the Iron Work's sawmill for lumber and building supplies. On his last trip he was able to hire two of the Iron Work's carpenters to help build the house. Nelson kept busy pushing aside thoughts of Spaid and his men. He couldn't worry about them coming back for him. He could only be ready for a fight if they did. During the first week of building, Mr. Oliver came looking for him and asked to talk to him alone.

"Mrs. Oliver and I noticed a couple of strangers riding through town along Yadkin Creek while you were gone with Miss Anne. They always rode up the hill checking on the school and the burnt out house. Then they rode on out of town after that," Mr. Oliver said, "I think they were looking for you?"

"It might be," Nelson said, "There are some men that don't like the fact that I'm back in Steelville."

"We're glad you're here," Mr. Oliver said. "Going to take all the help we can get to rebuild from this flood and war. Glad the boy could stay with us while you and Miss Anne were away. He kept wanting to run off after his dad again. We kept him busy helping to build our house."

"Thanks, Mr. Oliver. How's your house coming along?"

"Neighbors lent a hand. Moved what was left of it up the ridge away from the creek. It will be safe for us up there next time it floods."

Nelson thanked him again for keeping Joshua. Anne joined them to give Mr. Oliver a fresh loaf of bread she had baked on the stove Thomas had set up in the lot back of the barn.

"I don't know what we would have done if you wouldn't have taken care of Joshua while we were gone," Anne said.

"Glad to do it for our schoolteacher. I'm a little embarrassed to ask, Miss Anne, but is the nigger working here for you a slave?" Mr. Oliver asked.

"He was a slave, but he's a freedman now," Anne replied. "He's earning what we can pay him for helping us."

"That's good. I respect that. Some folk around here been talking, those folk having hoods hanging in their closets need your watching," Mr. Oliver said.

"Glad you let me know. I'm sure Thomas is aware of the hatred that exists and will do his best to avoid any trouble," Anne said, "Come back and bring Mrs. Oliver. We will put together what we can for a housewarming when the house is finished, you are both invited."

Nelson and the builders had the house ready for the roof to be put on when Dyer rode into Steelville. Before Anne could even greet him, he pointed his finger at her. "You almost got us killed, up there at the Hawksbill. Lucky Hagan let you ride out of there."

Anne didn't answer. She yelled to Joshua that his pa was there. The boy came around the house and ran to his father, grabbing him around the waist in a big hug.

The house sat ready for the roof, with all the material at hand and plenty of help. After talking it over with Anne, Nelson felt he could leave for a bit. He wasted no time before heading for Jefferson City. Nelson had a list of things he needed to do.

First, he needed a telegraph to send a notice to ship the printing press his deceased Saint Louis parents had willed to him. He worried the Army would be looking for him in

Jefferson City but felt sure the Saint Louis Army command had taken the heat off for the incidents with Turner. He had been given an open hand of cards to play—whatever it took, the General had told him. That was next on his list. He needed to notify the General about the fact that Turner was dead, and the pardons still needed to be awarded.

And finally, he was tired of Spaid riding around out of sight. Nelson wanted to finish this, and to do that, he needed to figure out which big-shot senator was in cahoots with Sheriff Spaid.

~ ~ ~ ~

Nelson always liked riding into Jefferson City, except today he knew Spaid worked for someone there in government and they could be out to kill him. From several miles away the granite capital always stood out, shining on the river bluff overlooking the Missouri River. He enjoyed watching the ferryboats make trips back and forth across the river. He didn't take time this trip to stop and enjoy the view. He rode on into town, early in the morning. He had to face his enemies and see what crawled out of the dirt.

Morning of April 15, 1865

After leaving his horse at a livery stable, he headed straight to the telegraph office. The operator arrived just as Nelson did and unlocked the building right at eight o'clock. The code key on the desk was clicking before the operator had a chance to sit down and lift his pencil to start writing. When the operator finished writing the incoming message, he sat staring at the piece of paper in his hand. Nelson tapped the counter trying to attract his attention. The operator stood and turned toward Nelson. His arms and hands shook as he announced to the only person there, that the president had been shoot — assassinated. He moved aside, in shock, as the operator bolted out the door, shouting to all, that Lincoln was dead.

CHAPTER 25

Nelson watched the still clicking telegraph key, continuing its message to the empty operator's chair.

He heard the shouting. Lincoln was dead!

"My God!" he said to the empty room. So many had died fighting for Lincoln's vision—United States of America free of slavery in both the north and south. Now he was dead! Lincoln was dead. Lincoln had never offered a compromise to the south. Surely, the vice president would not offer one now, Nelson reasoned.

Going north as a boy, fleeing for his life from the men in Steelville who wanted him dead for trying to save a slave girl, had put him in a different world. New people had taken him in. Even as a boy, he'd wanted to learn other ways than those he had witnessed from the men and women of the south.

Before noon the town's streets were flooded with wagons and buggies, people all trying to get the news and find out what had happened to the president. Missouri had its share of Lincoln haters, people that had wanted the war to go on and end with the state part of a new country, controlled by the Confederacy.

Certain that he blended well with the crowds, he went to the capital first. Climbing the five marble steps, he stopped to read the engraved letters high on the wall of the building. "Built in 1838." The five thirty-inch marble columns majestically supported the upper balcony over the entrance. He moved to the left and entered the door that had been left open by the frantic crowd that milled in the streets.

The nearly empty building offered Nelson an opportunity to observe the names and offices of the men in the Missouri Government. Climbing the steps to the second-floor corridor, he strolled passed the office doors, reading the names and titles of the men in power. He thought of the many debates and arguments that must have raged between them on how to shape Missouri's position in the war, and always how to keep the fight away from their own homes and families.

He stopped in an open space between the offices to look out the windows at the Missouri River down below. The ferryboat, J.W. Spencer, had reached the middle of the river, black smoke poured from the two smokestacks, a sure sign that the captain had a full load on board and was in a big hurry to reach the capital city. He could see more than a dozen wagons on the north side of the river still waiting for the boat to return. The news of Lincoln's death had gripped the countryside.

Walking on down the capital hall, two more offices remained and then the floor ended at a marble wall. The last office's door bore the name of a man he remembered and hated. He should have known—*Saunders.* Saunders, now a Senator. Nelson knew him as the vile Crawford County judge. Senator Saunders's door stood half open. He felt his gut wrench. This man was the judge in Steelville who had thrown him out of his chambers. He had stood before him to tell him that Mary, the slave girl, did not drown the Mockbee's baby. The judge's shouts still rang in Nelson's ears, "Get out! Get out, you nigger loving little bastard!"

He backed away from the office door and started back down the cold marble corridor of the Capital only to pause at hearing the laughter coming from the senator's office. Without a second thought, he turned, walked back and pushed the door open wide. An empty desk of a secretary guarded another door standing open to the Senator's inner sanctuary. He charged through the office to that doorway outlined in walnut and stopped. Neither man in the room acknowledged his presence. Certain the man pouring shots from a fifth of whiskey was the judge—senator—Nelson wasn't as sure about the man about to lift a glass. That was until the man turned toward him, and Nelson knew it was Spaid. It seemed these two were still thick as thieves after all these years.

Spaid pointed a finger at him, "Who the hell are you just waltzing through the senator's door?" He took a few steps toward Nelson, who didn't reply.

"I ain't gonna ask you again, mister." Spaid stood with his hand in his vest. Nelson was unarmed and naked. His weapon sat tucked away in the saddlebag at the stable.

"My name is Nelson Paintier, and you're Sheriff Spaid, and you"—he looked at Saunders—"are *Judge* Saunders. The two of you burned my father up in our Steelville cabin. Remember me now?"

The Senator had set the bottle of whiskey down and headed for his desk for his protection. Spaid had pulled a pistol and held it in his hand pointed at Nelson.

"You won't need that. I'm not here to kill either of you right now. I heard your party celebrating Lincoln's death and wanted to tell you about my written history of Steelville will be published soon. Your celebrating will be short lived, gentlemen." Nelson backed slowly out the open door.

"Kill that son of a bitch, Spaid," the Senator shouted, struggling to get his pistol cocked.

Spaid pointed a finger at the Senator, "Put the gun down. We'll both hang if he's killed here."

Spaid's words were the last Nelson heard from the Senator's office. His boots clicked on the marble floors and echoed off the ceiling as he hurried down the long corridor of the capital. Pushing his luck had never been a favorite thing for Nelson to do, but this time, he couldn't help himself. Today, he may have pushed it too far.

~ ~ ~ ~

Back on the street, he noticed the citizens had gathered in small groups, some talking softly, sadly, about the news of the day. Another group, mostly men, passed a flask from man to man. When he watched carefully, he could see the men tip the flask in a half-hidden salute. Their disrespect for the president shown on their faces in the smiles and pats on the backs of their fellow pro-Confederates. Several squads of Federal Troops marched by Nelson and took up guard positions along the Capital's front and the sidewalk leading there. They were there expecting trouble. Nelson felt the same way and made a stop at the stable to retrieve his two pistols from his saddlebags.

Halfway down the block, the doors to the Methodist Church stood wide open as he passed going south toward the Union Hotel. Nelson turned back to the church and went in. The pews were nearly full, the minister stood in the pulpit speaking of the great loss to the country and then, "A moment of silent prayer for our slain president." Nelson slid into the closest pew and bowed his head with the congregation. His memory of the tall slender man he had once seen standing near General Grant for a picture, brought him sadness for the terrible struggle the man would have endured since becoming president. He said a short prayer to himself, "God, let him rest in peace." When the minister asked the congregation to stand and sing, he got up and left the church.

The streets were crowded, but Nelson noticed a man fold his newspaper as he walked by. Half a block away, Nelson stopped to look in a store window and then glanced to check if he had been followed. The man made a half effort to stop and tie his shoe on an empty bench. The clerk at the desk of the Union Hotel asked no questions when Nelson signed in, handing him a key to a room on the second floor. No one had followed Nelson into the hotel, so he climbed the steps, went into his room, locking the door behind, and collapsed on the bed. No way would he sit another second, he finally had a bed to lie down. The first one in some time for the weary soldier.

It was past midnight when the soft knock at the door awoke him. Rolling off the bed he gripped one of the pistols he had brought and crouched at the side of the door. Another knock and, "Captain Paintier? Open the door, sir."

He expected a lot of things to come with the knock, but the words "Captain Paintier" and "sir" were not part of them. Opening the door could get him shot if he was wrong about who stood outside.

Carefully, without standing, he turned the key to unlock the door, and then slid along the floor to the side of a heavy dresser. If somebody wanted to kill him, they would have a fight on their hands in his dark room.

"I'm coming in, Captain Paintier. Carrying a lantern in one hand, the other is empty, sir."

Nelson had his pistol cocked and pointed directly at the heart of the man that came through the door into his room.

"Hold the lantern higher with both hands, I want to see your face," Nelson ordered before he moved from behind the dresser, "Shut the door behind you, lock it."

"Our General said you would show up in Jefferson City sooner or later. He also said you might be in over your head with things going on down south with Turner and all," the man said.

"Who are you?" Nelson asked, still pointing his pistol at the stranger.

"My name's Edwin. We don't use last names in the service branch I'm in."

"Ok, Edwin. Put the lantern on the table, I'll stand back a ways. Does Command know Turner's dead?"

"They thought that would be the case. Since you handed him over to Hagan and his men."

"Hagan hasn't taken the pardon yet, but most of his men are tired of the bushwhacker life."

"I had been expecting you to show up before this. Men were sent to watch for you in several cities. The General gave you orders to bring in Hagan one way or another and he still means it."

"Will Lincoln's death change anything with my orders?" Nelson dropped into the chair beside the Army agent.

"Nothing will change for a while. It will take a new president some time to get around to changing field officers." Edwin sat down in a chair across from Nelson.

"In your report, tell them state Senator Saunders has had men out to kill me. It has nothing to do with Hagan and the pardons, it's about the history I'm writing and the wrongs that happened in Steelville before the war. He sent a crooked sheriff to burn us out when I was a boy and killed my dad in the fight."

"We know about Senator Saunders. We know he and the sheriff you're talking about had been running guns south to the Confederates. Did you know he's got his name up to run for governor?"

"No. It doesn't surprise me. He may have to change his plans when I get my book published."

"I've been assigned here since the war started. I plan to keep an eye on Saunders and what he's up to," said Edwin, "It will be best if you put an end to Hagan and his raiding.

It would go a long way to explain your busting into the fort at Rolla."

Someone at Command wasn't happy about what he had done. He was certain getting the pardons signed would take away most of his problems, but he didn't intend to discuss it with Edwin.

"I'm heading back in the morning. I don't know if Hagan will be so easy to find this time. Tell Command I still understand the mission, and I know Hagan's heart isn't into the raiding anymore. He'll be willing to sign the pardon."

"Good luck, Captain." The man slipped out and quietly shut the door behind him. Nelson slid the lock in place before turning for his bed. He dropped into the feather mattress already asleep.

CHAPTER 26

With a cup of coffee, two eggs and a steak filling his belly, Nelson headed back for the telegraph office. Most of the local people that rushed to town at the word of Lincoln's death had gone home. Nearing the top of the steep hill that defined the downtown for Jefferson City, a squad of Federal troops passed him marching at double time headed for the Missouri River just down from his hotel. A lot of rush to get down there. He would need to find out why.

The telegraph operator sat at his code key clicking away trying to get caught up on the pile of messages he had waiting. One message on the top of the pile caught Nelson's attention. The message ran a full page of text, nothing in it made any sense, it was code, for sure. It was addressed to a name in St. Louis he remembered at Jefferson Barracks. It was signed simply "E." Edwin had relayed his information on to his General.

"Quite a stack of messages you got," Nelson said.

"Yep," the operator said, picking up the stack in front of Nelson and slipping them under his elbow. "Bunch of them came in late last night, spent the night here just trying to catch up."

"Going to leave one more for you," Nelson said, picking up a pencil and writing out the message to the Saint Louis shipping company that had been holding his printing press. "Dear Sir, please ship the Lombard Press you have been holding for me to Jefferson City by steam ship. Notify me by mail at Steelville, Mo when the shipment is to leave. Name of steamship and time of arrival in J.C. Sincerely Nelson Paintier."

"Is there any other news from Washington?" Nelson asked, handing his message to the telegraph operator with the required twenty-five cent fee.

"It must be crazy there. They're looking for an actor, named Booth, that shot Lincoln," the operator said, "Everyone's out to hang him."

"Stick this message on that pile under your arm," Nelson said, "Would like for it to remain private."

"I'd lose my job if I didn't," the operator said, turning back to the clattering code key.

With his goals met in Jefferson City, Nelson headed for his horse and the trip to Steelville. Halfway to the livery stable, he saw the Federal Troops coming back from the riverfront. They were carrying a stretcher with a body on it. He sidestepped off the boardwalk to get a glance at who they were carrying.

"Move off the street, mister," said a first sergeant leading the troops. "Man's about as dead as he can get."

Nelson saw the grey face of the body on the stretcher, a man he had just met last night. Edwin had been shot in the forehead and tossed in the river. Someone must have connected Edwin with his coming to town. It had gotten the secret federal agent killed. Spaid and the Senator's men would be waiting to ambush him when he went south. He hurried to the stable, checked that his weapons were working, saddled the big gelding, and headed for the river landing.

He had only one chance, catch the ferry and go north into Callaway County. With any luck, without them close on his heels, a turn to either the east or west would be possible. Ferryboats operated all up and down the Missouri River, so he could get back across the river later.

The ferry's pilot had just closed the gate when he reached Lohman's Landing. With the offer of a good tip, the gates were opened back up for him. Nelson led the horse to the back of the boat and watched the gates close and two riders rush up waving to the boat's captain trying to get on board. It was too late. The ferry had pulled away from the landing headed for the north bank of the river. He had his head start.

~ ~ ~ ~

When the ferry docked on the north shore of the river, Nelson headed across the mile-long stretch of Missouri River bottomland, headed for the bluff road. He had to head east and look for an out of the way river crossing somewhere around the mouth of the Osage River, or further east.

The roads along the north bluffs were well traveled so his tracks would be hard to follow there. He felt sure the men would be watching for him at the ferry crossing just out from the German settlement of Hermann, so he had to find a way across the Missouri River at another place, the river was way too wide and dangerous to try and swim the horse across. He would need a boat or raft to cross.

Ten miles from the Jefferson City ferry crossing he found the answer to getting across the river without being detected. Heavy logging of the timber along the river area had made it necessary to have a steam driven barge to push the logs across the river and up into the slower Osage River to a sawmill. He found the owner of the barge on the end of a bucksaw cutting a three-foot thick walnut log into sections for transporting.

"Hey there, mister. Heard from your neighbors that you might be planning a river crossing sometime today?" Nelson said.

"What's on your mind, young fellow?" the barge owner asked, stopping his sawing and wiping his forehead with the dirty towel draped over his shoulder.

"I need to be on the other side tonight and I'm willing to pay you for the trip." Nelson not wishing to say any more about his reasons for crossing the river.

"My log business has slowed down, the North was buying a lot of lumber to make boxcars from us, over in the town of Osage, but slowed down a lot since the war's ended. So how much you figure you could pay if we was willing to bring the steam up on the barge for you?"

Nelson didn't quibble. He took a gold piece from behind his gun belt and flipped it to the man.

"Get down, take a rest, steam be up in about an hour. We keep coals hot on her all the time. I planned on making another trip over to Osage this afternoon to see a gal anyway."

"The quicker you get going the better." He dismounted and led the mustang to the riverbank. The river looked like one huge muddy field, turning and boiling along the bank with whirlpools rising every few hundred feet. Nelson never wanted to be caught in a whirlpool again.

The little steam barge sat rope tied, front and back, to large river sycamore trees. A narrow board walkway was the only way to board it. He had crossed a lot of wooden bridges with the horse, so he didn't expect any problems getting him on board the boat.

"We going to need to hoist that horse on board?" the owner asked, pointing to the log lift rigged on the bank.

"Hope not, the horse will go wherever I go. The walkway's really narrow, but looks strong, so I'm just going to have to try."

"Go ahead. Get him on board if he'll go."

He looked again at the walkway. He wouldn't like making the twenty-foot walk over it any more than his horse. "Mister, could I use one of those bridles that you have up on your mule team?"

"You sure could, fellow."

"The big eyeshades on each side, will just let him look straight ahead," Nelson said.

With the workhorse bridle on the mustang, he led the horse to the front edge of the walkway. Without pausing, he stepped on the walk and never looked back. The big roan nearly ran over him pushing him to hurry across the walkway onto the barge.

"Get the horse settled down, the steam makes a lot of noise when she gets run up in the current," the owner said.

He sided the horse up against the three-foot-high rail on the ferry. Being at the front of the boat would give him a good view of where they would be landing. "Just stay off that whistle and he should be ok," Nelson told the owner.

With the steam pressure up, the owner's helper untied the ropes from the sycamores. The strong river current whipped the front of the barge from the bank and pointed it downstream. The barge's engine let out two bursts of steam before beginning to turn the paddlewheel at the stern. The slap-slap of the wheel digging into the muddy water slowly brought the front of the barge around and got it heading across the river. Nelson stood close with his hand rubbing the mustang's neck to help keep him calm.

Twenty minutes passed before the barge entered the mouth of the Osage River. Upstream a little less than a mile, the owner guided the barge up solid against a large dock. The town of Osage looked quiet. A couple teams of horses tied in front of what looked like the general store was all Nelson could see.

Walking the horse off the barge, Nelson thanked the

owner before riding through the town and onto a trail heading south to the Ozarks. He watched carefully behind him as he rode, after half a day's ride no one was following. The men would try and head him off somewhere before Steelville. He rode on.

Anyone that waited for him would expect him to ride in from the west or north, so he rode miles out of the way to approach Steelville from the east. The way was clear, he rode up to the back of the barn and the nearly complete house they were building for Anne. She saw him first and tossed a handful of laundry into the basket on the ground as she ran to wrap her arms around him.

"We heard this morning about the president being assassinated," she said, with her head pressed to his chest, "I was so worried about you."

"I missed you. I'm sorry I left so suddenly."

She took his hand and lead him toward the new house. "Come see the stove I found for the kitchen. A family left and said I could have it. It was too heavy for them to take in their wagon."

After Anne had a chance to show him the stove and house, they went to the front where Dyer and Thomas worked to add a small porch. Nelson was eager to explain what had happened in Jefferson City and tell them he knew they were all in danger.

"I got chased out of Jefferson City by two men. I'm sure they had orders to kill me. A lot more is going on in Jefferson City than just hatred for me. A senator and Sheriff Spaid are running stolen guns south, selling them to the bushwhackers and deserted Confederate soldiers. An agent from army command paid me a visit, he let me know command was aware of my capturing Turner, and they said I had the go ahead to do whatever it took to bring in Hagan. Spaid must have made the connection between the agent and me. Next morning the agent was found dead, floating in the river."

"Red come in with a message from Hagan while you were gone," Dyer said, "Hagan wants to know the terms of the pardon."

"That's the best news I've heard in a long while. Can you set up a meeting with him?" Nelson asked Dyer.

"Hagan's been moving back north after leaving Buffalo River. I expect we wouldn't have to travel very far to have a meeting," Dyer said. "I'll see if I can get word out to him."

"Settle down, Captain. You just rode in from one chase," Anne said. "Joshua wants to see you. Maybe not as much as I do, however."

Nelson pulled her into a hug, holding the side of his head to hers. She was right. He needed to get his priorities in order. Safety for Anne and the boy came first in his mind.

CHAPTER 27

Nelson stood in front of Anne's new house watching Joshua trudge up the long hill carrying his fishing pole and a stringer loaded with big bluegills. Joshua dropped the stringer on the hillside and ran to see him.

"Joshua, you look wetter than a snapping turtle that just crawled out of the water." Dyer laughed and pointed at the boy as he ran to give Nelson a hug.

"Afraid you wasn't coming back," Joshua said.

When Joshua's hug was short, he knew some of the little boy in Joshua had been wiped away by the things he had been through. "I'll always come back; this town is my home again." Nelson rubbed the boy's back with his hand.

"Now head back and get those fish, Anne will need them to cook for dinner tonight."

~ ~ ~ ~

With dinner over, Joshua pumped water from the well and carried it to wash the dishes. Together with Anne, Nelson walked down the hill, and through the flood damaged buildings that were part of the town's center.

"I always did like to walk along this creek," Anne said. "The flood didn't change my mind about that."

"Not many folks are going to rebuild down here. They're moving up on the north hillside it looks like," he said, lifting Anne in his arms and carrying her across the creek.

"Did you know they buried the slave girl up there. A rocky place near the edge of that bluff. No one ever marked her grave." Anne pointed to the bluff.

"I'd like to go up there some time soon. It will be a place for me to think about what I want to write about her and what happened," Nelson said.

"A bunch of the town hoodlums were up on the bluff last year. They burnt a cross near where she is buried. They claimed her ghost is haunting Steelville." Anne shook her head then pressed against Nelson's chest.

"The ghost of the girl that I write about in my book will haunt the guilty ones for a long time."

"Come on, mister, there's a little ledge that sticks out just up the way. We can sit there." Anne wiggled free, forcing him to put her on the ground.

Anne ran fast toward the ledge, he followed at a slow run, his leg had healed, and the exercise felt good. She encouraged him to hurry and join her on the ledge. He sat down on the rocks and pushed tightly against her side. His love for Anne had come on strong. He wanted to know all about her, and her life as a schoolteacher. They talked and talked on through the night, sharing feelings and their past, until they saw the first rays of the sun start to come over the east ridge. Morning found them back at the barn. She kissed him and left him to sleep on a cot set up for him in the barn.

~ ~ ~ ~

Collecting his notes and writing material, Nelson left in the afternoon for the hill across the creek. He explained to Anne where he was going to write. He climbed the steep north side of the valley and walked along the rim of the hill looking for Mary's grave. When he found part of the burnt cross, he guessed her grave would be close. Most of the rocks that had been covering the grave had been scattered in front of the cross. He spent the next hour placing them back on the desecrated grave of the slave girl.

He wasn't a man that stopped to pray a lot, but still, he stood silently remembering the hanging. It happening right before him, down there in the valley. He knelt alongside the rock pile, and then sat on the rocky hillside beside Mary's resting place and put his pencil to paper.

Her screams caused me to jump to my feet and rush around the brambles. She stumbled into me grabbing my arm and pulling me toward the place where the apron sat empty.

Mary covered her gasping mouth with one hand, the other pointed toward the cornhusk doll floating slowly in the current toward the spring pool rock dam. In the clear water under the doll, suspended just over the bottom of the pool I could see the baby's stark white arms and blond hair moving slowly with the flowing water. I couldn't move or speak, frozen from trying to save the baby. I watched the spring water coming toward my face covering my body, jarring me into doing something.

Mary screamed to save the baby and shoved me into the water. I tried to stand but slipped on the slime-covered rocks lining the spring's bottom and fell deep into the spring pool. My hand touched the baby's dress and I staggered to get a footing and lift the baby girl from the water. The baby slipped away turning face up. A white face turned blue with eyes that seemed to stare directly at me, my white face that had caused her to drown.

I climbed from the water and Mary was gone. I could hear her screams from up the hill, she had reached the cabin.

I ran the other way down the steep hill from the spring, crossing the creek at the bottom. I climbed halfway up the other side and dropped to the ground gasping for breath. I was choking on the tears and snot filling my mouth. Behind me at the spring pool I could hear a man yell and then the shrieks of the baby's mother.

Minutes later I snuck back across the branch and up through the trees so I could see the cabin. I looked for Mary. She lay on the ground beside the smoke house, crying out in short gasps of breath. A man I remembered seeing as he cut wood on the ridge carried the baby's body up the trail and stooped with it in his arms, reaching and yanking Mary's head up. "Look, you nigger bitch. You did this! Look, goddamn you!"

Mary cried out loudly, "No! No!"

Another man jerked Mary to her feet, dragging her to a hickory tree. "Turn around, you murdering nigger. Don't want no more 'No's' out of your black hide," he yelled. The first man had carried the baby's body into the cabin and came out carrying a rope and a whip. They tied Mary's hands forcing her upright. I tried to get up my courage and go out and tell them it was my fault. I peed my pants at just the thought. Her sack dress was ripped off and she stood naked. Naked against the savage torture. Naked against the words they kept shouting at her. "You drowned the baby. You murdering nigger!" The whip fell again and again. Each time the whip lashed the slave girl, she screamed the same words. "I don't drown no baby. No drown the baby!"

I had to stop her torture. I ran from the woods toward the two men. One saw me and picked up a rock, throwing it and hitting me in the leg. "Get out of here, boy. Don't want no white boy around this naked murdering nigger slave." I felt sure she would tell them it was my fault. My fault for dragging her behind the bramble bush. My fault for causing the baby to drown. A man yelled that she was a murderer and was going to hang for it. They built a fire and stoked it higher. Long into the night they beat the girl. I turned and ran like a coward into the blackness of the night.

Nelson returned the pencil to his pocket and folded the paper tablet he had been writing on. Writing the story came hard, the memories of what happened at the dogtrot cabin's spring pool before the war.

The snap of twigs behind him made him turn and look toward the tree line along the ridge. Only a movement there behind a tree, was it someone watching him or just an animal? He stood and looked again but saw no one. No threat came from the tree line now. A gut feeling told him someone had watched him sitting beside Mary's grave.

CHAPTER 28

The next morning, Nelson told Anne his plans to find a location for his newspaper shop, and then rode the mustang down the hill into the flood torn section of Steelville. He stopped first at the Olivers to thank them again for taking care of Joshua while they were gone. Mrs. Oliver came out of the partially rebuilt house to greet him.

"Wanted to stop by and thank you both for taking care of the boy," Nelson said, swinging down from the horse.

"That's all right. Mr. Oliver and I would do anything for Miss Anne. Folks here have a lot of respect for her, you know."

"I'm sure she is a fine teacher," Nelson said. "Or did you have something else to say?"

"Yes…folks are talking about you staying up there…going off together and all," Mrs. Oliver said, looking straight at him. "Just what do you intend to do to stop this talk, Mr. Paintier? You said yourself she is a schoolteacher!"

"With people out to kill me, things got a little crazy for

both of us," Nelson said, "Expect I wouldn't say this so loud she could hear me, but hope she'll have me for her husband someday soon."

"I hoped you would say that my boy. I always knew from the time you were a young boy you would turn out to be a fine man. You'll make Anne an honest woman."

With a red flush on his face, he thanked Mrs. Oliver and headed for the remains of the courthouse. Cleanup and rebuilding had been going on there since the flood. The half dozen men working on the building stopped when he rode up.

"Would you like to pitch in and help?" one of the men asked. He was wearing home sewn coveralls and no shirt.

"I would but I'm looking for someone that can help me with county records," Nelson said, walking over and offering a handshake and his name.

"Charles Link, County Clerk. Some records been coming back, what we found lying along the riverbanks after the flood. Drying them best we can. A lot of them can't be read, the ink's all washed away."

"Well, I'm looking to buy a couple acres, put up an office and start building a place to live."

"What's your last name, again?" the clerk asked.

"Paintier. I lived here before the war."

"Are you Levi Paintier's boy?" the clerk asked.

"Yes, he was my Pa. We lived about quarter mile up to the north of town, before our place burnt."

"I know your place, squatters were up there for a while, but the place is still there. If you pay a little tax on it and I think it would be yours again. The damn records are such a mess nobody else could claim it anyway."

"If you figure the taxes for me, I'll be back to pay them."

It came as a surprise to Nelson, having a chance to get his home place back, up on the north ridge above town. He left the courthouse and rode up the north hill, along the wagon trail that had first been cut by his father.

The rock chimney and fireplace were hidden by the brush and ivy vines. A closer look showed the black soot that covered the chimney and foundation. Charred timbers from the burned house filled the foundation and lay strewn over the rock walls.

He had got there that day to see flaming lanterns being thrown at both front windows of the house, the first lantern went through the window where his dad slept. His dad came out of the cabin door yelling and screaming with fire burning all over his body. Nelson ran toward him but turned in terror and bolted into the woods with the men shouting at him. He watched the riders, from the woods, when they came around the burning cabin. The leader's face burnt into Nelson's memory like the fire burned what remained of his father and their home.

Nelson walked around the charred remains, kicking a few of the burnt timbers back into the foundation walls. He would have to clean up what remained of his home before building anything else on the forty-four acres. Seeing the place where their house had stood made him feel at home again. Riding back to the courthouse, he paid the taxes that were due, and the land was his.

He rode up the south hill to the new home that was being completed for Anne with a renewed spirit that he could overcome all that faced him. Seeing the burnt-out house convinced him that he could never rest until he faced Spaid. The time had come to hunt him down.

Dyer saw him coming and walked out to meet him.

"Rider came in, Hagan wants to meet tomorrow. Told me where to take you," Dyer said.

"Sure, he's not just trying to draw me out?" Nelson asked, climbing from his saddle.

"All the men are tired of always being chased or having to steal from folks with nothin' left to steal," Dyer said, taking the reins of Nelson's horse.

"Do we need to leave tonight?" Nelson asked.

"It's about half a day's ride, so the morning's fine."

"Is Anne in the house?" Nelson asked, starting across the front porch of the nearly completed house.

"She walked down into town, a while ago, looking for a fiddler."

"A fiddler?"

"Yep, going to have some fiddling and singin' to celebrate the new house," Dyer said, leading the horse toward the barn to unsaddle.

~ ~ ~ ~

Dyer shook Nelson awake early the next morning. With a cook fire burning in the back-barn lot, Dyer fried up a dozen thick cuts of smoked bacon in a huge cast iron skillet. The four eggs frying in the bacon grease leavings came from the hen's nest Thomas found way in the back of the hayloft.

Thomas stood watching the eggs cook, "That chicken wantin' to go setting on them eggs. Flogged me all the ways to the front of the hayloft. Went back with the hayfork to gets them."

"That old hen's a mean one," Joshua said.

After a good laugh at Thomas's story, and the breakfast under their belt, Nelson kissed Anne goodbye and joined Dyer to head south. Dyer took the lead. Nelson felt Anne would be safe while he was away since he had hired two of the local men to help finish the house and to protect her.

Twice in the last few miles Dyer had pulled them up to a short stop. The last time he got off his horse and tightened the cinch on his saddle.

"Something bothering you?" Nelson asked, turning to check the trace they had been following.

"Someone is following us for sure."

"You hearing something behind us?"

"Not for sure. A couple times I thought I heard a horse whinny. Riding the bushes for months like I've been doing has taught me to trust my gut on this."

"I'll watch to make sure they don't close up on us." Nelson looked around the area. "We can pull up over by the cedars."

They didn't have to wait long. Hagan rode up from the south, Red came in behind them.

Hagan rode his horse right against the side of Nelson's mustang pushing against Nelson's leg and foot in the stirrup, "For a time there I wanted to kill both you and your woman," Hagan said, having to turn his horse to avoid the mustang's back feet about to come his way.

"She shot him, because she knew I was going to." Nelson rode back to the side of Hagan's horse.

"I thought you might try that," Hagan said, "Surprised the hell out of me when your schoolteacher shot him first. She saved your life, mister."

"You did ask me here to talk about the pardons, right?" Nelson asked, backing away from Hagan and swinging from the saddle to the ground. He stood with his back to a stand of cedar trees.

"The son-of-a-bitch Turner is dead as he can be, so is my boy," Hagan said, "Get on with it." Finding a couple fallen logs, they both sat looking at each other.

"The pardons would be for all your men. The raiding would have to stop after they sign them."

"Only a couple of them say they ain't signing. The rest are ready to quit this kind of life and go back home."

"You say where and when we can meet, and I'll bring the pardons to sign."

"Who signs for the army?" Hagan asked.

"After you and your men sign, the pardons go to the General at Jefferson Barracks to sign."

"I have to see him sign. I'm not going to put my trust in that happening down the road a piece." Hagan shook his head from side to side.

"All of you go in riding up to that fort would create quite a stir," Nelson said, "I've done some crazier things for you though."

"If that's the way it has to be, tell me when to meet you. It'll have to be on the edge of the timber outside Saint Louis. If anybody tries to spring a trap on us, there's going to be a lot of dead people."

"I'll meet you at the Meramec River outside of Saint Louis. One week from today, if that's not too soon for you to round up your boys?"

With the agreement reached, Hagan and Red headed west at a fast gallop, Nelson looked at Dyer asking for his opinion on the negotiations that were just about complete.

"Looking for my opinion, are you?" Dyer said, "Takin' that bunch into Jefferson Barracks will be like dancing barefoot on a rattlesnake."

"I'm going to lead them in there. They'll have to keep that damn black flag in their saddlebags. The command will be jarred up some."

"Let's get back to Steelville. That fiddler will be coming tonight, along with half the curious town folks," Dyer said.

"I expect most of them will like to hear some good fiddling music. It'll cheer them up after the flood and all they have been through," Nelson said.

CHAPTER 29

There were four lamps struck and lighting the front porch of the Anne's new house when folks began to arrive. The strains of Old Joe Tucker from Fiddlin' Tom's, gut-strung Ozark fiddle, could be heard clear across the Steelville valley. Anne set out the cookies and pies she had baked for the folks to eat. Being a schoolteacher, she had made sweet tea for them to drink instead of hard liquor. She stood at the door of the house greeting all the visitors, "The house is open, come on through. I'm glad to have you all here."

Nelson and Dyer stood in the door of the barn to keep an eye on who came up the hill. The smell of Anne's apple pies as they came out of the oven had them leave the barn and head down the hill to the front porch.

"Well, hello, Mr. Paintier and Mr. Spencer," Anne quipped, making a sweeping bow and motioning for them to join her for a look at the inside of the new house.

"Howdy, Miss Anne. Your house is looking mighty fine. The smell coming from those fresh baked apple pies catches a man's nose, and don't want to let go," Nelson said.

"Okay, boys. I understand what you're wanting. You both sit down on the edge of the porch and let's see what I can come up with," Anne said. "Both you boys are going to have to do a little jig to that fiddle tune, before you get any pie."

Dyer went first, hitting a solid lick with his foot behind and across the back of his knee. The fiddler must have liked the jigging. He bowed up the tempo faster and faster. Dyer slowed down a bit.

"I didn't know you had that jig stepping hiding in there," Anne said.

"It don't get to come out much, with the life I been leading," Dyer said, dropping to the porch out of breath.

"Now it's your turn, Mr. Paintier," Anne said, reaching to pull Nelson to his feet.

"Fiddlin' Tom, how about 'Mary of The Wild Moor'?" Nelson asked.

"Sorry don't know that one, but here's a little waltz been playing since I was a boy." Fiddlin' Tom cut into about the most beautiful waltz Nelson had ever heard.

"Dance with me, Miss Ruth Anne," Nelson said, bowing before taking a firm grip on her waist and turning with her to the one-two-three beat of the waltz.

"My goodness you're quite a dancing man, Mr. Paintier. You're going to have all those town folks standing there, staring at us and talking about me for a month, you know."

The music was getting louder with each of their turns. He slowed their turns and stopped their dance steps. Gently pulling her out of the waltz position and held her close with his mouth to her ear. "I love you schoolteacher. More than the music could ever sing out. There's something I want to ask you."

"The music is so loud, could you say what you just said again?" Anne looked into his eyes.

"I love—"

"I heard you the first time. I just wanted to be sure you meant it. Ask me now and I'll say yes. I love you too." Her interruption caught him off guard. It took a few seconds before he realized what she had just said. "You will marry me? You said yes?"

"Yes, yes, yes. A thousand yes's, sir. A thousand." He got kissed like never before, right there on the porch. They started again stepping one-two-three to a waltz he didn't even know the name of.

He waltzed Anne to the side of Fiddlin' Tom. The music trailed off on a squeak from the e string of the fiddle when Tom got the news first-hand from them. Tom's next note came right from the 'Wedding March'. Dyer and Joshua jumped to their feet, giving Anne and Nelson a what-just-happened look. Joshua started clapping first, then the circle of Steelville folks listening to the music joined in. Nelson saw the big smile on Mrs. Oliver's face as she and her husband clapped to the music.

"You know you might end up being sorry about marrying a schoolteacher." Anne said, still turning with him to the fiddle music.

"Never, since the schoolteacher I'm marrying is you."

"The town folks expect more from a teacher." Anne gave Nelson a big smile. "Things like helping with church, and town events."

"Good. We can both help." Nelson smiled broadly back at Anne. He really loved her.

"All right then, here's a kiss and a thousand more yes's I'll marry you!"

CHAPTER 30

The porch lamps had cooled and were stored away when Nelson left Anne and her new house to return to his bed in the horse barn. He walked up the hill, thinking of how she had accepted him to be her husband. He had realized the first time they meet that he wanted to be with her for all of his life. The clear night and full moon caused him to pause and turn back toward the house and Anne. The sound of running horses coming toward him in the dark caused him to reach for the pistol he wasn't wearing. He saw the muzzle flashes and heard the hiss of bullets flying around him from the riders on the horses.

He shouted, "Dyer, you in the barn?"

Dyer didn't answer but came running out of the barn carrying two rifles. He tossed one to Nelson and started firing at the other riders.

"Who the hell are they?" Dyer shouted.

"Get inside, before we both get shot!" Nelson ran past Dyer into the barn.

Dyer followed, joining Nelson behind a heavy stall wall.

"Keep some fire on them from here. I'm going out the back and get to Anne and the house." Nelson rushed toward the back of the barn. When the back door swung open, he got nicked in the face by flying wood chips.

"Damn, Dyer, they got us pinned in here!" He yelled, then set up to guard the back of the barn.

"There's a couple of them behind the rock wall across the road. From there it'll be easy to keep us pinned in here till morning." Dyer took another shot.

"If you see them move down the hill toward Anne and Joshua, I'm going to have to break out of here!" Nelson shot at a moving shadow behind the barn. He heard a groan and saw the man crawl to the other side of the garden.

"They're after me! It must be Spaid's men that have been running guns for the old judge from Crawford County." Nelson saw another target and shot again.

"What the hell did you do to have them want to kill you?" Dyer glanced two shots off the top of the rock wall, above the head of one of the shooters.

"Long story—It's more about what I'm going to do," Nelson said. "They're coming again, don't let them get in the barn."

"I've got two trying to come up here." Dyer reloaded his carbine.

Two shotgun blasts echoed from behind the men running at the barn, dropped them to their knees. The men turned around to fire at where the shots were coming from, only to see the burning powder from half a dozen other pistols and shotguns shooting at them.

"It looks like a couple of them are backing off here. We getting a lot of help from somebody," Dyer said.

"They're leaving faster than they came." Nelson pointed at the men running away. "Who's driving them off?"

"You okay in there, boys?" The friendly voice came from one of the men crossing the rock wall headed for the barn.

"We're fine," Dyer said, stepping out of the barn and into the road.

"Mr. Oliver, who all's with you?" Nelson asked. "They surprised us, got the drop on me when I was headed back from the house."

"Mr. Gunther saw something was up. He watched them circled up on the road when the fiddler finished playing," Mr. Oliver said, "He came got me, and the rest of the folks too."

"Mighty grateful to all you folks," Nelson said.

Anne came running from the house holding her rifle. "Is anybody hurt out there?"

"We're all okay. The town folk ran off some bad folks wanting to kill me, I think." Nelson held his arm out for Anne.

"I woke when I heard the first shots. I got the rifle ready in case anyone tried to get in the house."

He put his arm around her and held her in a quiet hug for a long moment.

"I'm sorry I'm causing this to be brought down on you and the boy." Nelson hugged her even tighter.

"Doesn't matter, we're all in this together now." She took his hand and gave Mr. Oliver and the town folk a big, sincere thank you.

Halfway up the hill, Anne stopped and grabbed him around the waist.

"We need to make all of this stop now," she pleaded.

"Oh, it's going to stop, and soon." Nelson took a deep breath. "Next week, Hagan and his men are riding into Saint Louis with me, and the pardons will be signed. Then I'm coming back here and tracking down Spaid to end this."

"Having the town folks coming out to help you says a lot."

"Might have something to do with their schoolteacher up here where all this shooting's going on. Don't you think?" Nelson smiled at the woman he loved.

~ ~ ~ ~

With a few days left before he planned to leave for Saint Louis, Nelson hired three men to help him start cleaning up his dad's house across the valley. With the charred remains of the timbers, and all the rock foundations removed, Nelson staked out the location for his print shop, and drew plans for a two-bedroom house that he would ask Anne to live in as his wife.

Finished with the first steps in building the shop and house, he needed to get ready for the trip to Saint Louis. He got out the captain's uniform he had been carrying in his saddlebags and brushed it clean. He and Dyer would leave in the morning.

~ ~ ~ ~

Both men were awake at daybreak and ready to travel. Nelson had carefully folded the uniform to keep it neat for the ride to the Jefferson Barracks Post.

When they reached a stand of heavy timber a few miles from the Meramec River meeting place, the first two of Hagan's men reined their horses out of the cover of the trees to join them.

"I didn't see any sign of you or your horses before you rode out," Nelson said, the men didn't answer.

"They learn to hide like that if they want to stay alive," Dyer said.

At the end of the next mile, Nelson and Dyer had eighteen riders along with Hagan and Red with them. They formed up four abreast through the south edges of Saint Louis.

"Are you going to stop and put on that uniform?" Dyer asked.

"I thought about wearing it when we ride in there today. I had to put it on again when we went into Rolla to get Turner, but I won't ever wear it again after killing the Union Soldier when we got ambushed."

"I wondered if killing the soldier still bothered you."

"Today I'll ride into the fort looking like the men alongside me."

Hagan rode up to the side of Nelson's horse. "Nelson, you do realize if this gets messed up today, there's going to be a lot of Yankees die. My men are carrying five to six firearms each, and they aim to empty them all before it ends."

"I understand, Hagan. Ask them to keep the pistols out of sight. There's going to be some excitement when they realize who's coming through the front gate of the fort. I don't know how this will set with the Federals. So, keep your men calm," Nelson said.

The closer they got to Jefferson Barracks, the more of a stir they were causing. The soldiers in blue they rode past, saw men dressed like they had been on a thousand-mile ride, unshaven with long beards draped down over their chests. Each of them wore a dark coat, long enough to cover the weapons they carried.

One of the troops of mounted soldiers they passed, redirected two of their riders. They sent them at a gallop back toward the fort.

"Going to be a welcoming committee now, I'm thinking," Hagan said.

"The gates are open up ahead. Follow my lead, ride right in there." Nelson indicated the gates ahead with a slight nod of his head toward them. "Stay formed up behind me."

"Ride proud, boys," Hagan ordered.

Riding in front of a notorious gang of bushwhackers and leading them into one of the major Union Army stations gave him chills. Each of the men behind him was armed to the teeth with enough bullets to kill dozens of Yankee troops standing guard. In turn, few of Hagan's men would make it out of Jefferson Barracks alive if things went south on them. The die had been cast and had to be played out.

When Nelson lifted his hand to stop in the middle of the fort's parade ground, Hagan's men broke the four-man formation and formed a circle with their horses, each rider facing outward protecting each other's back.

The troops standing at attention on the side of the parade ground came toward the circle with bayonets mounted. They formed a double layered circle around the riders, each taking aim at the bushwhacker in front.

At the first sight of the bayonets, Hagan's men drew a pistol to each hand and leveled them at the soldiers that would be the first to die.

"Hold it, damn it," shouted the powerful voice from the steps of the command barracks. "Paintier! You wanting to die, bringing those men in here?"

"Sir, all of them came to see you sign the pardons you sent me with, General," he said, offering the General a salute. "Sir."

"Troop commanders, have your men lower their weapons," the General ordered.

"Put them away, boys," Hagan said.

"I am going to guess this is Jim Hagan and his men you are riding with, Captain Paintier."

"That is correct, sir."

"Dismount and bring Hagan in." The General tilted his shoulders back a bit more.

Hagan followed him up the steps. His men held the circle, unbroken, with their weapons stowed.

The General stood behind his desk, facing Hagan, "I was sorry to hear what happened to your boy, Hagan."

Hagan didn't respond. The General looked at Nelson, "I'm not going to ask what happened to Turner. I won't have to deal with him. Correct, Captain?"

"Correct, sir." Nelson made sure his voice was

convincing.

~ ~ ~ ~

Each of Hagan's men took their turn to sign a pardon. Some could only make X's while others wrote out their names in crude broken letters. Nelson watched, making sure that each man's name or mark got written on a pardon. Hagan signed last, followed by the General of the Western Territory.

"Hagan, this pardon is unconditional and allows your men to leave here carrying their weapons. I am sending Captain Paintier back to southern Missouri with you. I'm holding your discharge, Paintier, until the raiding settles down. Ride home and keep track of these fellows. Any raiding, and I'll send in my troops to stop it. Gentlemen, we are finished. Good luck to you and your men, sir. You stay, Captain Paintier, I need to talk to you about another matter."

Hagan left the pardon signing and joined his men on the parade ground of the fort.

The general pulled Nelson aside. "Paintier, we captured a wagon of small arms headed south out of Jefferson City last week. We got the team driver to talk and found out they were headed for a meet with Confederate Scouts, still wanting to keep fighting, down on the Arkansas border." The General gave the desk a pound with his fist. "He wouldn't tell us who was backing the enterprise, but we have been watching a senator in the state government for some time now."

"That man happens to be from Steelville, sir," Nelson said, "The senator is Saunders."

"So, you have an idea or two on this, Paintier? We lost one of our agents in Jefferson City a few weeks ago, shot in the head. He had sent a telegram before he was killed. So, we knew you were connected."

"Yes, sir. He had been to see me in the middle of the night. Then the next morning I saw them carry him up out of the river."

"Keep an eye out, Paintier. Pass along anything you find out. Good work with the pardons." The General stepped around the desk and shook Nelson's hand. "Thank you, soldier."

Hagan and Dyer stood with the horses, waiting for Nelson. The other men had left the fort for home. He felt the three of them probably could use a stop in Saint Louis before making the ride home.

"Do you want to head up into Saint Louis? We could lift a couple before heading back. I have a little business to attend to there before heading home."

Dyer turned his horse, "I'm heading on for Steelville. I promised Anne to help with the last work on the house."

He didn't have to ask Hagan twice about stopping. They rode out of the fort and into Saint Louis. After the stop at the tavern, Nelson made one other stop in Saint Louis at the shipping company, then headed home, with Hagan at his side.

CHAPTER 31

"What's your plan, Hagan? Staying around Rolla or Springfield?" Nelson waited while Hagan considered his question.

"I rustled a lot of people around both of those places. Some are gonna to want payback from me. I understand their feeling's but won't be able to sit still for any payback."

"I've got some work, if you feel like staying for a while to help. I'm starting a newspaper in Steelville. Got plans for a printing shop building that's got to go up first." Nelson looked down while they crossed a low water crossing on the Meramec River.

They stopped to let their horses drink just off the crossing. He watched six men riding some expensively bred quarter horses cross downstream from them. Two of the men had stopped talking to each other and were paying too much attention to them. Something familiar about them bothered him. His time in Jefferson City came to mind.

He turned to Hagan, "You know those boys?"

"No, but they were sure as hell watching us."

"Just keep talking and we'll see where they head. They're riding some fancy stock, talks money to me."

"Broke as hell, me and all the boys. Never did have much more than something to eat. Some days not even that," Hagan said.

Nelson watched one of the riders lightly lift both of his pistols in their holsters and drop them back. Ready.

"Could stay around for a while. Get a couple of the boys to help build your shop. Bunch of them live close to here." He swung off his horse and stood on the opposite side from the riders just off the edge of the low water crossing. The riders kicked up their mounts and rode on.

"Those fellows must have known your reputation, Hagan. They didn't want to start something out here in the open. They sure as hell were watching us."

"Let's head on. We can stop once in a while and pull off the road to see if we're being followed." Hagan lifted quickly into the saddle and kicked his horse into a lope.

Nelson followed behind Hagan. Thirty miles out from Steelville he pulled to a stop. "Hagan, mind riding ahead? Somebody is getting close behind us."

"Stay together be better." Hagan pointed to the trees. "We can just fade into the timber, see who comes up."

"Lead away, mister," Nelson nodded.

Hagan pulled up on a ridge south of the trace. "Get a look from here and see what they are up to."

"I hear them coming hard now. They've lost sight of us on the trace," Nelson said. The six riders rode right on past where they had left the trace. Nelson heard them stop and turn back. Now they rode with three more men.

"They're going to find where we turned off soon." Hagan said, "Let's go."

Nelson didn't know where Hagan would lead, but with nine men chasing them, Hagan better get them to a spot where they could at least hold the riders off.

"Big...cave...couple miles ahead. If they follow, we can put up quite a fight from inside." Hagan pointed north.

Hagan and Nelson rode right into the mouth of the huge cavern, taking their horses around several turns and tying them in safety. Back at the mouth of the cave, Hagan motioned him to a rock wall. Hagan settled in alongside him in the dirt behind the wall.

"Piled this wall up about a year back. Never knew I would be behind it with a Yankee." Hagan slapped the top of the rocks.

"Glad you are." Nelson said.

"Do you know these bastards?"

"I think so. They're some of the men working for a Missouri Senator and his ex-sheriff sidekick. They have a big gun running operation going on and have been after me since I first came back to Steelville."

"I knowed about the gun running for a while now."

"Sheriff Spaid burned my dad up back before the war in Steelville in our cabin. So, we got a lot of cards between us to play."

"He's been a no-good son of a bitch for a long time. We knowed him some."

Both of them heard the riders cross between the cave and the Meramec River. The riders fanned out outside of the cave and started firing into the cave's darkness.

"Save your ammo, Nelson. They might keep us in here for quite a while. There's plenty of water back in the cave when we need a drink."

"I bet they're going to come charging up here after dark," Nelson said as he pointed at one of the riders. "That fellow riding the big pacer is Spaid."

"We can hold off an army behind this wall. They aren't likely to come all at once. He'll send a couple fools up first. Let them get close."

Twice in the late afternoon, Spaid and his men tested Nelson and Hagan's firepower with a burst of rifle fire and a move to get closer to the mouth of the cave. Nelson and Hagan returned fire and heard two of the men shout to Spaid they had been hit. As soon as darkness came, Nelson watched the flickering of a torch being lit off to the side of the cave. The man stayed out of sight but managed to fling the lit torch into the cave behind them.

"The bastards are trying to backlight us," Nelson said.

"Tries that again, I'm going to move over to side and drop him. That'll keep them from sneaking up on the side of the cave." Hagan moved past the rock wall and into a shallow rock depression that ran across the mouth of the cave. The next man carrying a torch died with it still in his hands. Hagan's shot knocked him backward onto the burning torch. The attacks slowed down after the torch throwing.

"I'll keep a watch on them, if you want to slip back and bring up some water to drink," Nelson said.

"Don't think they are going to try and rush us again tonight. They might have to try and starve us out." Hagan headed into the large cavern behind them.

The next afternoon, Nelson began thinking Hagan might have been right about them being starved out. Only a shot or two came from the men along the river all day. They were settled in for a long stay out there.

The third day brought only light firing to keep Nelson and Hagan pinned in the cave.

"This is getting old, Hagan. Think we should try and ride out of here?" Nelson waited for Hagan's response.

"Good way to get killed, I think. Hang on, things could change soon out there."

The fourth morning's dawn came with a downpour. From inside the cave both men watched the riders, moving about trying to get shelter from the rain.

"Chance to drop a couple out there, they are getting careless it looks like," Nelson said.

"You're right, likely get one before they drop out of

sight in the brush." Hagan sat more relaxed than Nelson ever could. The rain had started to let up when both of them heard the firing start up outside. No lead was coming their way.

"Took them longer to get here than I expected." Hagan smiled broadly. "Who? Your men?"

"Yep, they watch out for me. If I didn't show up in Steelville, some of them would come looking. Probably been watching what's going on out there for a few hours."

"Come on, let's give them a hand." Nelson left the rock wall and joined the push to drive off Spaid's men.

Six of Hagan's men, riding from the east, attacked the rain-soaked men. All six carried a pistol in each hand, firing them until empty and gripping another two from their belt to continue pumping lead at the riders. Hagan's men had the riders beat, the two who were left rode for their lives.

"Hey, Red, glad you came along," Hagan said. "Things were starting to look grim for us in there."

"Sorry, boss, couple of those men got away, rest of them look mighty dead." Red pointed at the men on the ground.

"Spaid's gone, got away," Nelson said, after he had a chance to look over the bodies for a familiar face.

"Want us to go after him?" Red asked.

"This is one score I'm going to have to settle on my own. He burned my dad alive about fifteen years ago." Nelson headed for his horse. "And I haven't had the chance to repay him. Until now."

CHAPTER 32

The trail Nelson followed led north from the Meramec River. He pushed the roan hard. Their tracks showed the men had ridden at a gallop for the first few miles, and then slowed, certain no one would follow after the fight on the Meramec River ended. He connected with his spurs twice and the big horse answered the call stretching the gallop. The soggy road hadn't filled the horse tracks he followed with water yet. They weren't far ahead.

"Come on, horse, show a little more of your mustang spirit and we'll have those bastards in our sights."

Another two miles and he saw them, turning their heads to see who had followed them. They didn't run, just stopped their horses and moved apart about eight feet, facing him. It gave Nelson two targets to shoot at instead of one. He pulled the roan up hard, before starting ahead at a slow walk, the men had their pistols drawn and they started toward him at a gallop.

Bushwhacker tactics came natural to him now, he had been taught well. He put his horse's reins in his mouth and charged the oncoming riders with a pistol in each hand.

They started firing wildly at first. Then one bullet came close enough that he heard the snap of it passing his right ear. He responded by blowing the man out of his saddle. The fellow about to pass him on his right was luckier, Nelson's shot had hit his left arm, the big slug knocked his pistol out of his hand and turned him half out of his saddle. He slipped down to the side of his horse. Nelson turned his horse and rode back to where the man's horse had stopped. The man let go of his grip on the saddle horn with his good hand and splashed into the mud. He reined the mustang up, ready to step on the man.

"Where's Spaid holed up, damn it?" Nelson demanded.

"Piss on you, Yankee shit," the wounded man said, trying to use his good hand to sit up in the mud.

Nelson dropped from the saddle and kicked the man's second pistol away. He set his boot hard into the man's chest, the mud oozed up around the back of his head and both of his ears.

"I'm going to ask you again, where can I find Spaid?"

"Spaid's going to kill you for this."

After that reply, Nelson left the man and went to his saddlebag, returning with heavy rope. He made a loop and dropped it around the man's neck.

"It doesn't matter to me; do you want to die here like your friend over there?" Nelson drew the loop tight and tossed the end of the rope over an overhanging limb.

"I'm tying this to my saddle horn, and I'm not going to look back at what happens to your neck."

The man didn't say any more until Nelson turned the mustang north and lifted the man to his feet.

"Stop! He...rode...away last night. He was sure we would kill you."

"Well, he was damn wrong, wasn't he? Where's he staying?"

"Place...of his down...loosen the damn rope...on the

Osage River near Vienna."

"I'm going to let you go. Get back on that horse. I want you to tell Spaid that Paintier is coming for him. Do you hear me?

The man rode slumped in the saddle, headed to the north at a slow walk. Nelson didn't waste time. He reined the mustang back south to the Saint Louis-Rolla trace. He was worried about Anne and wanted to get back to her. There would be time for Spaid later.

He found her that afternoon, at the new house.

"Dyer said you would be coming soon. I was so worried," Anne said, "Hagan came through here two hours ago. He told us what happened."

"I had Spaid in my sights but missed him. I ended up shooting two of his men. He got away during the night before Hagan's men got there."

"Why don't you clean up at the water tank and I'll fix you something to eat." Anne finally let go of the hug she had planted around Nelson when he arrived.

"You know I'll be going out after him again."

"I know, but I don't want to think about you in the middle of another shootout right now. You need to eat and get some rest."

"Be right in." He tried to reassure her with a smile, and a kiss on the lips.

After he watered his horse and dropped some hay from the loft, he stopped to talk to Thomas, who was in the garden. Thomas got up from his knees and set down the bag of seeds he had been planting.

"Think any of those seeds will sprout, up here in red clay, Thomas?"

"Yes, sir, they gonna grow. Went way out back there and got some buckets of that old horse manure, mixed it all in with this here clay. They's gonna grow all right."

"I'm going to start work soon on a place over across the valley. I would like to have your help over there." Nelson smiled at the man.

"Be proud to help you, sir," Thomas said.

"I'll have a place for you to live in the shop when it is finished."

"Is it up on the other ridge, sir?"

"Yes, years ago my dad and I lived up there. Our house got burned down."

"I walked up there before, saw you sitting alongside that pile of rock," Thomas said, "I didn't wanna bother you, when you writin' on that paper."

"It's just some words, Thomas. About a little slave girl. She is buried up there under those rocks. Her name was Mary."

"Can you show me some of them words?"

With the manuscript in his hand, Nelson asked Thomas to go with him to Mary's grave. Together they climbed the steep pathway to the top of the bluff.

"Sit here beside me, Thomas. I know you can't read all the words of Mary's story yet. So, I would like to read it to you."

"Thank you, sir."

Nelson unfolded his writings and read Thomas the story of Mary. Thomas didn't speak or stand while Nelson read. At the end, Nelson looked away as Thomas wiped the tears that stained his face. They sat, quiet without speaking for some time. Finally, Nelson broke the silence. "Thomas, you never told me why you came to the ironworks and the dogtrot cabin."

"I's told...you, sir, about spirits that came upon me," Thomas said. "Feels like it might be the spirit of my little Mary girl, master took away. And I feel that spirit I remember from her here by this pile of rocks. Them rocks sitting on my little dead girl, that everybody keeps bothering. Bothering her dead bones. She can't rest in peace here."

There was a pang in Nelson's heart. "Mary was your

daughter? Why didn't you say?"

Thomas nodded, hanging his head. "I wish I could have protected her all those years ago."

Nelson wished he could've protected her too. This was just another way he could try to make it right. "Is there someplace else we could take her?" he asked Thomas. "You're still her daddy. You should have a say in where her final resting place is."

"Yes, sir. I have a deed for that little place where she was born. Up to the north of the big river."

"I promise you; we can do something about that someday soon." Nelson took a deep breath.

"You'd help me move my Mary?" Thomas's eyes grew wide. "You'd do that for me?"

"For you and Mary. Once I settle things with the senator and Sheriff Spaid, get justice for your little girl, and make sure my loved ones are safe, we'll make sure Mary is buried where she was raised and loved."

Thomas only nodded; his eyes glistened.

Nelson patted his back. "Walk with me back?"

"If it's all right, I like to stay here for a bit," Thomas said. "Thank you, sir."

Nelson squeezed Thomas's shoulder gently and then quietly turned away.

CHAPTER 33

After breakfast, Anne called for a showdown. "Nelson, I decided I'm ready to be done living in fear. If you really have to, why don't you take Hagan and go finish Spaid, once you rest a few more days?" she said, standing behind Nelson with her hands on his shoulders.

"Hagan's men saved us on the Meramec, but I've got to finish this fight with Spaid on my own."

"Take someone to help."

"This is between me and him, plus that rotten Senator Saunders, who doesn't want the things I know about him to be published, including that they killed my father. This is personal." Nelson turned to face her. "And they're willing to kill to stop me."

"I still think this has all got to be more than that. All this over a book?"

"Even a few words can change history," Nelson said. "There are still a lot of folks that won't mind that he ran guns to support Confederate Troops turned bushwhackers. But they will care a lot more about how he murdered my father and hung an innocent slave girl. And when it's proved that the senator had Spaid murder a Federal Agent in Jefferson City, it will be over for both of them for sure."

Anne sighed and worry lines creased her face. "Rest a few days first. I'm sick over this. I know you need to go, but let's pretend this battle doesn't exist for a bit." She smiled. "I would like to know more about my husband to be."

"And what would the lady like to know about this worn-out old soldier?"

"Oh, I want to know about your father, about the dog-trot-cabin that you lived in up on the trace, and just where is it, that you are going to move me to?"

"Tomorrow, I'll take you across the valley to the place where my father's house stood and show you the land where we can build our home."

~ ~ ~ ~

With a good night's rest under his belt, he and Anne walked down the hill and waded Yadkin Creek. On the other side, Anne took him a quarter mile downstream to the place where her sister's home had stood.

"That night, the creek was running full when everyone went to bed. I remember hearing thunder and rain. Rain coming down so hard, like I couldn't ever remember."

"I rode through a lot of it, that night on the way here."

"It had to be a wall of water that ripped right through the stores and courthouse building. It took the houses from both sides of the creek," Anne said, "I ran down to warn them, the rushing water almost got me. The house was gone, I was too late."

"There was nothing you could do. The water tore the houses right off the foundations. It was a good thing Joshua, and his mother were sleeping upstairs when the water came." Nelson tried to reassure Anne it was not her fault and put her worries to rest, but he knew he might not ever be able to accomplish that.

"It still feels like it was my fault that I didn't go sooner."

"You're not to blame for your sister's death. Tell me what she was like?"

"She had a hard time with Dyer being gone, riding with the bushwhackers and all. She always did her best to protect Joshua. I saw her chase a gang of boys off with a club. They were tormenting him about his dad being a bushwhacker. When she would start to drink, Joshua would come over and stay with me. It got to the point she was drunk more often than not. I think she had just given up."

"She tried her best, out there on the roof, to save Joshua." Nelson took her hand. "She didn't see the limb coming that caught her up. It threw her into the currents. She was gone so quick. I might not have gotten out of that flood if it wasn't for her screaming for help on their house roof."

"Come on, no more sad talk. Show me your land. Lead the way, Mr. Paintier."

They climbed the north side of the valley, past the church where Nelson had found his father's grave, and up the hill to the land where he wanted their house to be built.

"We lived there, right in that stand of trees. They came in the night, throwing flaming lanterns in on the house. Then the shooting started. I was crying and had just come from the courthouse where Mary had been hanged. I ran through the trees and back into town to hide."

"You were there when they hanged her?"

"I hid out with the crowd out in front of the gallows until they covered her face."

"Did she see you, there in the crowd?"

"Her eyes were open wide with fright. She had to be looking for me, those staring eyes asking why you didn't tell them, why didn't you save me?" Nelson looked down. "Her face has haunted me."

"Nelson, you did all you could. Your book will tell what really happened at the spring pool," Anne said. "I'll help you...."

"I need to finish it, write the last chapter here, just down the hill where she is buried." Nelson pointed in front of them. "Then take it to Saint Louis to a friend in the printing business that's waiting to publish it. Then I can start work on the newspaper."

"What do we need to print the newspaper?" Anne looked at Nelson with a hopeful smile.

"I have a printing press coming by steamship soon. It's scheduled to be delivered in Jefferson City. That's never going to happen with Spaid and the Senator watching me. The ship will stop at Hermann for the ironworks deliveries, so I'll have an ore wagon and team up there to pick up the press."

Nelson and Anne walked over the forty-acre tract and talked about where Anne wanted their house to be built. She liked an open area near to the corner of the land facing the valley and he agreed. With their home location planned, they crossed the valley, to talk with Dyer about getting carpenters to start building.

"I need to go to the ironworks sawmill tomorrow. Would you like to go? We can stop by the dog-trot-cabin for you to see what we built years ago."

As they continued to walk, she hung on tightly to Nelson's hand. "Do you think Spaid, and his men might try to ambush us?"

"Dyer is going to ride out ahead of us to be sure it's safe. He wants to get supplies at the iron works anyway." He gave her hand a squeeze. "If you don't mind, I'd like to head up the creek hollow and see Spaid's sister on the way."

"Does she know where her brother's place is up on the Osage?"

"I don't know, but she told me she knew enough about

things he'd done for him to kill her. I want to see if she'll tell me what she knows."

CHAPTER 34

Driving a team of fine mules and a wagon Anne borrowed from the Olivers, Nelson and Anne started up the valley toward Jenny Spaid's cabin. Nelson's roan gelding trotted along tied behind. Less than halfway to the cabin they saw Jenny's sow and litter. The hog stopped in front of them and lifted its nose, grunting loudly.

"Sow's ranging a long way for food," Anne said.

"It's strange the pigs are this far from the cabin. Jenny had them penned up close when I came up here the first time."

"They must have found a hole in the fence."

"I need to get on up to Jenny's cabin fast and see what might be going on." Nelson handed the reins to Anne, then climbed down and untied his horse from the rear of the wagon.

As he got closer to the cabin, Nelson saw the rails around the hog pen had been broken, and the front door to the cabin stood open. He called out for the old woman, and then went to see if she was inside the cabin. When he came out Anne had the team of mules tied to the broken fence.

"She's not here. Check the shed out back, I'll go through the cabin again."

She ran around the cabin and shouted back, "Not here, either."

"There's no one inside the cabin. The place is all torn up like somebody was searching for something." Nelson stepped out the back of the cabin.

"The root cellar back here has been cleaned out also," Anne called.

"She's gone. He must have taken her. He tried to make it look like raiders did it." Nelson said, "She told me she had written down enough about Spaid to get him hung."

"Where would she hide something like that?" Anne asked.

"She's a stubborn old gal, even if he tortured her, she would never tell Spaid where she hid her writings about him." Nelson looked around but saw nothing that would help.

"I'll start searching in thc shed," Anne said.

"I'll go through the cabin; I really doubt if he found where she hid her papers." Nelson said, heading back into the cabin.

He climbed on a chair and searched high in the broken chinking between the logs. He found plenty of cow dung that had been used to plug holes, but no papers. After two hours of searching, he pulled the chairs up to the table and called Anne to come join him.

"When I came to see her the first time...something she said...about the papers she had written. She told me 'Gonna be a cold spring before he finds them.' We have to find the spring. There has to be a spring for drinking water, back on the hillside."

"There should be a heavy path where she walks to get water," Anne said. They both left the cabin and walked around to the back. "Here." Anne pointed at the path.

In less than a hundred yards up the valley, they found the rock-wall spring. He opened the wooden cover and reached to feel around the back wall, "She's got a jar tied up way in the back." He tried to pull the jug out.

"Hand it to me, if you can reach it."

"I can't, it's tied by a cord up through the back wall. See if you can cut it loose from up back. Here, take my knife."

Anne climbed over the back of the spring and cut the cord holding the jug.

"Got it." Nelson lifted the jug from the spring and handed it to Anne.

"Lordy, the top is rusted on tight. The sides all covered with some kind of slime," she said.

"Let me see if I can get it open." Nelson tapped the edge of the jug top with his knife. "There, the top's coming off."

Spaid's history of murder and robbery fell to the ground at their feet. Scraps of paper, each with places, dates, and crimes. He knelt and picked up the papers, unrolling some, and stopping to read the faint pencil marking on them.

"My God. Spaid did things that got blamed on Hagan and his men. He even committed some of the robberies that everyone thought Bloody Bill Anderson had done."

Anne picked up pieces of paper and read them. The expression on her face told him a lot about what Jenny had written.

"This tells a whole lot about some of the people round here that weren't heard from ever again," she said, "I want to just throw up all over these papers."

"Don't, we need them to make sure he hangs."

"Do you think Spaid took her, to stop her from telling what she knows?"

"From what she told me, he knew she had written it all down. Either he took her, or she got away, and hid in the hills. If she's hid, he'll be back to silence her."

"We need to get out of here, go get help." Anne tugged at Nelson's arm.

"You need to go," he said, "Don't send help, it might just scare him off. He'll be by himself if he comes. His men all got shot up back on the Meramec. Go. Take the team and wagon back to Steelville."

With Anne on the way to safety, Nelson stuffed the faded scraps of paper spelling out Spaid's crimes into his saddlebags before he led his horse up the valley, out of sight of the cabin and tied it to a stout tree limb. Walking back, he tried to think out a plan for when Sheriff Spaid showed up. It would be best to just shoot the son-of-a-bitch, rather than ask why he had killed his father. The guilt of his father dying raised up in his mind. It had been his fault his dad had been burned alive. He wiped tears from his face and headed for the cabin to wait. Back in the cabin, he picked a spot just off to the side of the cast iron cook stove and sat down, ready for what trouble would come.

Less than an hour had passed when it arrived, "Come out here, Paintier."

"Stay...there, Nelson!"

Damn, that was Anne's muffled voice.

He bolted to the door of the cabin to find Spaid sitting with Anne in front of him on his horse.

"Look what I found coming out of the valley, Paintier." Spaid slid off the side of his horse, pulling Anne with him, his pistol pointed at her neck.

"Let her go, Spaid. This fight is between you and me." He stepped through the open doorway with his pistol in his hand.

"Where's that old bitch sister of mine, Paintier?"

"I guess she knew you were coming back and left, Spaid," Nelson said, holding his pistol pointed at the floor.

"Get back in the cabin!" Spaid said, as he pushed Anne forward and forced Nelson into the cabin door.

"Let her go, Spaid."

"Throw that cannon you're holding over in the corner, Paintier, and I'll let her go."

With no option left, Nelson tossed his pistol into the back corner of the cabin.

"Let me go, you scum!" Anne sank her boot heel into Spaid's foot.

"You whore!" Spaid hit Anne in the side of the head with his pistol. She fell to the cabin floor at his feet.

"You're going to die for that, Spaid."

"It's funny you saying that, standing there empty handed." Spaid cocked the hammer and leveled his pistol at Nelson's head. "Should have gotten this done years ago."

An explosion came from behind Spaid. Smoke filled the doorway and swept around the sheriff. Yet he still stood. He spun to see what had just happened behind him. Nelson dove across the floor, sliding into the corner to grab his weapon. His shot hit Spaid square in the back of the head, knocking him out of the cabin door. Spaid fell dead right at the feet of a powder-covered old woman, trying to wipe the black soot from her eyes, and still holding what was left of her exploded blunderbuss.

"You throwing that revolver into the corner wasn't the smartest thing you ever did, boy," Jenny Spaid, said as she stepped across her dead brother's body. "I was watching through the window when you done it."

Nelson had rushed to lift Anne's head from the floor.

"I'll get some spring water for her face, that'll get her going," Jenny Spaid headed around the cabin.

"Had a feeling you might be around somewhere," shouted Nelson. "Lucky for us you hadn't been scared too far off."

Jenny Spaid quickly returned and poured most of the ladle of spring water over Anne's face. With the rest she wet her sleeve to wipe the burnt gunpowder off her own face.

"Anne, wake up!" Nelson used his hand to wipe the

water off her face.

Her eyes opened and she struggled to sit up. "Wh...wh...happened?"

"Jenny Spaid sneaked up and tried to shoot her brother."

"Jenny, where had you been?" asked Anne.

"Been hiding up on the mountain all along. Just waiting for him to come back." Jenny Spaid pointed at her dead brother's body.

"The old gun exploded in her face. It scared Spaid so bad he turned around to face her, gave me time to kill him," Nelson said. "I'd rather had shot him square in the face."

Anne gripped his arms and pulled them around her, "I was sure...he was...going to kill you."

"So was I." Nelson held her close, his eyes on Spaid's lifeless body. It didn't make him feel good to kill, but this time, he was glad to put this bad one down for good.

CHAPTER 35

Spaid's demise did little to satisfy Nelson. There was still justice to be served. It took two to kill Mary and his father, and Senator Saunders was next on his list. Plus, the senator had more to lose than the sheriff, which meant he'd stop at nothing to end Nelson before his book could be published.

The word was that Saunders was missing in action from the capitol. He must've heard about Spaid being taken out, or that the Army was onto his gun running operation— maybe both. Nelson had no doubt the senator was planning his next attack on him from wherever he was hiding. It turned out that Thomas knew a group of former slaves who'd escaped from a senator's farm. Nelson suspected that senator was Saunders, and they could have information that would lead them right to him.

The moonlight helped Nelson see to slide the harness over the backs of the two stout Missouri mules he had purchased for the trip. Thomas stood alongside the wagon keeping the doubletree hitch straight for Nelson to back the team into place. With the team hitched to the flatbed wagon, he left Thomas holding the mules and went to tell Anne they were leaving.

She hurried from the house, carrying a cup of hot cider. "Drink this. It will keep the cold away for a while."

He took a deep sip of the cider and gave a small cough. "Lady, that's hot. Come here."

She nestled close to him. "Are you sure about what Thomas told you about the slave camp?"

"Yes. He thinks there could be former slaves there that know where Saunders and his men could be hiding. I've got to finish this, Anne." He tried to keep his worry from showing.

The danger of Saunders men looking for him concerned him. He would keep weapons ready at his side.

~ ~ ~ ~

Both mules were reluctant to leave the barnyard where they had been feed the last few days. However, they drove out of the yard and worked together holding back the wagon and the empty coffin inside going down the hillside to cross Yadkin Creek. The mules paused at the creek's edge and then splashed in the foot-deep water before crossing. Nelson cracked the heavy trace lines across their backs and started the climb to the top of the Steelville ridge where Mary lay buried. The steep climb caused Thomas to shuffle in the wagon's seat to get a better grip on a side brace. The clatter of the mule's iron shoes on the rock street was loud, which bothered Nelson. He didn't want any visitors from town watching and tormenting them when they reached Mary's gravesite.

At the top of the hill he steered the team along the ridge top the short distance to the pile of rocks marking the slave's grave. With the team stopped and tied to a tree, Nelson and Thomas got down and lifted the coffin out. Setting the coffin to the side of the grave, they started removing the rock pile from the top with plans to rebury Mary in her rightful place after they finished the senator.

Nelson paused. "Thomas are you okay doing this? It would be all right if you waited at the wagon."

Thomas didn't answer. He finished pushing the rocks away and set the edge of his shovel into the outline the rocks had left. He pushed on the shovel with his shoe to break into the brick hard red clay of southern Missouri. Little of the clay moved.

"Let me, Thomas. My boots are tougher, and this shovel has a shaper edge."

Thomas stood back a few feet to let Nelson dig. With the outline of the grave cut into the ground, both men started working out slabs of the clay. With the tough two feet of the clay removed the digging got easier. Nelson stood on the edge of his shovel blade and pushed it a foot deeper into the dirt. He felt the shovel hit wood. He had reached the rotten top of a wooden box, he hoped she had been buried in. Certain only the bones of the girl would remain he pried away the broken box's cover. The bones lay drawn up in what looked like way more than a fetal position. Her back had been broken to force her to fit into the small box.

"Thomas, open the coffin." He wanted to curse the men that had shoved her remains into a small box that looked like it had been a hay box in a barn. A decayed dress draped from the girl's bones. Her black hair he had felt as a boy remained gracing her skull into a macabre portrait. The years since he had watched this same body drop through a trap door had done little to ease the pain of not being able to save her from the fate she met on that day. Reaching and starting to lift her bones from the box he fell back in dismay when only parts of the bones remained together. Thomas eased him aside.

"I do this for her, Mr. Nelson." Bone by bone Nelson watched the old slave lift his child from the disgraceful burial and place her into the coffin Thomas had made to carry her home.

With the bones laid out in the coffin he paused and then put on the wooden lid. He pulled the two leather straps on each side to fastened the lid in place. Together they carried the coffin with the child's bones to the waiting wagon.

Thomas didn't say anything, only started back for the grave site.

"Leave the grave open, Thomas. I want them to know someone took her. Took her to a better place where she had been loved by a mother and father."

~ ~ ~ ~

Leaving the bluff above the town, he quickly found the trace leading north toward Herman, Missouri and a ferry crossing to the north river bluff where Thomas said his plot of land would lie. The place to bury his child. On the way, they'd come to the slave camp where Nelson could hopefully find some answers about Saunders's whereabouts. They passed the dogtrot cabin where the girl had been beaten in the first light of the morning. Today, Nelson didn't stop.

"I'm sorry you had to take her from the grave." Nelson clucked to the mules and snapped the lead on their backs to hurry past the cabin and so many of his memories.

"When our master treats our dead babies like dead pigs, we do this same thing and move them when he ain't watchin'."

"I didn't know. I expect there's a lot about your life I don't know about."

"Some things you might not want to know, sir."

Setting up a tent and camp on the trip was out of the question. The dangers of sleeping along a trace still traveled by bands of guerrillas that would not know him and his connection to Hagan and his men was real. Thomas would be in danger, some of the bands were known for hanging x-slaves that they found. The first day found them stopped well after midnight along a running stream they would have to cross in the morning. With the mules hobbled to graze for a few hours they finished off some of the food Anne had prepared for their journey. Nelson sat on a blanket with his back to a tree and his rifle lying across his lap.

"It would be best if you sleep, Mr. Nelson," Thomas said as he paced limping along the edge of the wagon. Nelson recognized his uneasiness and pacing was to guard the bones of his child.

"There's a second rifle under the clapboard cover under the seat. I didn't hide it from you. It's only there if this one jams," Nelson told him.

"I killed a lot of men coming at us with a muzzle loader. Nigger learns to load a weapon fast when rebels are hell bent on killing him."

"I guess we needed to talk to each other more. You've surprised me, Thomas." Nelson stood and went quickly to the wagon to get the rifle. He handed Thomas the loaded rifle and then sat back down on the blanket. "Wake me in two hours and you can get some sleep too."

CHAPTER 36

Nelson awoke to the sound of one of the mules braying. He sat up, wiping his eyes. The sun had topped the trees to the east. He had slept too long. A lot more time than two hours had passed.

"Why didn't you wake me?" He stood and shook off the stiffness before walking to help Thomas harness the mules to the wagon. "You needed some sleep too."

"It's alright, Mr. Nelson. If you'll let me, I'll just lay down next to my little girl when we get going. I'll sleep a little there beside her." Thomas leaned over behind the mule and finished dropping the harness links into one of the doubletrees.

With the team ready and Thomas in the back of the wagon, Nelson lifted the reins and snapped them on the backs of the two mules. The wagon shuddered and then moved out to join the trace north. The old slave sat with the rifle in his hand and the casket against his back on four sacks of straw Nelson had put in the wagon earlier. He hoped Thomas would sleep so he would be rested to stay awake and guard them through the night.

Nelson figured it was around four o'clock when he slowed on a high ridge to study the valley ahead in his direction of travel. Much of the valley was covered with clouds of smoke. The wind had just brought the stink of smoldering wood up the steep hill ahead. He shook his head at the smell and tried to cover his nose with one hand. The path of the trace across the valley lay clear. All the burning had been off to the east of the trace.

"There could be trouble ahead. Keep that rifle ready and watch behind us for riders." Nelson clucked to the mules to start the wagon down the long hill.

Both mules shuffled sideways trying to turn away from going into the smoke smell. With a slap and a shout to get back in line he got them started down into the valley.

"Them mules might be smarter than us 'ins," Thomas said, sitting up on his knees to look over the wagon seat and down into the valley.

"You may be right," Nelson said, holding back the mules on the steep decent with his right foot pushing hard against the friction brake lever on the side of the wagon. The brake shoe caused the rear wheels to lock and drag screeching on the rocky path.

Near the bottom of the long decline, Nelson let off on the brake and gave the mule's their head. Their lightened load and coasting wagon only lasted a couple minutes. A low water creek crossing ahead was covered with fast moving water.

"Hang on back there." He cracked the reins on the mules. Both mules tried to jump the stream. Their surge cocked the wagon and slid the left side wheels up in the air. Nelson fought to keep from falling off the driver's seat. When the wheels came back down, the wagon was in midstream and sliding to the side with the strong current. Both mules had gathered themselves up from the jump and lunged ahead, getting the wagon the rest of the way across the stream. He turned to check on his passengers. Thomas lay straddled across the casket. One of his arms locked through the leather straps on it, the other holding on to the support of the driver's seat.

"I was afraid I had lost you both back there, Thomas." Nelson tried to get the reins straight across the backs of the two mules. "I don't know what's going on up ahead. But we need to get through here before dark." He lifted his rifle off the floor of the wagon and set it upright against the side of his right leg. "Keep ready back there."

Thomas knelt at the back of the wagon seat holding on with one hand, the other holding the rifle Nelson had given him. "We be real near the camp I told you about."

"Could the smoke be coming from a fire there?" Nelson pointed in the direction of all the smoke.

The sight of a negro woman and what looked to be her teenage daughter running toward the wagon from the woods caused the mules to shy off the trace.

"Whoa, mules!" Nelson pulled hard on the lines just before hitting a downed cedar tree lying across part of the trace. The woman ran to the back of the wagon and tried to help the girl up into the wagon bed.

"Hold on till I get stopped." He handed the reins to Thomas and jumped off the stopped wagon to help the woman.

"They gonna come back and get my girl," the woman said, finishing pushing the girl into the wagon's bed.

"Who's coming back?" Nelson took the woman's arm and helped her in the wagon.

"They came in the night and took my man and then killed Jobe."

She pointed toward a narrow wagon path leading toward where Nelson had seen the smoke rising. She seemed too frantic to provide more detailed information.

Back in the driver's seat, he steered the mules down the path toward the smoke. A quarter mile had passed before they broke out in an open field with smoldering tin covered sheds. He pulled up the team and jumped down from the wagon. The woman stood in the wagon pointing between two sheds.

"We drug him around there," she said, holding the girl tight behind her long clay-stained dress. The woman's hair was wrapped with bright cloth that might at one time have been a dress.

The woman got down from the wagon and led Nelson and Thomas around the ruins. Moisture in the still smoldering logs in the shed walls popped and blew out in small explosions. Nelson flinched at what sounded like distant gun shots. He stepped around three dead goats, all of them with blood spots on their carcasses. The bastards had shot them. When they reached a ragged quilt covering a body, he stood back and let Thomas lift it for them to see. It came clear to Nelson the dead negro man had been dragged before being shot in the middle of his forehead. His shirt was torn ragged and filled with fresh scrapped up clay.

"Do you know him, Thomas?"

"I knowed him some. He was owned by a farm up by Hermann—the senator's farm, that I was tellin' you about. He ran away and took some other slaves with him. It was a long time ago."

Nelson stopped on his way back to the wagon. He knelt running his finger along the edge of one of the killers' horse tracks. The horse was wearing new horseshoes. All four of the horse's hooves had on the premium shoes. It wasn't something a raider's horse would be wearing. These riders were backed by money.

The sun had just disappeared behind the hills to the west when he got the two shovels to bury the dead negro. He called off the digging when they had a shallow grave that would protect the body from animals. Together with Thomas, they laid the man to rest under three feet of red clay from the hillside. Thomas stood with the woman and child alongside the finished grave, all three with their heads down. Nelson stepped forward.

He bowed his head to remember the prayer he had to say so many times before on the battlefield.

"The Lord is my shepherd. I shall not want. He maketh me to lie down in green pastures. Amen," he recited, knowing full well he had shortened the psalm. He needed to be back on the trace before full darkness set in.

Going back to the wagon and mules, Nelson climbed into the driver's seat, Thomas followed into the wagon sitting with his back to Nelson and his hand on the coffin with Mary. The negro woman and girl stood across the trace as if they were about to go into the woods.

"Was that her husband?" Nelson asked.

"No, sir. The dead man was Jobe. When I lived in this camp, she lived in the shacks with a white man she was wed too. She said the raiders tied him up and led him away behind their horses. They left traveling north toward the river."

"We're not going to leave them, Thomas." Nelson looked at the woman. "Both of you get in the wagon. You're going with us."

The woman didn't move.

"What is she waiting for?"

"For her man to come back, I's reckon."

"Tell her we're going north where they took him. We'll look for him."

Thomas jumped from the wagon and went to the woman and girl. Nelson couldn't hear what he was telling her, but soon realized it had worked. The woman and girl crossed the trace. Thomas helped both of them into wagon and then climbed back on board himself. Nelson snapped the reins and the team moved out to the north toward Hermann and the Missouri River.

CHAPTER 37

The travel got slower as they approached the hills and deep valleys that would soon butt against the river.

Thomas leaned over the seat. "We going see that river soon, mister Nelson."

"Before noon I reckon." Nelson glanced back for a moment. "How's our two travelers doing? Did she tell you anything more?"

"Mother is sure quiet. Girl is speaking out some."

"Did she say her name?"

"Say's her name is Keziah. Her daddy is the white man I was tellin' you about. Ain't no secret who he used to work for at a farm just a ways from the town up ahead, near Hermann."

"A senator?"

"Mhm. Senator Saunders. The three of them escaped from his farm."

Nelson perked up. This could be his lead to the senator and an easier life after this battle was won. Still, he was cautious and nervous, knowing Saunders's men could be in the area while he was traveling with a mother, daughter, and Mary's bones. He ranked high on the list of people Saunders would want to kill, just as Saunders ranked high on his list.

As if on cue, running horses and riders came over a ridge behind them before either of them knew danger could be on them. Nelson dropped the trace lines after giving the mules a hard hit to move out. He lifted his rifle and loaded a shell. Thomas moved a little slower but did the same with his rifle.

A loud holler came from one of the two riders, "Hold up, Nelson." Both riders were at the wagon's rear. Thomas had his rifle leveled at the man in front.

"Whoa!" Nelson smiled, recognizing Hagan and Red before Thomas did. "It's all right, Thomas."

"Sorry, Mr. Hagan, sir," Thomas said as he lowered his rifle and Hagan and Red pulled up alongside the wagon.

"Anne told us you were going after the senator."

"We'll need all the guns we can get. Sure, glad to see you. Saunders's place is near here and his men have kidnapped this woman's husband. We ran into some of their killing yesterday."

"I've been aching to meet up with his boys again. Back in the days he ran guns to us. He stuck us with a wagon of bad rifles. Lots of the parts were gone out of the actions. They shot up two of my men getting away when we found out."

Nelson nodded and made the introductions. "You both know Thomas. The young woman is Keziah. Her mother hasn't been free with her name yet."

"Her name is Rossa. Find my daddy so I can kill the son-of-a-bitch, Saunders," Keziah said. "He been searching for me all over since I run off from his bed."

Her sudden outspokenness took Nelson by surprise. The frown of hate on Keziah's face was enough to convince anyone she meant what she had just said.

"The Senator's men killed a man yesterday and took off with Rossa's husband in chains. They're headed north toward the river." Nelson pointed in that direction.

"We'll ride point for you," Hagan said. They rode out from the wagon and kicked up their horses.

"We'll be a mile or so ahead," Red said, catching up to Hagan.

~ ~ ~ ~

The midday closed in on them quickly without hearing from Hagan and Red. They pulled up on a hill where the trace wound down into the small town of Hermann.

"Did those boys go in there and get into whores and drinking?" Thomas asked.

"It wouldn't be the first time for Red to do that." Nelson laughed. "Hang on. Riders coming up from the west side of town." Both Hagan and Red pulled up from a climb from the valley.

"The men we're after aren't down there now. They came through hours ago with a man hog tied onto a horse. They rode west from here. A couple of the old men said to look out about five miles along the river we would come to Senator Saunder's farm. They were mostly afraid to talk to us."

"Did they say how many of Saunders men went through?" Nelson stared at the men in front of him.

"There were six plus the man they had captive." Hagan looked at Nelson. "We're going after them, right?"

Nelson didn't hesitate. He started the team toward the west. They traveled along a ridgeline road until they pulled up on an overlook of a valley with a barn. Keziah stood behind the wagon seat and pointed out the two-story farmhouse where she'd apparently been held. Uncertain if Saunders would be there, Nelson had Red hold the team while he and Hagan crept closer to the rim of the valley.

"Looks like they're in front of the barn with a man they are about ready to hang." Nelson crept a bit closet to the edge. "We're going to have to come at them from the back of the barn."

"Red and I will try to get up into the loft. We can kick the fight off from there."

"I'm going to have Thomas stay with the women. He can handle a rifle if things get out of hand."

"If we go down the ridge about a hundred yards, we can work our way down from there. We better hurry. They're about to hang the man," Hagan said, standing with his rifle in his hand and motioning for Red to follow.

Leaving Thomas and the two women with a warning to stay put, Nelson followed the two men to a place on the ridge where their approach down the hill would be hidden from view. They went down sliding between small trees they grabbed to slow their decent. The three entered the door at the back of the barn unnoticed. At a barn ladder, Hagan and Red climbed into the loft. Nelson slipped along the edges of the horse stalls. The wide barn door at the front of the barn was open. Out front, Keziah's father was being tortured with a hangman noose around his neck. His count of men at the front got to five as he settled inside a stall with a full view of the outside of the barn. He heard a *tap-tap* from the loft just over his head. Hagan was ready.

A squeak of the stall door behind him startled him, and he turned ready to fire. Keziah stood with her finger over her lips. She pushed into the wall beside him carrying what he knew must've been Thomas's rifle.

"They going to hang my father." She cocked the rifle and aimed at one of the men.

He tried to push the girl with a gun back from the fight. She slipped past him and fired the first shot, hitting the man on the horse holding the end of the hanging rope. Keziah's mother ran from the side of the barn toward her husband. The men in front fired wildly, and Rossa fell quickly.

Keziah's father stood and started toward his wife and also went down in a hail of bullets. The gunfight had started so suddenly, it took Hagan and Red a second to open up on the five men.

Nelson's first shot hit one of the men in front of the barn running to get behind a log. The man went to his knees still pulling the trigger and shooting uncontrollably. Two other men fell from Hagan's and Red's firing. The two men left on their feet ran toward the farmhouse. One fell from a shot from the loft. He staggered a few steps and went down trying to hold his leg and wave a hand in surrender. The other man disappeared into the door of the farmhouse. Keziah ran from the stall to her father and mother and knelt beside them. She looked back at Nelson.

"Take care of them," she yelled, getting up and racing for the farmhouse. "I'm going to kill him if he in the house."

Nelson knew she meant Saunders. He stopped beside her father and mother and felt for their pulse. They were gone. He ran for the door Keziah had just gone in. Pushing the door open he stepped inside. Two shots rang out from somewhere in the house, and a man screamed. A third shot ended the screaming.

"Keziah, I'm coming inside. Don't shoot," Nelson said, going into the hallway.

The steps squeaked, and Keziah came down the stairs with the rifle in her right hand and a pistol in the other. "Saunders ain't here. I shot his right-hand man up there," she said, letting the end of the rifle barrel rest on the floor and leaning on it. "They's dead. Wasn't they?"

Nelson nodded. "I'm sorry."

"Did the man lying out there still alive, he do it?" she asked. "His name is Marvin." She strapped on a belt and stuck the pistol through it at the center of her tiny waist.

"I don't know, but don't kill him. He could know where Saunders might be."

Nelson led the way back out into the barnyard. Keziah followed, her long, hand sewn dress pulled tight around her waist by the leather belt. It was clear to him now that she wasn't a girl. She was a woman. She may have been Saunders's sex slave, but somehow, she'd watched and learned battle skills rarely known by other slaves. Her expression was stony. Could she have seen so much death that losing her mother and father hadn't sunk her into grief? Keziah was tougher than iron nails. He would handle her with caution.

The man on the ground held the palms of his hands out. "Don't shoot me, mister," he said. "I gave up."

"I'm not going to shoot you. She is. She just killed your comrade. Took a souvenir from him. She's wearing his belt," Nelson said, stepping aside to let Keziah point her rifle at the man.

"No. Keep Saunders's bitch away from me." He scooted back a few feet before slumping to grab his bleeding leg.

Keziah followed and pushed the barrel of the rifle into his chest, shoving him over on his back. "Where is he, Marvin? He can't help you now." She cocked the rifle and took aim.

"Wait! All I know is he left Hermann on a cargo steamer. He's probably in St. Louis."

"What else?" she demanded.

"All right, all right. He talked about a place he owns in New Orleans."

"Now?" she asked, looking at Nelson.

"No. He may remember something else. The local sheriff is going to want him for murder."

Keziah lowered the hammer on the rifle and turned away, then went to her mother's body. Thomas stood over the body and had covered it with a blanket. Keziah slipped the blanket off her mother's face, and on her knees sat running her hands through her mother's hair to untangle the strands. Nelson watched from a distance, helping Hagan bandage Marvin's leg wound. They would carry the other men's bodies into the house to await the sheriff.

With their wagon loaded with Keziah's parents' bodies and the wounded man, Thomas started the team toward Hermann. With several horses to choose from, Nelson saddled a paint for Keziah and a big sorrel for himself. Red dropped several forks of hay from the loft for the other horses they had turned loose. They rode out to follow Thomas.

~ ~ ~ ~

When they rode into Hermann, it created quite a stir. Old timers gracing the streets on the wooden porches in front of the stores came to the edges to look and point at Saunders's hogtied henchman and the bodies in the wagon. They turned the henchman over to the sheriff, and he was placed under arrest for the murder of Keziah's parents. Getting word to the Army Command in St. Louis came next. Nelson went to the telegraph office and sent word that Saunders had left the mid-Missouri area.

Nelson asked for a burial plot in the town cemetery for Keziah's mother and father. The town's elders stood alongside the wagon shaking their heads. There would be no way the negro woman could be buried with her white husband in the town's cemetery. Keziah's quick temper and dirty mouth didn't help to persuade the old white men to Nelson's cause.

He took a quieter approach, certain that cash would open a spot in the cemetery. A plot far in the back along a railroad track was finally offered for Keziah's parents.

~ ~ ~ ~

Thomas stood solemnly staring down at the two hastily built wooden coffins sitting alongside each other at the bottom of the grave.

Nelson asked Keziah, "Do you want to come stand over here with us?"

She shook her head sharply, refusing to do anything but stand alone with her head down, as if she would never take comfort from anyone ever again.

Nelson opened his mouth to say the words he'd said so many times before over his fallen troops, but he didn't have a chance.

"Amen," Keziah uttered and looked up. The funeral was over before it began.

~ ~ ~ ~

With the wagon and Mary's coffin safely rolled into the back of the town's stable, Thomas and Keziah each took blankets and found a corner of the stable to sleep in. Nelson promised to return with food, then took Hagan and Red to get rooms at the Hermann Inn.

Two hours had passed when he returned to the stable carrying a pot of beef stew and two bottles of home brew beer. Thomas greeted him at the door of the stable.

"She's gone, Mr. Nelson. Saddled up that paint horse and rode off into the night. She's going after Saunders, ain't she?"

"I'd say so, Thomas. And freedom—something she has never had in her life."

Sending Hagan and Red to bring her back would be useless. Keziah's quest to find and punish Saunders had begun. Nelson knew what it was like to have revenge burning on the heart. Plus, the girl had nothing left to lose. Silently, he wished her the best.

CHAPTER 38

The next morning, Hagan and Red sat on their horses at the ferryboat ramp, offering to go after Keziah if Nelson ordered. Thomas shook his head no at their offer.

"She ain't never going to stay. Even if you bring her back."

"Thomas is right. She's on a mission. If both of you would head back to Steelville and give the carpenters a hand with the new building for the newspaper, I'll stay with Thomas the rest of the way."

With a wave and a goodbye, the two men rode off to the south.

~ ~ ~ ~

After half a day of riding, Thomas pointed just ahead. "We will be turning off just up yonder. It a big hollow just up ahead."

Nelson pulled his horse up and hung back behind to see the turn's location. Nothing but a ditch lay along the right side of the wagon. Thomas slowed the mules and steered them to cross the ditch. The wagon bed squeaked at the twist between the front and back wheels from the uneven path. The wagon leaned and Mary's coffin strained against the leather ties holding it. Just across the ditch, a narrow field, four wagon widths wide, of tall prairie grass lay between them and the tall timbered woods.

"This was my garden," Thomas said, pointing in both directions along the strip of land now grown over.

The dark hollow lay before them. First growth trees rose from the sides of the small canyon-like hollow. Thomas reined the mules into a narrow-rutted wagon trail leading up and back into the flattest area of the hollow. Cracked and aged blackened logs made up the sides of two cabins built on the hollow's only flat spot. Nelson dismounted and walked to look in a cast-iron kettle the size of a washtub steaming with boiling cracklings from the scraped clean and gutted pig hanging from a tree limb. Thomas cupped his hands in front of his mouth and blew a call into them.

"Whoo whoo!" The sound echoed off the walls of the hollow.

Even before the call ended, Nelson heard the response from someone on a hillside above the hollow. "Who lives here?" Nelson went to stand by one of the cabins and peer in.

"I don't know for sure now. The white man gave all of us our freedom. Some left like me, looking for our families." Thomas got down from the wagon and went to the kettle. He lifted the long wooden carved handle sticking from the kettle and stirred the boiling cracklins'. "These needin' to come out soon."

A man and woman slid down one of the steep hollow slopes toward the cabins. They ran to within a few yards of them.

"Do you know them, Thomas?" Nelson asked.

"No, sir. I don't think I do."

"Uncle Thomas!" the man said. "I was a boy when you left here."

"My brother's children? Josie and John?" Thomas stepped closer to see them better, awe in his voice.

"I'm John. This woman is Sandra, my wife." The man's smile drooped. "Josie died when she was ten years old."

Thomas went to the man and gave him a hug, and the woman put her arms around both of the men.

"I never knew why you left your home place," John said.

"I went looking for my wife and little girl that got sold away years ago, before the war."

Nelson stood quietly listening, not wanting to intrude. He was as out of place at this homecoming as he could be.

Thomas turned toward him. "This here is Mr. Nelson. He has helped me bring my little dead girl home where I can bury her, where no one can bother her again."

Nelson offered a hello and a handshake to both before going and standing alongside the wagon and Mary's coffin with Thomas and his family. No one spoke for the longest time. They simply stood looking at the wooden coffin. To break the silence, Nelson offered a short prayer for Thomas's child, and all three of the Negros offered an amen when the prayer ended.

~ ~ ~ ~

At dawn, Nelson woke to see Thomas already coming down the back of the hollow, a rope drug behind him, tied to an empty, open coffin. The handle of a shovel hung over the back edge of the coffin. Meeting him at the open area around the cabins, Nelson saw the sadness painted across the old man's face. It blended with the scars he bore of his years of slavery.

"I took her bones from the box. Nobody else will ever find them now. They're buried deep in the ground with roots and stones all around them. Soon they will be dust," Thomas said, pulling the coffin next to the fire. He pushed it into the still smoldering coals.

They stood together watching the last of Mary's past burn away.

It was clear Thomas intended to spend the rest of his days in the hollow near Mary. He spoke of his garden, and soon, he would need to get it ready for another planting.

Nelson stood using the back of the wagon as a table to write a note.

"As a form of payment for his work on my home in Steelville, Missouri, I, Nelson Paintier, hereby pay to Thomas X this wagon and team of mules." He handed it to Thomas, along with a handshake, and began to read.

Thomas held up a hand. "It's all right, sir. Miss Anne taught me most of these here words. Will you thank her for me?"

CHAPTER 39

MORE THAN THREE MONTHS HAD PASSED SINCE
NELSON RETURNED FROM MARY'S HOLLOW. ANNE
HAD QUIT HER SCHOOL TEACHING TO HELP WITH THE
PRINTING AND PUBLICATION OF THEIR NEWSPAPER, THE
CRAWFORD JOURNAL. SHE ENJOYED SETTING TYPE FOR
THE NEWS ARTICLES THEY WROTE.

With that week's paper almost complete on the print table,
she held the last type piece in her hand.

"You might want to hold up on that," Nelson told her.
"The mail man's coming just down the road in an awful
hurry." He headed for the office's door to meet the mail
man.

"Hello, Sam. Good morning," Nelson said, reaching for
the envelop the man held out.

"I thought you might want this in a hurry. Came special
this morning."

"Thanks, Sam. Coffee before you go?"

"Got to hurry today." With that, he took off again.

Nelson turned and opened the letter. Pausing to read it before telling Anne the news. "I think she found him." His heart beat quick in his chest.

"Who found who?"

"Keziah, the slave girl I told you about. Senator Saunders was murdered in a brothel in New Orleans. The woman that did it was a light-skinned Negro. She got away clean. Keziah had found him."

"So, it's done," she said, both disbelief and relief in her tone. She went and wrapped her arms around him in a tight embrace. "I'm so glad for you."

She left him and went to change the type set for that week's newspaper.

Turning the press wheel to print the front page of the paper, Nelson swelled with a feeling of justice and pride. The senator—and former judge—had put Mary, the slave girl, to death, and now someone had done the same to him. He took the first page of the print and shook it to be sure it was dry before folding it twice. Anne followed him over to a desk stacked with the books, recently printed and published, that told Mary's story for all to read. Anne opened one to the inside cover, where he had signed his name, and helped him guide the folded newspaper into the book. He closed the cover, sealing the fate of the former judge of Crawford County, the murderer of Mary and his father. It seemed the final chapter of Mary's story and Nelson's quest for justice had come to a close.

ABOUT THE AUTHOR

From his deep-seated roots in the Ozarks and his love of all things outdoors Snelson's novels bring these feeling to the printed page around unforgettable characters. He has been published in national magazines and in the past published an International Newsletter on aviation and aircraft building. His novel Little Minnow is available on Amazon and online retailers everywhere.

He and his wife live on a ranch with their horses, where he continues to bring stories of meaning to life.

www.ingramcontent.com/pod-product-compliance
Lightning Source LLC
Chambersburg PA
CBHW060626260626
47161CB00008B/2812